MINISTRY OF DISTURBANCE

And Other SF

MINISTRY OF DISTURBANCE

And Other SF

H. Beam Piper

ÆGYPAN PRESS

Ministry of Disturbance and Other SF
A publication of
ÆGYPAN PRESS

www.aegypan.com

Table of Contents

Ministry of Disturbance

The symphony was ending, the final triumphant pæan soaring up and up, beyond the limit of audibility. For a moment, after the last notes had gone away, Paul sat motionless, as though some part of him had followed. Then he roused himself and finished his coffee and cigarette, looking out the wide window across the city below – treetops and towers, roofs and domes and arching skyways, busy swarms of aircars glinting in the early sunlight. Not many people cared for João Coelho's music, now, and least of all for the Eighth Symphony. It was the music of another time, a thousand years ago, when the Empire was blazing into being out of the long night and hammering back the Neobarbarians from world after world. Today people found it perturbing.

He smiled faintly at the vacant chair opposite him, and lit another cigarette before putting the breakfast dishes on the serving-robot's tray, and, after a while, realized that the robot was still beside his chair, waiting for dismissal. He gave it an instruction to summon the cleaning robots and sent it away. He could as easily have summoned them himself, or let the guards who would be in checking the room do it for him, but maybe it made a robot feel trusted and important to relay orders to other robots.

Then he smiled again, this time in self-derision. A robot couldn't feel important, or anything else. A robot was nothing but steel and plastic and magnetized tape and photo-micro-positronic circuits, whereas a man – His Imperial Majesty Paul XXII, for instance – was nothing but tissues and cells and colloids and electro-neuronic circuits. There was a difference; anybody knew that. The trouble was that he had never met anybody – which included physicists, biologists, psychologists, psionicists, philosophers and theologians – who could define the difference in satisfactorily exact terms. He watched the robot pivot on its treads and glide away, trailing steam from its coffee pot. It might be silly to treat robots like people, but that wasn't as bad as treating people like robots, an attitude which was becoming entirely too prevalent. If only so many people didn't act like robots!

He crossed to the elevator and stood in front of it until a tiny electroencephalograph inside recognized his distinctive brain-wave pattern. Across the room, another door was popping open in response to the robot's distinctive wave pattern. He stepped inside and flipped a switch – there were still a few things around that had to be manually operated – and the door closed behind him and the elevator gave him an instant's weightlessness as it started to drop forty floors.

When it opened, Captain-General Dorflay of the Household Guard was waiting for him, with a captain and ten privates. General Dorflay was human. The captain and his ten soldiers weren't. They wore helmets, emblazoned with the golden sun and superimposed black cogwheel of the Empire, and red kilts and black ankle boots and weapons belts, and the captain had a narrow gold-laced cape over his shoulders, but for the rest, their bodies were covered with a stiff mat of black hair, and their faces were slightly like terriers'. (For all his humanity, Captain-General Dorflay's face was more like a bulldog's.) They were hillmen from the southern hemisphere of Thor, and as a people they made excellent mercenaries. They were crack shots, brave and crafty fighters, totally uninterested in politics off their own planet, and, because they had grown up in a patriarchial-clan society, they were fanatically loyal to anybody whom they accepted as their chieftain. Paul stepped out and gave them an inclusive nod.

"Good morning, gentlemen."

"Good morning, Your Imperial Majesty," General Dorflay said, bowing the couple of inches consistent with military dignity. The Thoran captain saluted by touching his forehead, his heart, which was on the right side, and the butt of his pistol. Paul complimented him on the smart appearance of his detail, and the captain asked how it could be otherwise, with the example and inspiration of his imperial majesty. Compliment and response could have been a playback from every morning of the ten years of his reign. So could Dorflay's question: "Your Majesty will proceed to his study?"

He wanted to say, "No, to Niffelheim with it; let's get an aircar and fly a million miles somewhere," and watch the look of shocked incomprehension on the captain-general's face. He couldn't do that, though; poor old Harv Dorflay might have a heart attack. He nodded slowly.

"If you please, general."

Dorflay nodded to the Thoran captain, who nodded to his men. Four of them took two paces forward; the rest, unslinging weapons, went scurrying up the corridor, some posting themselves along the way and the rest continuing to the main hallway. The captain and two of his men started forward slowly; after they had gone twenty feet, Paul and General Dorflay fell in behind them, and the other two brought up the rear.

"Your Majesty," Dorflay said, in a low voice, "let me beg you to be most cautious. I have just discovered that there exists a treasonous plot against your life."

Paul nodded. Dorflay was more than due to discover another treasonous plot; it had been ten days since the last one.

"I believe you mentioned it, general. Something about planting loose strontium-90 in the upholstery of the Audience Throne, wasn't it?"

And before that, somebody had been trying to smuggle a fission bomb into the Palace in a wine cask, and before that, it was a booby trap in the elevator, and before that, somebody was planning to build a submachine gun into the viewscreen in the study, and –

"Oh, no, Your Majesty; that was – Well, the persons involved in that plot became alarmed and fled the planet before I could arrest them. This is something different, Your Majesty. I have learned that unauthorized alterations have been made on one of the cooking-robots in your private kitchen, and I am positive that the object is to poison Your Majesty."

They were turning into the main hallway, between the rows of portraits of past emperors, Paul and Rodrik, Paul and Rodrik, alternating over and over on both walls. He felt a smile growing on his face, and banished it.

"The robot for the meat sauces, wasn't it?" he asked.

"Why – ! Yes, Your Majesty."

"I'm sorry, general. I should have warned you. Those alterations were made by roboticists from the Ministry of Security; they were installing an adaptation of a device used in the criminalistics-labs, to insure more uniform measurements. They'd done that already for Prince Travann, the Minister, and he'd recommended it to me."

That was a shame, spoiling poor Harv Dorflay's murder plot. It had been such a nice little plot, too; he must have had a lot of fun inventing it. But a line had to be drawn somewhere. Let him turn the Palace upside down hunting for bombs; harass ladies-in-waiting whose lovers he suspected of being hired assassins; hound musicians into whose instruments he imagined firearms had been built; the emperor's private kitchen would have to be off limits.

Dorflay, who should have been looking crestfallen but relieved, stopped short – shocking breach of Court etiquette – and was staring in horror.

"Your Majesty! Prince Travann did that openly and with your consent? But, Your Majesty, I am convinced that it is Prince Travann himself who is the instigator of every one of these diabolical schemes. In the case of the elevator, I became suspicious of a man named Samml Ganner, one of Prince Travann's secret police agents. In the case of the gun in the viewscreen, it was a technician whose sister is a member of the household of Countess Yirzy, Prince Travann's mistress. In the case of the fission bomb –"

The two Thorans and their captain had kept on for some distance before they had discovered that they were no longer being followed, and were returning. He put his hand on General Dorflay's shoulder and urged him forward.

"Have you mentioned this to anybody?"

"Not a word, Your Majesty. This Court is so full of treachery that I can trust no one, and we must never warn the villain that he is suspected –"

"Good. Say nothing to anybody." They had reached the door of the study, now. "I think I'll be here until noon. If I leave earlier, I'll flash you a signal."

He entered the big oval room, lighted from overhead by the great star-map in the ceiling, and crossed to his desk, with the viewscreens and reading screens and communications screens around it, and as he sat down, he cursed angrily, first at Harv Dorflay and then, after a moment's reflection, at himself. He was the one to blame; he'd known Dorflay's paranoid condition for years. Have to do something about it. Any psychomedic would certify him; be no problem at all to have him put away. But be blasted if he'd do that. That was no way to repay loyalty, even insane loyalty. Well, he'd find a way.

He lit a cigarette and leaned back, looking up at the glowing swirl of billions of billions of tiny lights in the ceiling. At least, there were supposed to be billions of billions of them; he'd never counted them, and neither had any of the seventeen Rodriks and sixteen Pauls before him who had sat under them. His hand moved to a control button on his chair arm, and a red patch, roughly the shape of a pork chop, appeared on the western side.

That was the Empire. Every one of the thousand three hundred and sixty-five inhabited worlds, a trillion and a half intelligent beings, fourteen races – fifteen if you counted the Zarathustran Fuzzies, who were almost able to qualify under the talk-and-build-a-fire rule. And that had been the Empire when Rodrik VI had seen the map completed, and when Paul II had built the Palace, and when Stevan IV, the grandfather of Paul I, had proclaimed Odin the Imperial planet and Asgard the capital city. There had been some excuse for staying inside that patch of stars then; a newly won Empire must be consolidated within before it can safely be expanded. But that had been over eight centuries ago.

He looked at the Daily Schedule, beautifully embossed and neatly slipped under his desk glass. Luncheon on the South Upper Terrace, with the Prime Minister and the Bench of Imperial Counselors. Yes, it was time for that again; that happened as inevitably and regularly as Harv Dorflay's murder plots. And in the afternoon, a Plenary Session, Cabinet and Counselors. Was he going to have to endure the Bench of Counselors twice in the same day? Then the vexation was washed out of his face by a spreading grin. Bench of Counselors; that was the answer! Elevate Harv Dorflay to the Bench. That was what the Bench was for, a gold-plated dustbin for the disposal of superannuated dignitaries. He'd do no harm there, and a touch of outright lunacy might enliven and even improve the Bench.

And in the evening, a banquet, and a reception and ball, in honor of His Majesty Ranulf XIV, Planetary King of Durendal, and First Citizen Zhorzh Yaggo, People's Manager-in-Chief of and for the Planetary Commonwealth of Aditya. Bargain day; two planetary chiefs of state in one big combination deal. He wondered what sort of prizes he had drawn this time, and closed his eyes, trying to remember. Durendal, of course, was one of the Sword-Worlds, settled by refugees from the losing side of the System States War in the time of the old Terran Federation, who had reappeared in Galactic history a few centuries later as the Space Vikings. They all had monarchial and rather picturesque governments; Durendal, he seemed to recall, was a sort of quasi-feudalism. About Aditya he was less sure. Something unpleasant, he thought; the titles of the government and its head were suggestive.

He lit another cigarette and snapped on the reading screen to see what they had piled onto him this morning, and then swore when a graph chart, with jiggling red and blue and green lines, appeared. Chart day, too. Everything happens at once.

It was the interstellar trade situation chart from Economics. Red line for production, green line for exports, blue for imports, sectioned vertically for the ten Viceroyalties and sub-sectioned for the Prefectures, and with the magnification and focus controls he could even get data for individual planets. He didn't bother with that, and wondered why he bothered with the charts at all. The stuff was all at least twenty days behind date, and not uniformly so, which accounted for much of the jiggling. It had been transmitted from Planetary Proconsulate to Prefecture, and from Prefecture to Viceroyalty, and from there to Odin, all by ship. A ship on hyperdrive could log light-years an hour, but radio waves still had to travel 186,000 mps. The supplementary chart for the past five centuries told the real story – three perfectly level and perfectly parallel lines.

It was the same on all the other charts. Population fluctuating slightly at the moment, completely static for the past five centuries. A slight decrease in agriculture, matched by an increase in synthetic food production. A slight population movement toward the more urban planets and the more densely populated centers. A trend downward in employment – nonworking population increasing by about .0001 percent annually. Not that they were building better robots; they were just building them faster than they wore out. They all told the same story – a stable economy, a static population, a peaceful and undisturbed Empire; eight centuries, five at least, of historyless tranquility. Well, that was what everybody wanted, wasn't it?

He flipped through the rest of the charts, and began getting summarized Ministry reports. Economics had denied a request from the Mining Cartel to authorize operations on a couple of uninhabited planets; danger of local market gluts and overstimulation of manufacturing. Permission granted to Robotics Cartel to —— Request from planetary government of Durendal for increase of cereal export quotas under consideration – they wouldn't want to turn that down while King Ranulf was here. Impulsively, he punched out a combination on the communication screen and got Count Duklass, Minister of Economics.

Count Duklass had thinning red hair and a plump, agreeable, extrovert's face. He smiled and waited to be addressed.

"Sorry to bother Your Lordship," Paul greeted him. "What's the story on this export quota request from Durendal? We have their king here, now. Think he's come to lobby for it?"

Count Duklass chuckled. "He's not doing anything about it, himself. Have you met him yet, sir?"

"Not yet. He's to be presented this evening."

"Well, when you see him – I think the masculine pronoun is permissible – you'll see what I mean, sir. It's this Lord Koreff, the Marshal. He came here on business, and had to bring the king along, for fear somebody else would grab him while he was gone. The whole object of Durendalian politics, as I understand, is to get possession of the person of the king. Koreff was on my screen for half an hour; I just got rid of him. Planet's pretty heavily agricultural, they had a couple of very good crop years in a row, and now they have grain running out their ears, and they want to export it and cash in."

"Well?"

"Can't let them do it, Your Majesty. They're not suffering any hardship; they're just not making as much money as they think they ought to. If they start dumping their surplus into interstellar trade, they'll cause all kinds of dislocations on other agricultural planets. At least, that's what our computers all say."

And that, of course, was gospel. He nodded.

"Why don't they turn their surplus into whisky? Age it five or six years and it'd be on the luxury goods schedule and they could sell it anywhere."

Count Duklass' eyes widened. "I never thought of that, Your Majesty. Just a microsec; I want to make a note of that. Pass it down to somebody who could deal with it. That's a wonderful idea, Your Majesty!"

He finally got the conversation to an end, and went back to the reports. Security, as usual, had a few items above the dead level of bureaucratic procedure. The planetary king of Excalibur had been assassinated by his brother and two nephews, all three of whom were now fighting among themselves. As nobody had anything to fight with except small arms and a few light cannon, there would be no intervention. There had been intervention on Behemoth, however, where a whole continent had tried to secede from the planetary republic and the Imperial Navy had been requested to send a task force. That was all right, in both cases. No interference with anything that passed for a planetary government, but only one sovereignty on any planet with nuclear weapons, and only one supreme sovereignty in a galaxy with hyperdrive ships.

And there was rioting on Amaterasu, because of public indignation over a fraudulent election. He looked at that in incredulous delight. Why, here on Odin there hadn't been an election in the past six centuries that hadn't been utterly fraudulent. Nobody voted except the nonworkers, whose votes were bought and sold wholesale, by gangster bosses to pressure groups, and no decent person would be caught within a hundred yards of a polling place on an election day. He called the Minister of Security.

Prince Travann was a man of his own age – they had been classmates at the University – but he looked older. His thin face was lined, and his hair was almost completely white. He was at his desk, with the Sun and Cogwheel of the Empire on the wall behind him, but on the breast of his black tunic he wore the badge of his family, a silver planet with three silver moons. Unlike Count Duklass, he didn't wait to be spoken to.

"Good morning, Your Majesty."

"Good morning, Your Highness; sorry to bother you. I just caught an interesting item in your report. This business on Amaterasu. What sort of a planet is it, politically? I don't seem to recall."

"Why, they have a republican government, sir; a very complicated setup. Really, it's a junk heap. When anything goes badly, they always build something new into the government, but they never abolish anything. They have a president, a premier, and an executive cabinet, and a tricameral legislature, and two complete and distinct judiciaries. The premier is always the presidential candidate getting the next highest number of votes. In the present instance, the president, who controls the planetary militia, is accusing the premier, who controls the police, of fraud in the election of the middle house of the legislature. Each is supported by the judiciary he controls. Practically every citizen belongs either to the militia or the police auxiliaries. I am looking forward to further reports from Amaterasu," he added dryly.

"I daresay they'll be interesting. Send them to me in full, and red-star them, if you please, Prince Travann."

He went back to the reports. The Ministry of Science and Technology had sent up a lengthy one. The only trouble with it was that everything reported was duplication of work that had been done centuries before. Well, no. A Dr. Dandrik, of the physics department of the Imperial University here in Asgard announced that a definite limit of accuracy in measuring the velocity of accelerated subnucleonic particles had been established – 16.067543333 – times light-speed. That seemed to be typical; the frontiers of science, now, were all decimal points. The Ministry of Education had a little to offer; historical scholarship was still active, at least. He was reading about a new trove of source-material that had come to light on Uller, from the Sixth Century Atomic Era, when the door screen buzzed and flashed.

He lit it, and his son Rodrik appeared in it, with Snooks, the little red hound, squirming excitedly in the Crown Prince's arms. The dog began barking at once, and the boy called through the phone:

"Good morning, father; are you busy?"

"Oh, not at all." He pressed the release button. "Come on in."

Immediately, the little hound leaped out of the princely arms and came dashing into the study and around the desk, jumping onto his lap. The boy followed more slowly, sitting down in the deskside chair and drawing his foot up under him. Paul greeted Snooks first – people can wait, but for little dogs everything has to be right now – and rummaged in a drawer until he found some wafers, holding one for Snooks to nibble. Then he became aware that his son was wearing leather shorts and tall buskins.

"Going out somewhere?" he asked, a trifle enviously.

"Up in the mountains, for a picnic. Olva's going along."

And his tutor, and his esquire, and Olva's companion-lady, and a dozen Thoran riflemen, of course, and they'd be in continuous screen-contact with the Palace.

"That ought to be a lot of fun. Did you get all your lessons done?"

"Physics and math and galactiography," Rodrik told him. "And Professor Guilsan's going to give me and Olva our history after lunch."

They talked about lessons, and about the picnic. Of course, Snooks was going on the picnic, too. It was evident, though, that Rodrik had something else on his mind. After a while, he came out with it.

"Father, you know I've been a little afraid, lately," he said.

"Well, tell me about it, son. It isn't anything about you and Olva, is it?"

Rod was fourteen; the little Princess Olva thirteen. They would be marriageable in six years. As far as anybody could tell, they were both quite happy about the marriage which had been arranged for them years ago.

"Oh, no; nothing like that. But Olva's sister and a couple others of mother's ladies-in-waiting were to a psi-medium, and the medium told them that there were going to be changes. Great and frightening changes was what she said."

"She didn't specify?"

"No. Just that: great and frightening changes. But the only change of that kind I can think of would be . . . well, something happening to you."

Snooks, having eaten three wafers, was trying to lick his ear. He pushed the little dog back into his lap and pummeled him gently with his left hand.

"You mustn't let mediums' gabble worry you, son. These psi-mediums have real powers, but they can't turn them off and on like a water tap. When they don't get anything, they don't like to admit it, and they invent things. Always generalities like that; never anything specific."

"I know all that." The boy seemed offended, as though somebody were explaining that his mother hadn't really found him out in the rose garden. "But they talked about it to some of their friends, and it seems that other mediums are saying the same thing. Father, do you remember when the Haval Valley reactor blew up? All over Odin, the mediums had been talking about a terrible accident, for a month before that happened."

"I remember that." Harv Dorflay believed that somebody had been falsely informed that the emperor would visit the plant that day. "These great and frightening changes will probably turn out to be a new fad in abstract sculpture. Any change frightens most people."

They talked more about mediums, and then about aircars and aircar racing, and about the Emperor's Cup race that was to be flown in a month. The communications screen began flashing and buzzing, and after he had silenced it with the busy-button for the third time, Rodrik said that it was time for him to go, came around to gather up Snooks, and went out, saying that he'd be home in time for the banquet. The screen began to flash again as he went out.

It was Prince Ganzay, the Prime Minister. He looked as though he had a persistent low-level toothache, but that was his ordinary expression.

"Sorry to bother Your Majesty. It's about these chiefs-of-state. Count Gadvan, the Chamberlain, appealed to me, and I feel I should ask your advice. It's the matter of precedence."

"Well, we have a fixed rule on that. Which one arrived first?"

"Why, the Adityan, but it seems King Ranulf insists that he's entitled to precedence, or, rather, his Lord Marshal does. This Lord Koreff insists that his king is not going to yield precedence to a commoner."

"Then he can go home to Durendal!" He felt himself growing angry – all the little angers of the morning were focusing on one spot. He forced the harshness out of his voice. "At a court function, somebody has to go first, and our rule is order of arrival at the Palace. That rule was established to avoid violating the principle of equality to all civilized peoples and all planetary governments. We're not going to set it aside for the King of Durendal, or anybody else."

Prince Ganzay nodded. Some of the toothache expression had gone out of his face, now that he had been relieved of the decision.

"Of course, Your Majesty." He brightened a little. "Do you think we might compromise? Alternate the precedence, I mean?"

"Only if this First Citizen Yaggo consents. If he does, it would be a good idea."

"I'll talk to him, sir." The toothache expression came back. "Another thing, Your Majesty. They've both been invited to attend the Plenary Session, this afternoon."

"Well, no trouble there; they can enter by different doors and sit in visitors' boxes at opposite ends of the hall."

"Well, sir, I wasn't thinking of precedence. But this is to be an Elective Session – new Ministers to replace Prince Havaly, of Defense, deceased, and Count Frask, of Science and Technology, elevated to the Bench. There seems to be some difference of opinion among some of the Ministers and Counselors. It's very possible that the Session may degenerate into an outright controversy."

"Horrible," Paul said seriously. "I think, though, that our distinguished guests will see that the Empire can survive difference of opinion, and even outright controversy. But if you think it might have a bad effect, why not postpone the election?"

"Well – It's been postponed three times, already, sir."

"Postpone it permanently. Advertise for bids on two robot Ministers, Defense, and Science and Technology. If they're a success, we can set up a project to design a robot emperor."

The Prime Minister's face actually twitched and blanched at the blasphemy. "Your Majesty is joking," he said, as though he wanted to be reassured on the point.

"Unfortunately, I am. If my job could be robotized, maybe I could take my wife and my son and our little dog and go fishing for a while."

But, of course, he couldn't. There were only two alternatives: the Empire or Galactic anarchy. The galaxy was too big to hold general elections, and there had to be a supreme ruler, and a positive and automatic – which meant hereditary – means of succession.

"Whose opinion seems to differ from whose, and about what?" he asked.

"Well, Count Duklass and Count Tammsan want to have the Ministry of Science and Technology abolished, and its functions and personnel distributed. Count Duklass means to take over the technological sections under Economics, and Count Tammsan will take over the science part under Education. The proposal is going to be introduced at this Session by Count Guilfred, the Minister of Health and Sanity. He hopes to get some of the bio-and psychoscience sections for his own Ministry."

"That's right. Duklass gets the hide, Tammsan gets the head and horns, and everybody who hunts with them gets a cut of the meat. That's good sound law of the chase. I'm not in favor of it, myself. Prince Ganzay, at this session, I wish you'd get Captain-General Dorflay nominated for the Bench. I feel that it is about time to honor him with elevation."

"General Dorflay? But why, Your Majesty?"

"Great galaxy, do you have to ask? Why, because the man's a raving lunatic. He oughtn't even to be trusted with a sidearm, let alone five companies of armed soldiers. Do you know what he told me this morning?"

"That somebody is training a Nidhog swamp-crawler to crawl up the Octagon Tower and bite you at breakfast, I suppose. But hasn't that been going on for quite a while, sir?"

"It was a gimmick in one of the cooking robots, but that's aside from the question. He's finally named the mastermind behind all these nightmares of his, and who do you think it is? Yorn Travann!"

The Prime Minister's face grew graver than usual. Well, it was something to look grave about; some of these days –

"Your Majesty, I couldn't possibly agree more about the general's mental condition, but I really should say that, crazy or not, he is not alone in his suspicions of Prince Travann. If sharing them makes me a lunatic, too, so be it, but share them I do."

Paul felt his eyebrows lift in surprise. "That's quite too much and too little, Prince Ganzay," he said.

"With your permission, I'll elaborate. Don't think that I suspect Prince Travann of any childish pranks with elevators or viewscreens or cooking-robots," the Prime Minister hastened to disclaim, "but I definitely do suspect him of treasonous ambitions. I suppose Your Majesty knows that he is the first Minister of Security in centuries who has assumed personal control of both the planetary and municipal police, instead of delegating his *ex officio* powers.

"Your Majesty may not know, however, of some of the peculiar uses he has been making of those authorities. Does Your Majesty know that he has recruited the Security Guard up to at least ten times the strength needed to meet any conceivable peace-maintenance problem on this planet, and that he has been piling up huge quantities of heavy combat equipment – guns up to 200-millimeter, heavy contragravity, even gun-cutters and bomb-and-rocket boats? And does Your Majesty know that most of this armament is massed within fifteen minutes' flight-time of this Palace? Or that Prince Travann has at his disposal from two and a half to three times, in men and firepower, the combined strength of the Planetary Militia and the Imperial Army on this planet?"

"I know. It has my approval. He's trying to salvage some of the young nonworkers through exposing them to military discipline. A good many of them, I believe, have gone off-planet on their discharge from the SG and hired as mercenaries, which is a far better profession than vote selling."

"Quite a plausible explanation: Prince Travann is nothing if not plausible," the Prime Minister agreed. "And does Your Majesty know that, because of repeated demands for support from the Ministry of Security, the Imperial Navy has been scattered all over the Empire, and that there is not a naval craft bigger than a scout-boat within fifteen hundred light-years of Odin?"

That was absolutely true. Paul could only nod agreement. Prince Ganzay continued:

"He has been doing some peculiar things as Police Chief of Asgard, too. For instance, there are two powerful nonworkers' voting-bloc bosses, Big Moogie Blisko and Zikko the Nose – I assure Your Majesty that I am not inventing these names; that's what the persons are actually called – who have been enjoying the favor and support of Prince Travann. On a number of occasions, their smaller rivals, leaders of less important gangs, have been arrested, often on trumped-up charges, and held incommunicado until either Moogie or Zikko could move into their territories and annex their nonworker followers. These two bloc-bosses are subsidized, respectively, by the Steel and Shipbuilding Cartels and by the Reaction Products and Chemical Cartels, but actually, they are controlled by Prince Travann. They, in turn, control between them about seventy percent of the nonworkers in Asgard."

"And you think this adds up to a plot against the Throne?"

"A plot to seize the Throne, Your Majesty."

"Oh, come, Prince Ganzay! You're talking like Dorflay!"

"Hear me out, Your Majesty. His Imperial Highness is fourteen years old; it will be eleven years before he will be legally able to assume the powers of emperor. In the dreadful event of your immediate death, it would mean a regency for that long. Of course, your Ministers and Counselors would be the ones to name the Regent, but I know how they would vote with Security Guard bayonets at their throats. And regency might not be the limit of Prince Travann's ambitions."

"In your own words, quite plausible, Prince Ganzay. It rests, however, on a very questionable foundation. The assumption that Prince Travann is stupid enough to want the Throne."

He had to terminate the conversation himself and blank the screen. Viktor Ganzay was still staring at him in shocked incredulity when his image vanished. Viktor Ganzay could not imagine anybody not wanting the Throne, not even the man who had to sit on it.

He sat, for a while, looking at the darkened screen, a little worried. Viktor Ganzay had a much better intelligence service than he had believed. He wondered how much Ganzay had found out that he hadn't mentioned. Then he went back to the reports. He had gotten down to the Ministry of Fine Arts when the communications screen began calling attention to itself again.

When he flipped the switch, a woman smiled out of it at him. Her blond hair was rumpled, and she wore a dressing gown; her smile brightened as his face appeared in her screen.

"Hi!" she greeted him.

"Hi, yourself. You just get up?"

She raised a hand to cover a yawn. "I'll bet you've been up reigning for hours. Were Rod and Snooks in to see you yet?"

He nodded. "They just left. Rod's going on a picnic with Olva in the mountains." How long had it been since he and Marris had been on a picnic – a real picnic, with less than fifty guards and as many courtiers along? "Do you have much reigning to do, this afternoon?"

She grimaced. "Flower Festivals. I have to make personal tri-di appearances, live, with messages for the loving subjects. Three minutes on, and a two-minute break between. I have forty for this afternoon."

"Ugh! Well, have a good time, sweetheart. All I have is lunch with the Bench, and then this Plenary Session." He told her about Ganzay's fear of outright controversy.

"Oh, fun! Maybe somebody'll pull somebody's whiskers, or something. I'm in on that, too."

The call-indicator in front of him began glowing with the code-symbol of the Minister of Security.

"We can always hope, can't we? Well, Yorn Travann's trying to get me, now."

"Don't keep him waiting. Maybe I can see you before the Session." She made a kissing motion with her lips at him, and blanked the screen.

He flipped the switch again, and Prince Travann was on the screen. The Security Minister didn't waste time being sorry to bother him.

"Your Majesty, a report's just come in that there's a serious riot at the University; between five and ten thousand students are attacking the Administration Center, lobbing stench bombs into it, and threatening to hang Chancellor Khane. They have already overwhelmed and disarmed the campus police, and I've sent two companies of the Gendarme riot brigade, under an officer I can trust to handle things firmly but intelligently. We don't want any indiscriminate stunning or tear-gassing or shooting; all sorts of people can have sons and daughters mixed up in a student riot."

"Yes. I seem to recall student riots in which the sons of his late Highness Prince Travann and his late Majesty Rodrik XXI were involved." He deliberated the point for a moment, and added: "This scarcely sounds like a frat-fight or a panty-raid, though. What seems to have triggered it?"

"The story I got – a rather hysterical call for help from Khane himself – is that they're protesting an action of his in dismissing a faculty member. I have a couple of undercovers at the University, and I'm trying to contact them. I sent more undercovers, who could pass for students, ahead of the Gendarmes to get the student side of it and the names of the ring-leaders." He glanced down at the indicator in front of him, which had begun to glow. "If you'll pardon me, sir, Count Tammsan's trying to get me. He may have particulars. I'll call Your Majesty back when I learn anything more."

There hadn't been anything like that at the University within the memory of the oldest old grad. Chancellor Khane, he knew, was a stupid and arrogant old windbag with a swollen sense of his own importance. He made a small bet with himself that the whole thing was Khane's fault, but he wondered what lay behind it, and what would come out of it. Great plagues from little microbes start. Great and frightening changes –

The screen got itself into an uproar, and he flipped the switch. It was Viktor Ganzay again. He looked as though his permanent toothache had deserted him for the moment.

"Sorry to bother Your Majesty, but it's all fixed up," he reported. "First Citizen Yaggo agreed to alternate in precedence with King Ranulf, and Lord Koreff has withdrawn all his objections. As far as I can see, at present, there should be no trouble."

"Fine. I suppose you heard about the excitement at the University?"

"Oh, yes, Your Majesty. Disgraceful affair!"

"Simply shocking. What seems to have started it, have you heard?" he asked. "All I know is that the students were protesting the dismissal of a faculty member. He must have been exceptionally popular, or else he got a more than ordinary raw deal from Khane."

"Well, as to that, sir, I can't say. All I learned was that it was the result of some faculty squabble in one of the science departments; the grounds for the dismissal were insubordination and contempt for authority."

"I always thought that when authority began inspiring contempt, it had stopped being authority. Did you say science? This isn't going to help Duklass and Tammsan any."

"I'm afraid not, Your Majesty." Ganzay didn't look particularly regretful. "The News Cartel's gotten hold of it and are using it; it'll be all over the Empire."

He said that as though it meant something. Well, maybe it did; a lot of Ministers and almost all the Counselors spent most of their time worrying about what people on planets like Chermosh and Zarathustra and Deirdre and Quetzalcoatl might think, in ignorance of the fact that interest in Empire politics varied inversely as the square of the distance to Odin and the level of corruption and inefficiency of the local government.

"I notice you'll be at the Bench luncheon. Do you think you could invite our guests, too? We could have an informal presentation before it starts. Can do? Good. I'll be seeing you there."

When the screen was blanked, he returned to the reports, ran them off hastily to make sure that nothing had been red-starred, and called a robot to clear the projector. After a while, Prince Travann called again.

"Sorry to bother Your Majesty, but I have most of the facts on the riot, now. What happened was that Chancellor Khane sacked a professor, physics department, under circumstances which aroused resentment among the science students. Some of them walked out of class and went to the stadium to hold a protest meeting, and the thing snowballed until half the students were in it. Khane lost his head and ordered the campus police to clear the stadium; the students rushed them and swamped them. I hope, for their sakes, that none of my men ever let anything like that happen. The man I sent, a Colonel Handrosan, managed to talk the students into going back to the stadium and continuing the meeting under Gendarme protection."

"Sounds like a good man."

"Very good, Your Majesty. Especially in handling disturbances. I have complete confidence in him. He's also investigating the background of the affair. I'll give Your Majesty what he's learned, to date. It seems that the head of the physics department, a Professor Nelse Dandrik, had been conducting an experiment, assisted by a Professor Klenn Faress, to establish more accurately the velocity of subnucleonic particles, beta micropositos, I believe. Dandrik's story, as relayed to Handrosan by Khane, is that he reached a limit and the apparatus began giving erratic results."

Prince Travann stopped to light a cigarette. "At this point, Professor Dandrik ordered the experiment stopped, and Professor Faress insisted on continuing. When Dandrik ordered the apparatus dismantled, Faress became rather emotional about it – obscenely abusive and threatening, according to Dandrik. Dandrik complained to Khane, Khane ordered Faress to apologize, Faress refused, and Khane dismissed Faress. Immediately, the students went on strike. Faress confirmed the whole story, and he added one small detail that Dandrik hadn't seen fit to mention. According to him, when these micropositos were accelerated beyond sixteen and a fraction times light-speed, they began registering at the target before the source registered the emission."

"Yes, I – *What did you say?*"

Prince Travann repeated it slowly, distinctly and tonelessly.

"That was what I thought you said. Well, I'm going to insist on a complete investigation, including a repetition of the experiment. Under direction of Professor Faress."

"Yes, Your Majesty. And when that happens, I mean to be on hand personally. If somebody is just before discovering time-travel, I think Security has a very substantial interest in it."

The Prime Minister called back to confirm that First Citizen Yaggo and King Ranulf would be at the luncheon. The Chamberlain, Count Gadvan, called with a long and dreary problem about the protocol for the banquet. Finally, at noon, he flashed a signal for General Dorflay, waited five minutes, and then left his desk and went out, to find the mad general and his wirehaired soldiers drawn up in the hall.

There were more Thorans on the South Upper Terrace, and after a flurry of porting and presenting and ordering arms and hand-saluting, the Prime Minister advanced and escorted him to where the Bench of Counselors, all thirty of them, total age close to twenty-eight hundred years, were drawn up in a rough crescent behind the three distinguished guests. The King of Durendal wore a cloth-of-silver leotard and pink tights, and a belt of gold links on which he carried a jeweled dagger only slightly thicker than a knitting needle. He was slender and willowy, and he had large and soulful eyes, and the royal beautician must have worked on him for a couple of hours. Wait till Marris sees this; oh, brother!

Koreff, the Lord Marshal, wore what was probably the standard costume of Durendal, a fairly long jerkin with short sleeves, and knee-boots, and his dress dagger looked as though it had been designed for use. Lord Koreff looked as though he would be quite willing and able to use it; he was fleshy and full-faced, with hard muscles under the flesh.

First Citizen Yaggo, People's Manager-in-Chief of and for the Planetary Commonwealth of Aditya, wore a one-piece white garment like a mechanic's coveralls, with the emblem of his government and the numeral 1 on his breast. He carried no dagger; if he had worn a dress weapon, it would probably have been a slide rule. His head was completely shaven, and he had small, pale eyes and a rat-trap mouth. He was regarding the Durendalians with a distaste that was all too evidently reciprocated.

King Ranulf appeared to have won the toss for first presentation. He squeezed the Imperial hand in both of his and looked up adoringly as he professed his deep honor and pleasure. Yaggo merely clasped both his hands in front of the emblem on his chest and raised them quickly to the level of his chin, saying: "At the service of the Imperial State," and adding, as though it hurt him, "Your Imperial Majesty." Not being a chief of state, Lord Koreff came third; he merely shook hands and said, "A great honor, Your Imperial Majesty, and the thanks, both of myself and my royal master, for a most gracious reception." The attempt to grab first place having failed, he was more than willing to forget the whole subject. There was a chance that finding a way to dispose of the grain surplus might make the difference between his staying in power at home or not.

Fortunately, the three guests had already met the Bench of Counselors. Immediately after the presentation of Lord Koreff, they all started the two hundred yards march to the luncheon pavilion, the King of Durendal clinging to his left arm and First Citizen Yaggo stumping dourly on his right, with Prince Ganzay beyond him and Lord Koreff on Ranulf's left.

"Do you plan to stay long on Odin?" he asked the king.

"Oh. I'd *love* to stay for simply *months!* Everything is so *wonderful,* here in Asgard; it makes our little capital of Roncevaux seem so *utterly* provincial. I'm going to tell Your Imperial Majesty a secret. I'm going to see if I can lure some of your *wonderful* ballet dancers back to

Durendal with me. Aren't I *naughty,* raiding Your Imperial Majesty's theaters?"

"In keeping with the traditions of your people," he replied gravely. "You Sword-Worlders used to raid everywhere you went."

"I'm afraid those bad old days are long past, Your Imperial Majesty," Lord Koreff said. "But we Sword-Worlders got around the galaxy, for a while. In fact, I seem to remember reading that some of our brethren from Morglay or Flamberge even occupied Aditya for a couple of centuries. Not that you'd guess it to look at Aditya now."

It was First Citizen Yaggo's turn to take precedence – the seat on the right of the throne chair. Lord Koreff sat on Ranulf's left, and, to balance him, Prince Ganzay sat beyond Yaggo and dutifully began inquiring of the People's Manager-in-Chief about the structure of his government, launching him on a monologue that promised to last at least half the luncheon. That left the King of Durendal to Paul; for a start, he dropped a compliment on the cloth-of-silver leotard.

King Ranulf laughed dulcetly, brushed the garment with his fingertips, and said that it was just a simple thing patterned after the Durendalian peasant costume.

"You have peasants on Durendal?"

"Oh, *dear,* yes! Such quaint, *charming* people. Of course, they're all poor, and they wear such *funny* ragged clothes, and travel about in rackety old aircars, it's a wonder they don't fall apart in the air. But they're so *wonderfully* happy and carefree. I often wish I were one of them, instead of king."

"Nonworking class, Your Imperial Majesty," Lord Koreff explained.

"On Aditya," First Citizen Yaggo declared, "there are no classes, and on Aditya everybody works. 'From each according to his ability; to each according to his need.'"

"On Aditya," an elderly Counselor four places to the right of him said loudly to his neighbor, "they don't call them classes, they call them sociological categories, and they have nineteen of them. And on Aditya, they don't call them nonworkers, they call them occupational reservists, and they have more of them than we do."

"But of course, I was born a king," Ranulf said sadly and nobly. "I have a duty to my people."

"No, they don't vote at all," Lord Koreff was telling the Counselor on his left. "On Durendal, you have to pay taxes before you can vote."

"On Aditya the crime of taxation does not exist," the First Citizen told the Prime Minister.

"On Aditya," the Counselor four places down said to his neighbor, "there's nothing to tax. The state owns all the property, and if the Imperial Constitution and the Space Navy let them, the State would own all the people, too. Don't tell me about Aditya. First big-ship command I had was the old *Invictus*, 374, and she was based on Aditya for four years, and I'd sooner have spent that time in orbit around Niffelheim."

Now Paul remembered who he was; old Admiral – now Prince-Counselor – Gaklar. He and Prince-Counselor Dorflay would get along famously. The Lord Marshal of Durendal was replying to some objection somebody had made:

"No, nothing of the sort. We hold the view that every civil or political right implies a civil or political obligation. The citizen has a right to protection from the Realm, for instance; he therefore has the obligation to defend the Realm. And his right to participate in the government of the Realm includes his obligation to support the Realm financially. Well, we tax only property; if a nonworker acquires taxable property, he has to go to work to earn the taxes. I might add that our nonworkers are very careful to avoid acquiring taxable property."

"But if they don't have votes to sell, what do they live on?" a Counselor asked in bewilderment.

"The nobility supports them; the landowners, the trading barons, the industrial lords. The more nonworking adherents they have, the greater their prestige." And the more rifles they could muster when they quarreled with their fellow nobles, of course. "Beside, if we didn't do that, they'd turn brigand, and it costs less to support them than to have to hunt them out of the brush and hang them."

"On Aditya, brigandage does not exist."

"On Aditya, all the brigands belong to the Secret Police, only on Aditya they don't call them Secret Police, they call them Servants of the People, Ninth Category."

A shadow passed quickly over the pavilion, and then another. He glanced up quickly, to see two long black troop carriers, emblazoned with the Sun and Cogwheel and armored fist of Security, pass back of the Octagon Tower and let down on the north landing stage. A third followed. He rose quickly.

"Please remain seated, gentlemen, and continue with the luncheon. If you will excuse me for a moment, I'll be back directly." I hope, he added mentally.

Captain-General Dorflay, surrounded by a dozen officers, Thoran and human, had arrived on the lower terrace at the base of the Octagon Tower. They had a full Thoran rifle company with them. As he went down to them, Dorflay hurried forward.

"It has come, Your Majesty!" he said, as soon as he could make himself heard without raising his voice. "We are all ready to die with Your Majesty!"

"Oh, I doubt it'll come quite to that, Harv," he said. "But just to be on the safe side, take that company and the gentlemen who are with you and get up to the mountains and join the Crown Prince and his party. Here." He took a notepad from his belt pouch and wrote rapidly, sealing the note and giving it to Dorflay. "Give this to His Highness, and place yourself under his orders. I know; he's just a boy, but he has a good head. Obey him exactly in everything, but under no circumstances return to the Palace or allow him to return until I call you."

"Your Majesty is ordering me away?" The old soldier was aghast.

"An emperor who has a son can be spared. An emperor's son who is too young to marry can't. You know that."

Harv Dorflay was only mad on one subject, and even within the frame of his madness he was intensely logical. He nodded. "Yes, Your Imperial Majesty. We both serve the Empire as best we can. And I will guard the little Princess Olva, too." He grasped Paul's hand, said, "Farewell, Your Majesty!" and dashed away, gathering his staff and the company of Thorans as he went. In an instant, they had vanished down the nearest rampway.

The emperor watched their departure, and, at the same time, saw a big black aircar, bearing the three-mooned planet, argent on sable, of Travann, let down onto the south landing stage, and another troop carrier let down after it. Four men left the aircar – Yorn, Prince Travann, and three officers in the black of the Security Guard. Prince Ganzay had also left the table: he came from one direction as Prince Travann advanced from the other. They converged on the emperor.

"What's happening here, Prince Travann?" Prince Ganzay demanded. "Why are you bringing all these troops to the Palace?"

"Your Majesty," Prince Travann said smoothly, "I trust that you will pardon this disturbance. I'm sure nothing serious will happen, but I didn't dare take chances. The students from the University are marching on the Palace – perfectly peaceful and loyal procession; they're bringing a petition for Your Majesty – but on the way, while passing through a nonworkers' district, they were attacked by a gang of hooligans connected with a voting-bloc boss called Nutchy the Knife. None of the students were hurt, and Colonel Handrosan got the procession out of the district promptly, and then dropped some of his men, who have since been re-enforced, to deal with the hooligans. That's still going on, and these riots are like forest fires; you never know when they'll shift and get out of control. I hope the men I brought won't be needed here. Really, they're a reserve for the riot work; I won't commit them, though, until I'm sure the Palace is safe."

He nodded. "Prince Travann, how soon do you estimate that the student procession will arrive here?" he asked.

"They're coming on foot, Your Majesty. I'd give them an hour, at least."

"Well, Prince Travann, will you have one of your officers see that the public-address screen in front is ready; I'll want to talk to them when they arrive. And meanwhile, I'll want to talk to Chancellor Khane, Professor Dandrik, Professor Faress and Colonel Handrosan, together. And Count Tammsan, too; Prince Ganzay, will you please screen him and invite him here immediately?"

"Now, Your Majesty?" At first, the Prime Minister was trying to suppress a look of incredulity; then he was trying to keep from showing comprehension. "Yes, Your Majesty; at once." He frowned slightly when he saw two of the Security Güard officers salute Prince Travann instead of the emperor before going away. Then he turned and hurried toward the Octagon Tower.

The officer who had gone to the aircar to use the radio returned and reported that Colonel Handrosan was bringing the Chancellor and both professors from the University in his command-car, having anticipated that they would be wanted. Paul nodded in pleasure.

"You have a good man there, Prince," he said. "Keep an eye on him."

"I know it, Your Majesty. To tell the truth, it was he who organized this march. Thought they'd be better employed coming here to petition you than milling around the University getting into further mischief."

The other officer also returned, bringing a portable viewscreen with him on a contragravity-lifter. By this time, the Bench of Counselors and the three off-planet guests had become anxious and left the luncheon pavilion in a body. The Counselors were looking about uneasily, noticing the black uniformed Security Guards who had left the troop carrier and were taking position by squads all around the emperor. First Citizen Yaggo, and King Ranulf and Lord Koreff, also seemed uneasy. They were avoiding the proximity of Paul as though he had the green death.

The viewscreen came on, and in it the city, as seen from an aircar at two thousand feet, spread out with the Palace visible in the distance, the golden pile of the Octagon Tower jutting up from it. The car carrying the pickup was behind the procession, which was moving toward the Palace along one of the broad skyways, with Gendarmes and Security Guards leading, following and flanking. There were a few Imperial and planetary and school flags, but none of the quantity-made banners and placards which always betray a planned demonstration.

Prince Ganzay had been gone for some time, now. When he returned, he drew Paul aside.

"Your Majesty," he whispered softly, "I tried to summon Army troops, but it'll be hours before any can get here. And the Militia can't be mobilized in anything less than a day. There are only five thousand Army Regulars on Odin, now, anyhow."

And half of them officers and noncoms of skeleton regiments. Like the Navy, the Army had been scattered all over the Empire – on Behemoth and Amida and Xipetotec and Astarte and Jotunnheim – in response to calls for support from Security.

"Let's have a look at this rioting, Prince Travann," one of the less decrepit Counselors, a retired general, said. "I want to see how your people are handling it."

The officers who had come with Prince Travann consulted briefly, and then got another pickup on the screen. This must have been a regular public pickup, on the front of a tall building. It was a couple of miles farther away; the Palace was visible only as a tiny glint from the Octagon Tower, on the skyline. Half a dozen Security aircars were darting about, two of them chasing a battered civilian vehicle and firing at it. On rooftops and terraces and skyways, little clumps of Security Guards were skirmishing, dodging from cover to cover, and sometimes individuals or groups in civilian clothes fired back at them. There was a surprising absence of casualties.

"Your Majesty!" the old general hissed in a scandalized whisper. "That's nothing but a big fake! Look, they're all firing blanks! The rifles hardly kick at all, and there's too much smoke for propellant-powder."

"I noticed that." This riot must have been carefully prepared, long in advance. Yet the student riot seemed to have been entirely spontaneous. That puzzled him; he wished he knew just what Yorn Travann was up to. "Just keep quiet about it," he advised.

More aircars were arriving, big and luxurious, emblazoned with the arms of some of the most distinguished families in Asgard. One of the first to let down bore the device of Duklass, and from it the Minister of Economics, the Minister of Education, and a couple of other Ministers, alighted. Count Duklass went at once to Prince Travann, drawing him away from King Ranulf and Lord Koreff and talking to him rapidly and earnestly. Count Tammsan approached at a swift half-run.

"Save Your Majesty!" he greeted, breathlessly. "What's going on, sir? We heard something about some petty brawl at the University, that Prince Ganzay had become alarmed about, but now there seems to be fighting all over the city. I never saw anything like it; on the way here we had to go up to ten thousand feet to get over a battle, and there's a vast crowd on the Avenue of the Arts, and –" He took in the Security Guards. "Your Majesty, just what *is* going on?"

"Great and frightening changes." Count Tammsan started; he must have been to a psi-medium, too. "But I think the Empire is going to survive them. There may even be a few improvements, before things are done."

A blue-uniformed Gendarme officer approached Prince Travann, drawing him away from Count Duklass and speaking briefly to him. The Minister of Security nodded, then turned back to the Minister of Economics. They talked for a few moments longer, then clasped hands, and Travann left Duklass with his face wreathed in smiles. The Gendarme officer accompanied him as he approached.

"Your Majesty, this is Colonel Handrosan, the officer who handled the affair at the University."

"And a very good piece of work, colonel." He shook hands with him. "Don't be surprised if it's remembered next Honors Day. Did you bring Khane and the two professors?"

"They're down on the lower landing-stage, Your Majesty. We're delaying the students, to give Your Majesty time to talk to them."

"We'll see them now. My study will do." The officer saluted and went away. He turned to Count Tammsan. "That's why I asked Prince Ganzay to invite you here. This thing's become too public to be ignored; some sort of action will have to be taken. I'm going to talk to the students; I want to find out just what happened before I commit myself to anything. Well, gentlemen, let's go to my study."

Count Tammsan looked around, bewildered. "But I don't understand –" He fell into step with Paul and the Minister of Security; a squad of Security Guards fell in behind them. "I don't understand what's happening," he complained.

An emperor about to have his throne yanked out from under him, and a minister about to stage a *coup d'état,* taking time out to settle a trifling academic squabble. One thing he did understand, though, was that the Ministry of Education was getting some very bad publicity at a time when it could be least afforded. Prince Travann was telling him about the hooligans' attack on the marching students, and that worried him even more. Nonworking hooligans acted as voting-bloc bosses ordered; voting-bloc bosses acted on orders from the political manipulators of Cartels and pressure-groups, and action downward through the nonworkers was usually accompanied by action upward through influences to which ministers were sensitive.

There were a dozen Security Guards in black tunics, and as many Household Thorans in red kilts, in the hall outside the study, fraternizing amicably. They hurried apart and formed two ranks, and the Thoran officer with them saluted.

Going into the study, he went to his desk; Count Tammsan lit a cigarette and puffed nervously, and sat down as though he were afraid the chair would collapse under him. Prince Travann sank into another chair and relaxed, closing his eyes. There was a bit of wafer on the floor by Paul's chair, dropped by the little dog that morning. He stooped and picked it up, laying it on his desk, and sat looking at it until the door screen flashed and buzzed. Then he pressed the release button.

Colonel Handrosan ushered the three University men in ahead of him – Khane, with a florid, arrogant face that showed worry under the arrogance; Dandrik, grey-haired and stoop-shouldered, looking irritated; Faress, young, with a scrubby red mustache, looking bellicose. He greeted them collectively and invited them to sit, and there was a brief uncomfortable silence which everybody expected him to break.

"Well, gentlemen," he said, "we want to get the facts about this affair in some kind of order. I wish you'd tell me, as briefly and as completely as possible, what you know about it."

"There's the man who started it!" Khane declared, pointing at Faress.

"Professor Faress had nothing to do with it," Colonel Handrosan stated flatly. "He and his wife were in their apartment, packing to move out, when it started. Somebody called him and told him about the fighting at the stadium, and he went there at once to talk his students into dispersing. By that time, the situation was completely out of hand; he could do nothing with the students.

"Well, I think we ought to find out, first of all, why Professor Faress was dismissed," Prince Travann said. "It will take a good deal to convince me that any teacher able to inspire such loyalty in his students is a bad teacher, or deserves dismissal."

"As I understand," Paul said, "the dismissal was the result of a disagreement between Professor Faress and Professor Dandrik about an experiment on which they were working. I believe, an experiment to fix more exactly the velocity of accelerated subnucleonic particles. Beta micropositos, wasn't it, Chancellor Khane?"

Khane looked at him in surprise. "Your Majesty, I know nothing about that. Professor Dandrik is head of the physics department; he came to me, about six months ago, and told me that in his opinion this experiment was desirable. I simply deferred to his judgment and authorized it."

"Your Majesty has just stated the purpose of the experiment," Dandrik said. "For centuries, there have been inaccuracies in mathematical descriptions of subnucleonic events, and this experiment was undertaken in the hope of eliminating these inaccuracies." He went into a lengthy mathematical explanation.

"Yes, I understand that, professor. But just what was the actual experiment, in terms of physical operations?"

Dandrik looked helpless for a moment. Faress, who had been choking back a laugh, interrupted:

"Your Majesty, we were using the big turbo-linear accelerator to project fast micropositos down an evacuated tube one kilometer in length, and clocking them with light, the velocity of which has been established almost absolutely. I will say that with respect to the light, there were no observable inaccuracies at any time, and until the micropositos were accelerated to 16.067543333-1/3 times light-speed, they registered much as expected. Beyond that velocity, however, the target for the micropositos began registering impacts before the source registered emission, although the light target was still registering normally. I notified Professor Dandrik about this, and –"

"You notified him. Wasn't he present at the time?"

"No, Your Majesty."

"Your Majesty, I am head of the physics department of the University. I have too much administrative work to waste time on the technical aspects of experiments like this," Dandrik interjected.

"I understand. Professor Faress was actually performing the experiment. You told Professor Dandrik what had happened. What then?"

"Why, Your Majesty, he simply declared that the limit of accuracy had been reached, and ordered the experiment dropped. He then reported the highest reading before this anticipation effect was observed as the newly established limit of accuracy in measuring the velocity of accelerated micropositos, and said nothing whatever in his report about the anticipation effect."

"I read a summary of the report. Why, Professor Dandrik, did you omit mentioning this slightly unusual effect?"

"Why, because the whole thing was utterly preposterous, that's why!" Dandrik barked; and then hastily added, "Your Imperial Majesty." He turned and glared at Faress; professors do not glare at galactic emperors. "Your Majesty, the limit of accuracy had been reached. After that, it was only to be expected that the apparatus would give erratic reports."

"It might have been expected that the apparatus would stop registering increased velocity relative to the light-speed standard, or that it would begin registering disproportionately," Faress said. "But, Your Majesty, I'll submit that it was not to be expected that it would register impacts before emissions. And I'll add this. After registering this slight apparent jump into the future, there was no proportionate increase in anticipation with further increase of acceleration. I wanted to find out why. But when Professor Dandrik saw what was happening, he became almost hysterical, and ordered the accelerator shut down as though he were afraid it would blow up in his face."

"I think it has blown up in his face," Prince Travann said quietly. "Professor, have you any theory, or supposition, or even any wild guess, as to how this anticipation effect occurs?"

"Yes, Your Highness. I suspect that the apparent anticipation is simply an observational illusion, similar to the illusion of time-reversal experienced when it was first observed, though not realized, that positrons sometimes exceeded light-speed."

"Why, that's what I've been saying all along!" Dandrik broke in. "The whole thing is an illusion, due –"

"To having reached the limit of observational accuracy; I understand, Professor Dandrik. Go on, Professor Faress."

"I think that beyond 16.067543333-1/3 times light-speed, the micropositos ceased to have any velocity at all, velocity being defined as rate of motion in four-dimensional space-time. I believe they moved through the three spatial dimensions without moving at all in the fourth, temporal, dimension. They made that kilometer from source to target, literally, in nothing flat. Instantaneity."

That must have been the first time he had actually come out and said it. Dandrik jumped to his feet with a cry that was just short of being a shriek.

"He's crazy! Your Majesty, you mustn't . . . that is, well, I mean – Please, Your Majesty, don't listen to him. He doesn't know what he's saying. He's raving!"

"He knows perfectly well what he's saying, and it probably scares him more than it does you. The difference is that he's willing to face it and you aren't."

The difference was that Faress was a scientist and Dandrik was a science teacher. To Faress, a new door had opened, the first new door in eight hundred years. To Dandrik, it threatened invalidation of everything he had taught since the morning he had opened his first class. He could no longer say to his pupils, "You are here to learn from me." He would have to say, more humbly, "*We* are here to learn from the Universe."

It had happened so many times before, too. The comfortable and established Universe had fitted all the known facts – and then new facts had been learned that wouldn't fit it. The third planet of the Sol system had once been the center of the Universe, and then Terra, and Sol, and even the galaxy, had been forced to abdicate centricity. The atom had been indivisible – until somebody divided it. There had been intangible substance that had permeated the Universe, because it had been necessary for the transmission of light – until it was demonstrated to be unnecessary and nonexistent. And the speed of light had been the ultimate velocity, once, and could be exceeded no more than the atom could be divided. And light-speed had been constant, regardless of distance from source, and the Universe, to explain certain observed phenomena, had been believed to be expanding simultaneously in all directions. And the things that had happened in psychology, when psi-phenomena had become too obvious to be shrugged away.

"And then, when Dr. Dandrik ordered you to drop this experiment, just when it was becoming interesting, you refused?"

"Your Majesty, I couldn't stop, not then. But Dr. Dandrik ordered the apparatus dismantled and scrapped, and I'm afraid I lost my head. Told him I'd punch his silly old face in, for one thing."

"You admit that?" Chancellor Khane cried.

"I think you showed admirable self-restraint in not doing it. Did you explain to Chancellor Khane the importance of this experiment?"

"I tried to, Your Majesty, but he simply wouldn't listen."

"But, Your Majesty!" Khane expostulated. "Professor Dandrik is head of the department, and one of the foremost physicists of the Empire, and this young man is only one of the junior assistant-professors. Isn't even a full professor, and he got his degree from some school away off-planet. University of Brannerton on Gimli."

"Were you a pupil of Professor Vann Evaratt?" Prince Travann asked sharply.

"Why, yes, sir. I –"

"Ha, no wonder!" Dandrik crowed. "Your Majesty, that man's an out-and-out charlatan! He was kicked out of the University here ten years ago, and I'm surprised he could even get on the faculty of a school like Brannerton, on a planet like Gimli."

"Why, you stupid old fool!" Faress yelled at him. "You aren't enough of a physicist to oil robots in Vann Evaratt's lab!"

"There, Your Majesty," Khane said. "You see how much respect for authority this hooligan has!"

On Aditya, such would be unthinkable; on Aditya, everybody respects authority. Whether it's respectable or not.

Count Tammsan laughed, and he realized that he must have spoken aloud. Nobody else seemed to have gotten the joke.

"Well, how about the riot, now?" he asked. "Who started that?"

"Colonel Handrosan made an investigation on the spot," Prince Travann said. "May I suggest that we hear his report?"

"Yes indeed. Colonel?"

Handrosan rose and stood with his hands behind his back, looking fixedly at the wall behind the desk.

"Your Majesty, the students of Professor Faress' advanced subnuclear physics class, postgraduate students, all of them, were told of Professor Faress' dismissal by a faculty member who had taken over the class this morning. They all got up and walked out in a body, and gathered outdoors on the campus to discuss the matter. At the next class break, they were joined by other science students, and they went into the stadium, where they were joined, half an hour later, by more students who had learned of the dismissal in the meantime. At no time was the gathering disorderly. The stadium is covered by a viewscreen pickup which is fitted with a recording device; there is a complete audio-visual of the whole thing, including the attack on them by the campus police.

"This attack was ordered by Chancellor Khane, at about 1100; the chief of the campus police was told to clear the stadium, and when he asked if he was to use force, Chancellor Khane told him to use anything he warned to."

"I did not! I told him to get the students out of the stadium, but –"

"The chief of campus police carries a personal wire recorder," Handrosan said, in his flat monotone. "He has a recording of the order, in Chancellor Khane's own voice. I heard it myself. The police," he continued, "first tried to use gas, but the wind was against them. They then tried to use sono-stunners, but the students rushed them and overwhelmed them. If Your Majesty will permit a personal opinion, while I do not sympathize with their subsequent attack on the Administration Center, they were entirely within their rights in defending themselves in the stadium, and it's hard enough to stop trained and disciplined troops when they are winning. After defeating the police, they simply went on by what might be called the momentum of victory."

"Then you'd say that it's positively established that the students were behaving in a peaceable and orderly manner in the stadium when they were attacked, and that Chancellor Khane ordered the attack personally?"

"I would, emphatically, Your Majesty."

"I think we've done enough here, gentlemen." He turned to Count Tammsan. "This is, jointly, the affair of Education and Security. I would suggest that you and Prince Travann join in a formal and public inquiry, and until all the facts have been established and recorded and action decided upon, the dismissal of Professor Faress be reversed and he be restored to his position on the faculty."

"Yes, Your Majesty," Tammsan agreed. "And I think it would be a good idea for Chancellor Khane to take a vacation till then, too."

"I would further suggest that, as this microposito experiment is crucial to the whole question, it should be repeated. Under the personal direction of Professor Faress."

"I agree with that, Your Majesty," Prince Travann said. "If it's as important as I think it is, Professor Dandrik is greatly to be censured for ordering it stopped and for failing to report this anticipation effect."

"We'll consult about the inquiry, including the experiment, tomorrow, Your Highness," Tammsan told Travann.

Paul rose, and everybody rose with him. "That being the case, you gentlemen are all excused. The students' procession ought to be arriving, now, and I want to tell them what's going to be done. Prince Travann, Count Tammsan; do you care to accompany me?"

Going up to the central terrace in front of the Octagon Tower, he turned to Count Tammsan.

"I notice you laughed at that remark of mine about Aditya," he said. "Have you met the First Citizen?"

"Only on screen, sir. He was at me for about an hour, this morning. It seems that they are reforming the educational system on Aditya. On Aditya, everything gets reformed every ten years, whether it needs it or not. He came here to find somebody to take charge of the reformation."

He stopped short, bringing the others to a halt beside him, and laughed heartily.

"Well, we'll send First Citizen Yaggo away happy; we'll make him a present of the most distinguished educator on Odin."

"Khane?" Tammsan asked.

"Khane. Isn't it wonderful; if you have a few problems, you have trouble, but if you have a whole lot of problems, they start solving each other. We get a chance to get rid of Khane and create a vacancy that can be filled by somebody big enough to fill it; the Ministry of Education gets out from under a nasty situation; First Citizen Yaggo gets what he thinks he wants –"

"And if I know Khane and if I know the People's Commonwealth of Aditya, it won't be a year before Yaggo has Khane shot or stuffs him into jail, and then the Space Navy will have an excuse to visit Aditya, and Aditya'll never be the same afterward," Prince Travann added.

The students massed on the front lawns were still cheering as they went down after addressing them. The Security Guards were conspicuously absent and it was a detail of red-kilted Thoran riflemen who met them as they entered the hall to the Session Chamber. Prince Ganzay approached, attended by two Household Guard officers, a human and a Thoran. Count Tammsan looked from one to the other of his companions, bewildered. The bewildering thing was that everything was as it should be.

"Well, gentlemen," Paul said, "I'm sure that both of you will want to confer for a moment with your colleagues in the Rotunda before the Session. Please don't feel obliged to attend me further."

Prince Ganzay approached as they went down the hall. "Your Majesty, what *is* going on here?" he demanded querulously. "Just who is in control of the Palace – you or Prince Travann? And where is His Imperial Highness, and where is General Dorflay?"

"I sent Dorflay to join Prince Rodrik's picnic party. If you're upset about this, you can imagine what he might have done here."

Prince Ganzay looked at him curiously for a moment. "I thought I understood what was happening," he said. "Now I – This business about the students, sir; how did it come out?"

Paul told him. They talked for a while, and then the Prime Minister looked at his watch, and suggested that the Session ought to be getting started. Paul nodded, and they went down the hall and into the Rotunda.

The big semicircular lobby was empty, now, except for a platoon of Household Guards, and the Empress Marris and her ladies-in-waiting. She advanced as quickly as her sheath gown would permit, and took his arm; the ladies-in-waiting fell in behind her, and Prince Ganzay went ahead, crying: "My Lords, Your Venerable Highnesses, gentlemen; His Imperial Majesty!"

Marris tightened her grip on his arm as they started forward. "Paul!" she hissed into his ear. "What is this silly story about Yorn Travann trying to seize the Throne?"

"Isn't it? Yorn's been too close the Throne for too long not to know what sort of a seat it is. He'd commit any crime up to and including genocide to keep off it."

She gave a quick skip to get into step with him. "Then why's he filled the Palace with these blackcoats? Is Rod all right?"

"Perfectly all right; he's somewhere out in the mountains, keeping Harv Dorflay out of mischief."

They crossed the Session Hall and took their seats on the double throne; everybody sat down, and the Prime Minister, after some formalities, declared the Plenary Session in being. Almost at once, one of the Prince-Counselors was on his feet begging His Majesty's leave to interrogate the Government.

"I wish to ask His Highness the Minister of Security the meaning of all this unprecedented disturbance, both here in the Palace and in the city," he said.

Prince Travann rose at once. "Your Majesty, in reply to the question of His Venerable Highness," he began, and then launched himself into an account of the student riot, the march to petition the emperor, and the clash with the nonworking class hooligans. "As to the affair at the University, I hesitate to speak on what is really the concern of His Lordship the Minister of Education, but as to the fighting in the city, if it is still going on, I can assure His Venerable Highness that the Gendarmes and Security Guards have it well in hand; the persons responsible are being rounded up, and, if the Minister of Justice concurs, an inquiry will be started tomorrow."

The Minister of Justice assured the Minister of Security that his Ministry would be quite ready to co-operate in the inquiry. Count Tammsan then got up and began talking about the riot at the University.

"What did happen, Paul?" Marris whispered.

"Chancellor Khane sacked a science professor for being too interested in science. The students didn't like it. I think Khane's successor will rectify that. Have a good time at the Flower Festivals?"

She raised her fan to hide a grimace. "I made my schedule," she said. "Tomorrow, I have fifty more booked."

"Your Imperial Majesty!" The Counselor who had risen paused, to make sure that he had the Imperial attention, before continuing: "Inasmuch as this question also seems to involve a scientific experiment, I would suggest that the Ministry of Science and Technology is also interested and since there is at present no Minister holding that portfolio, I would suggest that the discussion be continued after a Minister has been elected."

The Minister of Health and Sanity jumped to his feet.

"Your Imperial Majesty; permit me to concur with the proposal of His Venerable Highness, and to extend it with the subproposal that the Ministry of Science and Technology be abolished, and its functions and personnel divided among the other Ministries, specifically those of Education and of Economics."

The Minister of Fine Arts was up before he was fully seated.

"Your Imperial Majesty; permit me to concur with the proposal of Count Guilfred, and to extend it further with the proposal that the Ministry of Defense, now also vacant, be likewise abolished, and its functions and personnel added to the Ministry of Security under His Highness Prince Travann."

So that was it! Marris, beside him, said, "Well!" He had long ago discovered that she could pack more meaning into that monosyllable than the average counselor could into a half-hour's speech. Prince Ganzay was thunderstruck, and from the Bench of Counselors six or eight voices were babbling loudly at once. Four Ministers were on their feet clamoring for recognition; Count Duklass of Economics was yelling the loudest, so he got it.

"Your Imperial Majesty; it would have been most unseemly in me to have spoken in favor of the proposal of Count Guilfred, being an interested party, but I feel no such hesitation in concurring with the proposal of Baron Garatt, the Minister of Fine Arts. Indeed, I consider it a most excellent proposal –"

"And I consider it the most diabolically dangerous proposal to be made in this Hall in the last six centuries!" old Admiral Gaklar shouted. "This is a proposal to concentrate all the armed force of the Empire in the hands of one man. Who can say what unscrupulous use might be made of such power?"

"Are you intimating, Prince-Counselor, that Prince Travann is contemplating some tyrannical or subversive use of such power?" Count Tammsan, of all people, demanded.

There was a concerted gasp at that; about half the Plenary Session were absolutely sure that he was. Admiral Geklar backed quickly away from the question.

"Prince Travann will not be the last Minister of Security," he said.

"What I was about to say, Your Majesty, is that as matters stand, Security has a virtual monopoly on armed power on this planet. When these disorders in the city – which Prince Travann's men are now bringing under control – broke out, there was, I am informed, an order sent out to bring Regular Army and Planetary Militia into Asgard. It will be hours before any of the former can arrive, and at least a day before the latter can even be mobilized. By the time any of them get here, there will be nothing for them to do. Is that not correct, Prince Ganzay?"

The Prime Minister looked at him angrily, stung by the realization that somebody else had a personal intelligence service as good as his own, then swallowed his anger and assented.

"Furthermore," Count Duklass continued, "the Ministry of Defense, itself, is an anachronism, which no doubt accounts for the condition in which we now find it. The Empire has no external enemies whatever; all our defense problems are problems of internal security. Let us therefore turn the facilities over to the Ministry responsible for the tasks."

The debate went on and on; he paid less and less attention to it, and it became increasingly obvious that opposition to the proposition was dwindling. Cries of, "Vote! Vote!" began to be heard from its supporters. Prince Ganzay rose from his desk and came to the throne.

"Your Imperial Majesty," he said softly. "I am opposed to this proposition, but I am convinced that enough favor it to pass it, even over Your Majesty's veto. Before the vote is called, does Your Majesty wish my resignation?"

He rose and stepped down beside the Prime Minister, putting an arm over Prince Ganzay's shoulder.

"Far from it, old friend," he said, in a distinctly audible voice. "I will have too much need for you. But, as for the proposal, I don't oppose it. I think it an excellent one; it has my approval." He lowered his voice. "As soon as it's passed, place General Dorflay's name in nomination."

The Prime Minister looked at him sadly for a moment, then nodded, returning to his desk, where he rapped for order and called for the vote.

"Well, if you can't lick them, join them," Marris said as he sat down beside her. "And if they start chasing you, just yell, 'There he goes; follow me!'"

The proposal carried, almost unanimously. Prince Ganzay then presented the name of Captain-General Dorflay for elevation to the Bench of Counselors, and the emperor decreed it. As soon as the Session was adjourned and he could do so, he slipped out the little door behind the throne, into an elevator.

In the room at the top of the Octagon Tower, he laid aside his belt and dress dagger and unfastened his tunic, than sat down in his deep chair and called a serving robot. It was the one which had brought him his breakfast, and he greeted it as a friend; it lit a cigarette for him, and poured a drink of brandy. For a long time he sat, smoking and sipping and looking out the wide window to the west, where the orange sun was firing the clouds behind the mountains, and he realized that he was abominably tired. Well, no wonder; more Empire history had been made today than in the years since he had come to the Throne.

Then something behind him clicked. He turned his head, to see Yorn Travann emerge from the concealed elevator. He grinned and lifted his drink in greeting.

"I thought you'd be a little late," he said. "Everybody trying to climb onto the bandwagon?"

Yorn Travann came forward, unbuckling his belt and laying it with Paul's; he sank into the chair opposite, and the robot poured him a drink.

"Well, do you blame them? What would it have looked like to you, in their place?"

"A *coup d'état.* For that matter, wasn't that what it was? Why didn't you tell me you were springing it?"

"I didn't spring it; it was sprung on me. I didn't know a thing about it till Max Duklass buttonholed me down by the landing stage. I'd intended fighting this proposal to partition Science and Technology, but this riot blew up and scared Duklass and Tammsan and Guilfred and the rest of them. They weren't too sure of their majority – that's why they had the election postponed a couple of times – but they were sure that the riot would turn some of the undecided Counselors against them. So they offered to back me to take over Defense in exchange for my supporting their proposal. It looked too good to pass up."

"Even at the price of wrecking Science and Technology?"

"It was wrecked, or left to rust into uselessness, long ago. The main function of Technology has been to suppress anything that might threaten this state of economic *rigor mortis* that Duklass calls stability, and the function of Science has been to let muttonheads like Khane and Dandrik dominate the teaching of science. Well, Defense has its own scientific and technical sections, and when we come to carving the bird, Duklass and Tammsan are going to see a lot of slices going onto my plate."

"And when it's all cut up, it will be discovered that there is no provision for original research. So it will please My Majesty to institute an Imperial Office of Scientific Research, independent of any Ministry, and guess who'll be named to head it."

"Faress. And, by the way, we're all set on Khane, too. First Citizen Yaggo is as delighted to have him as we are to get rid of him. Why don't we get Vann Evaratt back, and give him the job?"

"Good. If he takes charge there at the opening of the next academic year, in ten years we'll have a thousand young men, maybe ten times that many, who won't be afraid of new things and new ideas. But the main thing is that now you have Defense, and now the plan can really start firing all jets."

"Yes." Yorn Travann got out his cigarettes and lit one. Paul glanced at the robot, hoping that its feelings hadn't been hurt. "All these native uprisings I've been blowing up out of inter-tribal knife fights, and all these civil wars my people have been manufacturing; there'll be more of them, and I'll start yelling my head off for an adequate Space Navy, and after we get it, these local troubles will all stop, and then what'll we be expected to do? Scrap the ships?"

They both knew what would be done with some of them. It would have to be done stealthily, while nobody was looking, but some of those ships would go far beyond the boundaries of the Empire, and new things would happen. New worlds, new problems. Great and frightening changes.

"Paul, we agreed upon this long ago, when we were still boys at the University. The Empire stopped growing, and when things stop growing, they start dying, the death of petrifaction. And when petrifaction is complete, the cracking and the crumbling starts, and there's no way of stopping it. But if we can get people out onto new planets, the Empire won't die; it'll start growing again."

"You didn't start that thing at the University, this morning, yourself, did you?"

"Not the student riot, no. But the hooligan attack, yes. That was some of my own men. The real hooligans began looting after Handrosan had gotten the students out of the district. We collared all of them, including their boss, Nutchy the Knife, right away, and as soon as we did that, Big Moogie and Zikko the Nose tried to move in. We're cleaning them up now. By tomorrow morning there won't be one of these nonworkers' voting blocks left in Asgard, and by the end of the week they'll be cleaned up all over Odin. I have discovered a plot, and they're all involved in it."

"Wait a moment." Paul got to his feet. "That reminds me; Harv Dorflay's hiding Rod and Olva out in the mountains. I wanted him out of here while things were happening. I'll have to call him and tell him it's safe to come in, now."

"Well, zip up your tunic and put your dagger on; you look as though you'd been arrested, disarmed and searched."

"That's right." He hastily repaired his appearance and went to the screen across the room, punching out the combination of the screen with Rodrik's picnic party.

A young lieutenant of the Household Troops appeared in it, and had to be reassured. He got General Dorflay.

"Your Majesty! You are all right?"

"Perfectly all right, general, and it's quite safe to bring His Imperial Highness in. The conspiracy against the Throne has been crushed."

"Oh, thank the gods! Is Prince Travann a prisoner?"

"Quite the contrary, general. It was our loyal and devoted subject, Prince Travann, who crushed the conspiracy."

"But – But, Your Majesty – !"

"You aren't to be blamed for suspecting him, general. His agents were working in the very innermost councils of the conspirators. Every one of the people whom you suspected – with excellent reason – was actually working to defeat the plot. Think back, general; the scheme to put the gun in the viewscreen, the scheme to sabotage the elevator, the scheme to introduce assassins into the orchestra with guns built into their trumpets – every one came to your notice because of what seemed to be some indiscretion of the plotters, didn't it?"

"Why . . . why, yes, Your Majesty!" By this time tomorrow, he would have a complete set of memories for each one of them. "You mean, the indiscretions were deliberate?"

"Your vigilance and loyalty made it necessary for them to resort to these fantastic expedients, and your vigilance defeated them as fast as they came to your notice. Well, today, Prince Travann and I struck back. I may tell you, in confidence, that every one of the conspirators is dead. Killed in this afternoon's rioting – which was incited for that purpose by Prince Travann."

"Then – Then there will be no more plots against your life?" There was a note of regret in the old man's voice.

"No more, Your Venerable Highness."

"But – What did Your Majesty call me?" he asked incredulously.

"I took the honor of being the first to address you by your new title, Prince-Counselor Dorflay."

He left the old man overcome, and blubbering happily on the shoulder of the Crown Prince, who winked at his father out of the screen. Prince Travann had gotten a couple of fresh drinks from the robot and handed one to him when he returned to his chair.

"He'll be finding the Bench of Counselors riddled with treason inside a week," Travann said. "You handled that just right, though. Another case of making problems solve each other."

"You were telling me about a plot you'd discovered."

"Oh, yes: this is one to top Dorflay's best efforts. All the voting-bloc bosses on Odin are in a conspiracy to start a civil war to give them a chance to loot the planet. There isn't a word of truth in it, of course, but it'll do to arrest and hold them for a few days, and by that time some of my undercovers will be in control of every nonworker vote on the planet. After all, the Cartels put an end to competition in every other business; why not a Voting Cartel, too? Then, whenever there's an election, we just advertise for bids."

"Why, that would mean absolute control –"

"Of the nonworking vote, yes. And I'll guarantee, personally, that in five years the politics of Odin will have become so unbearably corrupt and abusive that the intellectuals, the technicians, the business people, even the nobility, will be flocking to the polls to vote, and if only half of them turn out, they'll snow the nonworkers under. And that'll mean, eventually, an end to vote-selling, and the nonworkers'll have to find work. We'll find it for them."

"Great and frightening changes." Yorn Travann laughed; he recognized the phrase. Probably started it himself. Paul lifted his glass. "To the Minister of Disturbance!"

"Your Majesty!" They drank to each other, and then Yorn Travann said, "We had a lot of wild dreams, when we were boys; it looks as though we're starting to make some of them come true. You know, when we were in the University, the students would never have done what they did today. They didn't even do it ten years ago, when Vann Evaratt was dismissed."

"And Van Evaratt's pupil came back to Odin and touched this whole thing off." He thought for a moment. "I wonder what Faress has, in that anticipation effect."

"I think I can see what can come out of it. If he can propagate a wave that behaves like those micropositos, we may not have to depend on ships for communication. We may be able, some day, to screen Baldur or Vishnu or Aton or Thor as easily as you screened Dorflay, up in the mountains." He thought silently for a moment. "I don't know whether that would be good or bad. But it would be new, and that's what matters. That's the only thing that matters."

"Flower Festivals," Paul said, and, when Yorn Travann wanted to know what he meant, he told him. "When Princess Olva's Empress, she's going to curse the name of Klenn Faress. Flower Festivals, all around the galaxy, without end."

A Slave Is a Slave

Jurgen, Prince Trevannion, accepted the coffee cup and lifted it to his lips, then lowered it. These Navy robots always poured coffee too hot; spacemen must have collapsium-lined throats. With the other hand, he punched a button on the robot's keyboard and received a lighted cigarette; turning, he placed the cup on the command-desk in front of him and looked about. The tension was relaxing in Battle-Control, the purposeful pandemonium of the last three hours dying rapidly. Officers of both sexes, in red and blue and yellow and green coveralls, were rising from seats, leaving their stations, gathering in groups. Laughter, a trifle loud; he realized, suddenly, that they had been worried, and wondered if he should not have been a little so himself. No. There would have been nothing he could have done about anything, so worry would not have been useful. He lifted the cup again and sipped cautiously.

"That's everything we can do now," the man beside him said. "Now we just sit and wait for the next move."

Like all the others, Line-Commodore Vann Shatrak wore shipboard battle-dress; his coveralls were black, splashed on breast and between shoulders with the gold insignia of his rank. His head was completely bald, and almost spherical; a beaklike nose carried down the curve of his brow, and the straight lines of mouth and chin chopped under it enhanced rather than spoiled the effect. He was getting coffee; he gulped it at once.

"It was very smart work, Commodore. I never saw a landing operation go so smoothly."

"Too smooth," Shatrak said. "I don't trust it." He looked suspiciously up at the row of viewscreens.

"It was absolutely unnecessary!"

That was young Obray, Count Erskyll, seated on the commodore's left. He was a generation younger than Prince Trevannion, as Shatrak was a generation older; they were both smooth-faced. It was odd, how beards went in and out of fashion with alternate generations. He had been worried, too, during the landing, but for a different reason from the others. Now he was reacting with anger.

"I told you, from the first, that it was unnecessary. You see? They weren't even able to defend themselves, let alone. . . ."

His personal communication-screen buzzed; he set down the coffee and flicked the switch. It was Lanze Degbrend. On the books, Lanze was carried as Assistant to the Ministerial Secretary. In practice, Lanze was his chess-opponent, conversational foil, right hand, third eye and ear, and, sometimes, trigger-finger. Lanze was now wearing the combat coveralls of an officer of Navy Landing-Troops; he had a steel helmet with a transpex visor shoved up, and there was a carbine slung over his shoulder. He grinned and executed an exaggeratedly military salute. He chuckled.

"Well, look at you; aren't you the perfect picture of correct diplomatic dress?"

"You know, sir, I'm afraid I am, for this planet," Degbrend said. "Colonel Ravney insisted on it. He says the situation downstairs is still fluid, which I take to mean that everybody is shooting at everybody. He says he has the main telecast station, in the big building the locals call the Citadel."

"Oh, good. Get our announcement out as quickly as you can. Number Five. You and Colonel Ravney can decide what interpolations are needed to fit the situation."

"Number Five; the really tough one," Degbrend considered. "I take it that by interpolations you do not mean dilutions?"

"Oh, no; don't water the drink. Spike it."

Lanze Degbrend grinned at him. Then he snapped down the visor of his helmet, unslung his carbine, and presented it. He was still standing at present arms when Trevannion blanked the screen.

"That still doesn't excuse a wanton and unprovoked aggression!" Erskyll was telling Shatrak, his thin face flushed and his voice quivering with indignation. "We came here to help these people, not to murder them."

"We didn't come here to do either, Obray," he said, turning to face the younger man. "We came here to annex their planet to the Galactic Empire, whether they wish it annexed or not. Commodore Shatrak used the quickest and most effective method of doing that. It would have done no good to attempt to parley with them from off-planet. You heard those telecasts of theirs."

"Authoritarian," Shatrak said, then mimicked pompously: "'Everybody is commanded to remain calm; the Mastership is taking action. The Convocation of the Lords-Master is in special session; they will decide how to deal with the invaders. The administrators are directed to reassure the supervisors; the overseers will keep the workers at their tasks. Any person disobeying the orders of the Mastership will be dealt with most severely.'"

"Static, too. No spaceships into this system for the last five hundred years; the Convocation – equals Parliament, I assume – hasn't been in special session for two hundred and fifty."

"Yes. I've taken over planets with that kind of government before," Shatrak said. "You can't argue with them. You just grab them by the center of authority, quick and hard."

Count Erskyll said nothing for a moment. He was opposed to the use of force. Force, he believed, was the last resort of incompetence; he had said so frequently enough since this operation had begun. Of course, he was absolutely right, though not in the way he meant. Only the incompetent wait until the last extremity to use force, and by then, it is usually too late to use anything, even prayer.

But, at the same time, he was opposed to authoritarianism, except, of course, when necessary for the real good of the people. And he did not like rulers who called themselves Lords-Master. Good democratic rulers called themselves Servants of the People. So he relapsed into silence and stared at the viewscreens.

One, from an outside pickup on the *Empress Eulalie* herself, showed the surface of the planet, a hundred miles down, the continent under them curving away to a distant sun-reflecting sea; beyond the curved horizon, the black sky was spangled with unwinking stars. Fifty miles down, the sun glinted from the three thousand foot globes of the two transport-cruisers, *Canopus* and *Mizar.*

Another screen, from *Mizar,* gave a clearer if more circumscribed view of the surface – green countryside, veined by rivers and wrinkled with mountains; little towns that were mere dots; a scatter of white clouds. Nothing that looked like roads. There had been no native sapient race on this planet, and in the thirteen centuries since it had been colonized the Terro-human population had never completely lost the use of contragravity vehicles. In that screen, farther down, the four destroyers, *Irma, Irene, Isobel* and *Iris,* were tiny twinkles.

From *Irene,* they had a magnified view of the city. On the maps, none later than eight hundred years old, it was called Zeggensburg; it had been built at the time of the first colonization under the old Terran Federation. Tall buildings, rising from wide interspaces of lawns and parks and gardens, and, at the very center, widely separated from anything else, the mass of the Citadel, a huge cylindrical tower rising from a cluster of smaller cylinders, with a broad circular landing stage above, topped by the newly raised flag of the Galactic Empire.

There was a second city, a thick crescent, to the south and east. The old maps placed the Zeggensburg spaceport there, but not a trace of that remained. In its place was what was evidently an industrial district, located where the prevailing winds would carry away the dust and smoke. There was quite a bit of both, but the surprising thing was the streets, long curved ones, and shorter ones crossing at regular intervals to form blocks. He had never seen a city with streets before, and he doubted if anybody else on the Empire ships had. Long boulevards to give unobstructed passage to low-level air-traffic, of course, and short winding walkways, but not things like these. Pictures, of course, of native cities on planets colonized at the time of the Federation, and even very ancient ones of cities on pre-Atomic Terra. But these people had contragravity; the towering, wide-spaced city beside this cross-gridded anachronism proved that.

They knew so little about this planet which they had come to bring under Imperial rule. It had been colonized thirteen centuries ago, during the last burst of expansion before the System States War and the disintegration of the Terran Federation, and it had been named Aditya, in the fashion of the times, for some forgotten deity of some obscure and ancient polytheism. A century or so later, it had seceded from or been abandoned by the Federation, then breaking up. That much they had gleaned from old Federation records still existing on Baldur. After that, darkness, lighted only by a brief flicker when more records had turned up on Morglay.

Morglay was one of the Sword-Worlds, settled by refugee rebels from the System States planets. Mostly they had been soldiers and spacemen; there had been many women with them, and many were skilled technicians, engineers, scientists. They had managed to carry off considerable equipment with them, and for three centuries they had lived in isolation, spreading over a dozen hitherto undiscovered planets. Excalibur, Tizona, Gram, Morglay, Durendal, Flamberge, Curtana, Quernbiter; the names were a roll-call of fabulous blades of Old Terran legend.

Then they had erupted, suddenly and calamitously, into what was left of the Terran Federation as the Space Vikings, carrying pillage and destruction, until the newborn Empire rose to vanquish them. In the sixth Century Pre-Empire, one of their fleets had come from Morglay to Aditya.

The Adityans of that time had been near-barbarians; the descendants of the original settlers had been serfs of other barbarians who had come as mercenaries in the service of one or another of the local chieftains and had remained to loot and rule. Subjugating them had been easy; the Space Vikings had taken Aditya and made it their home. For several centuries, there had been communication between them and their home planet. Then Morglay had become involved in one of the interplanetary dynastic wars that had begun the decadence of the Space Vikings, and again Aditya dropped out of history.

Until this morning, when history returned in the black ships of the Galactic Empire.

He stubbed out the cigarette and summoned the robot to give him another. Shatrak was speaking:

"You see, Count Erskyll, we really had to do it this way, for their own good." He wouldn't have credited the commodore with such guile; anything was justified, according to Obray of Erskyll, if done for somebody else's good. "What we did, we just landed suddenly, knocked out their army, seized the center of government, before anybody could do anything. If we'd landed the way you'd wanted us to, somebody would have resisted, and the next thing, we'd have had to kill about five or six thousand of them and blow down a couple of towns, and we'd have lost a lot of our own people doing it. You might say, we had to do it to save them from themselves."

Obray of Erskyll seemed to have doubts, but before he could articulate them, Shatrak's communication-screen was calling attention to itself. The commodore flicked the switch, and his executive officer, Captain Patrique Morvill, appeared in it.

"We've just gotten reports, sir, that some of Ravney's people have captured a half-dozen missile-launching sites around the city. His air-reconn tells him that that's the lot of them. I have an officer of one of the parties that participated. You ought to hear what he has to say, sir."

"Well, good!" Vann Shatrak whooshed out his breath. "I don't mind admitting, I was a little on edge about that."

"Wait till you hear what Lieutenant Carmath has to say." Morvill seemed to be strangling a laugh. "Ready for him, Commodore?"

Shatrak nodded; Morvill made a hand-signal and vanished in a flicker of rainbow colors; when the screen cleared, a young Landing-Troop lieutenant in battle-dress was looking out of it. He saluted and gave his name, rank and unit.

"This missile-launching site I'm occupying, sir; it's twenty miles northwest of the city. We took it thirty minutes ago; no resistance whatever. There are four hundred or so people here. Of them, twelve, one dozen, are soldiers. The rest are civilians. Ten enlisted men, a non-com of some sort, and something that appears to be an officer. The officer had a pistol, fully loaded. The non-com had a submachine gun, empty, with two loaded clips on his belt. The privates had rifles, empty, and no ammunition. The officer did not know where the rifle ammunition was stored."

Shatrak swore. The second lieutenant nodded. "Exactly my comment when he told me, sir. But this place is beautifully kept up. Lawns all mowed, trees neatly pruned, everything policed up like inspection morning. And there is a headquarters office building here adequate for an army division. . . ."

"How about the armament, Lieutenant?" Shatrak asked with forced patience.

"Ah, yes; the armament, sir. There are eight big launching cradles for panplanetary or off-planet missiles. They are all polished up like the Crown Jewels. But none, repeat none, of them is operative. And there is not a single missile on the installation."

Shatrak's facial control didn't slip. It merely intensified, which amounted to the same thing.

"Lieutenant Carmath, I am morally certain I heard you correctly, but let's just check. You said. . . ."

He repeated the lieutenant back, almost word for word. Carmath nodded.

"That was it, sir. The missile-crypts are stacked full of old photoprints and recording and microfilm spools. The sighting-and-guidance systems for all the launchers are completely missing. The letoff mechanisms all lack major parts. There is an elaborate set of detection equipment, which will detect absolutely nothing. I saw a few pairs of binoculars about; I suspect that that is what we were first observed with."

"This office, now; I suppose all the paperwork is up to the minute in quintulplicate, and initialed by everybody within sight or hearing?"

"I haven't checked on that yet, sir. If you're thinking of betting on it, please don't expect me to cover you, though."

"Well, thank you, Lieutenant Carmath. Stick around; I'm sending down a tech-intelligence crew to look at what's left of the place. While you're waiting, you might sort out whoever seems to be in charge and find out just what in Nifflheim he thinks that launching-station was maintained for."

"I think I can tell you that, now, Commodore," Prince Trevannion said as Shatrak blanked the screen. "We have a petrified authoritarianism. Quite likely some sort of an oligarchy; I'd guess that this Convocation thing they talk about consists of all the ruling class, everybody has equal voice, and nobody will take the responsibility for doing anything. And the actual work of government is probably handled by a corps of bureaucrats entrenched in their jobs, unwilling to exert any effort and afraid to invite any criticism, and living only to retire on their pensions. I've seen governments like that before." He named a few. "One thing; once a government like that has been bludgeoned into the Empire, it rarely makes any trouble later."

"Just to judge by this missileless non-launching station," Shatrak said, "they couldn't even decide on what kind of trouble to make, or how to start it. I think you're going to have a nice easy Proconsulate here, Count Erskyll."

Count Erskyll started to say something. No doubt he was about to tell Shatrak, cuttingly, that he didn't want an easy Proconsulate, but an opportunity to help these people. He was saved from this by the buzzing of Shatrak's communication-screen.

It was Colonel Pyairr Ravney, the Navy Landing-Troop commander. Like everybody else who had gone down to Zeggensburg, he was in battle-dress and armed; the transpex visor of his helmet was pushed up. Between Shatrak's generation and Count Erskyll's, he sported a pointed mustache and a spiky chin-beard, which, on his thin and dark-eyed face, looked distinctly Mephistophelean. He was grinning.

"Well, sir, I think we can call it a done job," he said. "There's a delegation here who want to talk to the Lords-Master of the ships on behalf of the Lords-Master of the Convocation. Two of them, with about a dozen portfolio-bearers and note-takers. I'm not too good in Lingua Terra, outside Basic, at best, and their brand is far from that. I gather that they're some kind of civil-servants, personal representatives of the top Lords-Master."

"Do we want to talk to them?" Shatrak asked.

"Well, we should only talk to the actual, titular, heads of the government – Mastership," Erskyll, suddenly protocol-conscious, objected. "We can't negotiate with subordinates."

"Oh, who's talking about negotiating; there isn't anything to negotiate. Aditya is now a part of the Galactic Empire. If this present regime assents to that, they can stay in power. If not, we will toss them out and install a new government. We will receive this delegation, inform them to that effect, and send them back to relay the information to their Lords-Master." He turned to the Commodore. "May I speak to Colonel Ravney?"

Shatrak assented. He asked Ravney where these Lords-Master were.

"Here in the Citadel, in what they call the Convocation Chamber. Close to a thousand of them, screaming recriminations at one another. Sounds like feeding time at the Imperial Zoo. I think they all want to surrender, but nobody dares propose it first. I've just put a cordon around it and placed it off limits to everybody. And everything outside off limits to the Convocation."

"Well thought of, Colonel. I suppose the Citadel teems with bureaucrats and such low life-forms?"

"Bulging with them. Literally thousands. Lanze Degbrend and Commander Douvrin and a few others are trying to get some sensible answers out of some of them."

"This delegation; how had you thought of sending them up?"

"Landing-craft to *Isobel*; *Isobel* will bring them the rest of the way."

He looked at his watch. "Well, don't be in too much of a rush to get them here, Colonel. We don't want them till after lunch. Delay them on *Isobel*; the skipper can see that they have their own lunch aboard. And entertain them with some educational films. Something to convince them that there is slightly more to the Empire than one ship-of-the-line, two cruisers and four destroyers."

Count Erskyll was dissatisfied about that, too. He wanted to see the delegation at once and make arrangements to talk to their superiors. Count Erskyll, among other things, was zealous, and of this he disapproved. Zealous statesmen perhaps did more mischief than anything in the Galaxy – with the possible exception of procrastinating soldiers. That could indicate the fundamental difference between statecraft and war. He'd have to play with that idea a little.

An Empire ship-of-the-line was almost a mile in diameter. It was more than a battle-craft; it also had political functions. The grand salon, on the outer zone where the curvature of the floors was less disconcerting, was as magnificent as any but a few of the rooms of the Imperial Palace at Asgard on Odin, the floor richly carpeted and the walls alternating mirrors and paintings. The movable furniture varied according to occasion; at present, it consisted of the bare desk at which they sat, the three chairs they occupied, and the three secretary-robots, their rectangular black casts blazened with the Sun and Cogwheel of the Empire. It faced the door, at the far end of the room; on either side, a rank of spacemen, in dress uniform and under arms, stood.

In principle, annexing a planet to the Empire was simplicity itself, but like so many things simple in principle, it was apt to be complicated in practice, and to this, he suspected, the present instance would be no exception.

In principle, one simply informed the planetary government that it was now subject to the sovereignty of his Imperial Majesty, the Galactic Emperor. This information was always conveyed by a Ministerial Secretary, directly under the Prime Minister and only one more step down from the Emperor, in the present instance Jurgen, Prince Trevannion. To make sure that the announcement carried conviction, the presumedly glad tidings were accompanied by the Imperial Space Navy, at present represented by Commodore Vann Shatrak and a seven ship battle-line unit, and two thousand Imperial Landing-Troops.

When the locals had been properly convinced – with as little bloodshed as necessary, but always beyond any dispute – an Imperial Proconsul, in this case Obray, Count Erskyll, would be installed. He would by no means govern the planet. The Imperial Constitution was definite on that point; every planetary government should be sovereign as to intraplanetary affairs. The Proconsul, within certain narrow and entirely inelastic limits, would merely govern the government.

Unfortunately, Obray, Count Erskyll, appeared not to understand this completely. It was his impression that he was a torch-bearer of Imperial civilization, or something equally picturesque and metaphorical. As he conceived it, it was the duty of the Empire, as represented by himself, to make over backward planets like Aditya in the image of Odin or Marduk or Osiris or Baldur or, preferably, his own home world of Aton.

This was Obray of Erskyll's first proconsular appointment, it was due to family influence, and it was a mistake. Mistakes, of course, were inevitable in anything as large and complex as the Galactic Empire, and any institution guided by men was subject to one kind of influence or another, family influence being no worse than any other kind. In this case, the ultra-conservative Erskylls of Aton, from old Errol, Duke of

Yorvoy, down, had become alarmed at the political radicalism of young Obray, and had, on his graduation from the University of Nefertiti, persuaded the Prime Minister to appoint him to a Proconsulate as far from Aton as possible, where he would not embarrass them. Just at that time, more important matters having been gotten out of the way, Aditya had come up for annexation, and Obray of Erskyll had been named Proconsul.

That had been the mistake. He should have been sent to some planet which had been under Imperial rule for some time, where the Proconsulate ran itself in a well-worn groove, and where he could at leisure learn the procedures and unlearn some of the unrealisms absorbed at the University from professors too well insulated from the realities of politics.

There was a stir among the guards; helmet-visors were being snapped down; feet scuffed. They stiffened to attention, the great doors at the other end of the grand salon slid open, and the guards presented arms as the Adityan delegation was ushered in.

There were fourteen of them. They all wore ankle-length gowns, and they all had shaven heads. The one in the lead carried a staff and wore a pale green gown; he was apparently a herald. Behind him came two in white gowns, their empty hands folded on their breasts; one was a huge bulk of obesity with a bulging brow, protuberant eyes and a pursey little mouth, and the other was thin and cadaverous, with a skull-like, almost fleshless face. The ones behind, in dark green and pale blue, carried portfolios and slung sound-recorder cases. There was a metallic twinkle at each throat; as they approached, he could see that they all wore large silver gorgets. They came to a halt twenty feet from the desk. The herald raised his staff.

"I present the Admirable and Trusty Tchall Hozhet, personal chief-slave of the Lord-Master Olvir Nikkolon, Chairman of the Presidium of the Lords-Master's Convocation, and Khreggor Chmidd, chief-slave in office to the Lord-Master Rovard Javasan, Chief of Administration of Management of the Mastership," he said. Then he stopped, puzzled, looking from one to another of them. When his eyes fell on Vann Shatrak, he brightened.

"Are you," he asked, "the chief-slave of the chief Lord-Master of this ship?"

Shatrak's face turned pink; the pink darkened to red. He used a word; it was a completely unprintable word. So, except for a few scattered pronouns, conjunctions and prepositions, were the next fifty words he used. The herald stiffened. The two delegates behind him were aghast. The subordinate burden-bearers in the rear began looking around apprehensively.

"I," Shatrak finally managed, "am an officer of his Imperial Majesty's Space Navy. I am in command of this battle-line unit. I am *not*" – he reverted briefly to obscenity – "a slave."

"You mean, you are a Lord-Master, too?" That seemed to horrify the herald even more that the things Shatrak had been calling him. "Forgive me, Lord-Master. I did not think. . . ."

"That's right; you didn't," Shatrak agreed. "And don't call me Lord-Master again, or I'll. . . ."

"Just a moment, Commodore." He waved the herald aside and addressed the two in white gowns, shifting to Lingua Terra. "This is a ship of the Galactic Empire," he told them. "In the Empire, there are no slaves. Can you understand that?"

Evidently not. The huge one, Khreggor Chmidd, turned to the skull-faced Tchall Hozhet, saying: "Then they must all be Lords-Master." He saw the objection to that at once. "But how can one be a Lord-Master if there are no slaves?"

The horror was not all on the visitors' side of the desk, either. Obray of Erskyll was staring at the delegation and saying, "Slaves!" under his breath. Obray of Erskyll had never, in his not-too-long life, seen a slave before.

"They can't be," Tchall Hozhet replied. "A Lord-Master is one who owns slaves." He gave that a moment's consideration. "But if they aren't Lords-Master, they must be slaves, and. . . ." No. That wouldn't do, either. "But a slave is one who belongs to a Lord-Master."

Rule of the Excluded Third; evidently Pre-Atomic formal logic had crept back to Aditya. Chmidd, looking around, saw the ranks of spacemen on either side, now at parade-rest.

"But aren't they slaves?" he asked.

"They are spacemen of the Imperial Navy," Shatrak roared. "Call one a slave to his face and you'll get a rifle-butt in yours. And I shan't lift a finger to stop it." He glared at Chmidd and Hozhet. "Who had the infernal impudence to send slaves to deal with the Empire? He needs to be taught a lesson."

"Why, I was sent by the Lord-Master Olvir Nikkolon, and. . . ."

"Tchall!" Chmidd hissed at him. "We cannot speak to Lords-Master. We must speak to their chief-slaves."

"But they have no slaves," Hozhet objected. "Didn't you hear the . . . the one with the small beard . . . say so?"

"But that's ridiculous, Khreggor. Who does the work, and who tells them what to do? Who told these people to come here?"

"Our Emperor sent us. That is his picture, behind me. But we are not his slaves. He is merely the chief man among us. Do your Masters not have one among them who is chief?"

"That's right," Chmidd said to Hozhet. "In the Convocation, your Lord-Master is chief, and in the Mastership, my Lord-Master, Rovard Javasan, is chief."

"But they don't tell the other Lords-Master what to do. In Convocation, the other Lords-Master tell them. . . ."

"That's what I meant about an oligarchy," he whispered, in Imperial, to Erskyll.

"Suppose we tell Ravney to herd these Lords-Master onto a couple of landing-craft and bring them up here?" Shatrak suggested. He made the suggestion in Lingua Terra Basic, and loudly.

"I think we can manage without that." He raised his voice, speaking in Lingua Terra Basic:

"It does not matter whether these slaves talk to us or not. This planet is now under the rule of his Imperial Majesty, Rodrik III. If this Mastership wants to govern the planet under the Emperor, they may do so. If not, we will make an end of them and set up a new government here."

He paused. Chmidd and Hozhet were looking at one another in shocked incredulity.

"Tchall, they mean it," Chmidd said. "They can do it, too."

"We have nothing more to say to you slaves," he continued. "Hereafter, we will speak directly to the Lords-Master."

"But. . . . The Lords-Master never do business directly," Hozhet said. "It is un-Masterly. Such discussions are between chief-slaves."

"This thing they call the Convocation," Shatrak mentioned. "I wonder if the members have the business done entirely through their slaves."

"Oh, no!" That shocked Chmidd into direct address. "No slave is allowed in the Convocation Chamber."

He wondered how they kept the place swept out. Robots, no doubt. Or else, what happened when the Masters weren't there didn't count.

"Very well. Your people have recorders; are they on?"

Hozhet asked Chmidd; Chmidd asked the herald, who asked one of the menials in the rear, who asked somebody else. The reply came back through the same channels; they were.

"Very well. At this time tomorrow, we will speak to the Convocation of Lords-Master. Commodore Shatrak, see to it that Colonel Ravney has them in the Convocation Chamber, and that preparations in the room are made, so that we may address them in the dignity befitting representatives of his Imperial Majesty." He turned to the Adityan slaves. "That is all. You have permission to go."

They watched the delegation back out, with the honor-guard following. When the doors had closed behind them, Shatrak ran his hand over his bald head and laughed.

"Shaved heads, every one of them. That's probably why they thought I was your slave. Bet those gorgets are servile badges, too." He touched the Knight's Star of the Order of the Empire at his throat. "Probably thought that was what this was. We would have to draw something like this!"

"They simply can't imagine anybody not being either a slave or a slave-owner," Erskyll was saying. "That must mean that there is no free non-slave-holding class at all. Universal slavery! Well, we'll have to do something about that. Proclaim total emancipation, immediately."

"Oh, no; we can't do anything like that. The Constitution won't permit us to. Section Two, Article One: *Every Empire planet shall be self-governed as to its own affairs, in the manner of its own choice, and without interference.*"

"But slavery. . . . Section Two, Article Six," Erskyll objected. *"There shall be no chattel slavery or serfdom anywhere in the Empire; no sapient being of any race whatsoever shall be the property of any being but himself."*

"That's correct," he agreed. "If this Mastership intends to remain the planetary government under the Empire, they will be obliged to abolish slavery, but they will have to do it by their own act. We cannot do it for them."

"You know what I'd do, Prince Trevannion?" Shatrak said. "I'd just heave this Mastership thing out, and set up a nice tight military dictatorship. We have the planet under martial rule now; let's just keep it that way for about five years, till we can train a new government."

That suggestion seemed to pain Count Erskyll almost as much as the existing situation.

They dined late, in Commodore Shatrak's private dining room. Beside Shatrak, Erskyll and himself, there were Lanze Degbrend, and Count Erskyll's chargé d'affaires, Sharll Ernanday, and Patrique Morvill and Pyairr Ravney and the naval intelligence officer, Commander

Andrey Douvrin. Ordinarily, he deplored serious discussion at meals, but under the circumstances it was unavoidable; nobody could think or talk of anything else. The discussion which he had hoped would follow the meal began before the soup-course.

"We have a total population of about twenty million," Lanze Degbrend reported. "A trifle over ten thousand Masters, all ages and both sexes. The remainder are all slaves."

"I find that incredible," Erskyll declared promptly. "Twenty million people, held in slavery by ten thousand! Why do they stand for it? Why don't they rebel?"

"Well, I can think of three good reasons," Douvrin said. "Three square meals a day."

"And no responsibilities; no need to make decisions," Degbrend added. "They've been slaves for seven and a half centuries. They don't even know the meaning of freedom, and it would frighten them if they did."

"Chain of command," Shatrak said. When that seemed not to convey any meaning to Erskyll, he elaborated: "We have a lot of dirty-necked working slaves. Over every dozen of them is an overseer with a big whip and a stungun. Over every couple of overseers there is a guard with a submachine gun. Over them is a supervisor, who doesn't need a gun because he can grab a handphone and call for troops. Over the supervisors, there are higher supervisors. Everybody has it just enough better than the level below him that he's afraid of losing his job and being busted back to fieldhand."

"That's it exactly, Commodore," Degbrend said. "The whole society is a slave hierarchy. Everybody curries favor with the echelon above, and keeps his eye on the echelon below to make sure he isn't being undercut. We have something not too unlike that, ourselves. Any organizational society is, in some ways, like a slave society. And everything is determined by established routine. The whole thing has simply been running on momentum for at least five centuries, and if we hadn't come smashing in with a situation none of the routines covered, it would have kept on running for another five, till everything wore out and stopped. I heard about those missile-stations, by the way. They're typical of everything here."

"That's another thing," Erskyll interrupted. "These Lords-Master are the descendants of the old Space-Vikings, and the slaves of the original inhabitants. The Space Vikings were a technologically advanced people; they had all the old Terran Federation science and technology, and a lot they developed for themselves on the Sword-Worlds."

"Well? They still had a lot of it, on the Sword-Worlds, two centuries ago when we took them over."

"But technology always drives out slavery; that's a fundamental law of socio-economics. Slavery is economically unsound; it cannot compete with power-industry, let alone cybernetics and robotics."

He was tempted to remind young Obray of Erskyll that there were no such things as fundamental laws of socio-economics; merely usually reliable generalized statements of what can more or less be depended upon to happen under most circumstances. He resisted the temptation. Count Erskyll had had enough shocks, today, without adding to them by gratuitous blasphemy.

"In this case, Obray, it worked in reverse. The Space Vikings enslaved the Adityans to hold them in subjugation. That was a politico-military necessity. Then, being committed to slavery, with a slave population who had to be made to earn their keep, they found cybernetics and robotics economically unsound."

"And almost at once, they began appointing slave overseers, and the technicians would begin training slave assistants. Then there would be slave supervisors to direct the overseers, slave administrators to direct them, slave secretaries and bookkeepers, slave technicians and engineers."

"How about the professions, Lanze?"

"All slave. Slave physicians, teachers, everything like that. All the Masters are taught by slaves; the slaves are educated by apprenticeship. The courts are in the hands of slaves; cases are heard by the chief slaves of judges who don't even know where their own courtrooms are; every Master has a team of slave lawyers. Most of the lawsuits are estate-inheritance cases; some of them have been in litigation for generations."

"What do the Lords-Master do?" Shatrak asked.

"Masterly things," Degbrend replied. "I was only down there since noon, but from what I could find out, that consists of feasting, making love to each other's wives, being entertained by slave performers, and feuding for social precedence like wealthy old ladies on Odin."

"You got this from the slaves? How did you get them to talk, Lanze?"

Degbrend and Ravney exchanged amused glances. Ravney said:

"Well, I detailed a sergeant and six privates to accompany Honorable Degbrend," Ravney said. "They. . . . How would you put it, Lanze?"

"I asked a slave a question. If he refused to answer, somebody knocked him down with a rifle-butt," Degbrend replied. "I never had to do that more than once in any group, and I only had to do it three times in all. After that, when I asked questions, I was answered promptly and fully. It is surprising how rapidly news gets around the Citadel."

"You mean you had those poor slaves beaten?" Erskyll demanded.

"Oh, no. Beating implies repeated blows. We only gave one to a customer; that was enough."

"Well, how about the army, if that's what those people in the long red-brown coats were?" Shatrak changed the subject by asking Ravney.

"All slave, of course, officers and all. What will we do about them, sir? I have about three thousand, either confined to their barracks or penned up in the Citadel. I requisitioned food for them, paid for it in chits. There were a few isolated companies and platoons that gave us something of a fight; most of them just threw away their weapons and bawled for quarter. I've segregated the former; with your approval, I'll put them under Imperial officers and noncoms for a quickie training in our tactics, and then use them to train the rest."

"Do that, Pyairr. We only have two thousand men of our own, and that's not enough. Do you think you can make soldiers out of any of them?"

"Yes, I believe so, sir. They are trained, organized and armed for civil-order work, which is what we'll need them for ourselves. In the entire history of this army, all they have done has been to overawe unarmed slaves; I am sure they have never been in combat with regular troops. They have an elaborate set of training and field regulations for the sort of work for which they were intended. What they encountered today was entirely outside those regulations, which is why they behaved as they did."

"Did you have any trouble getting cooperation from the native officers?" Shatrak asked.

"Not in the least. They cooperated quite willingly, if not always too intelligently. I simply told them that they were now the personal property of his Imperial Majesty, Rodrik III. They were quite flattered by the change of ownership. If ordered to, I believe that they would fire on their former Lords-Master without hesitation."

"You told those slaves that they . . . *belonged* . . . to the *Emperor?*"

Count Erskyll was aghast. He stared at Ravney for an instant, then snatched up his brandy-glass – the meal had gotten to that point – and drained it at a gulp. The others watched solicitously while he coughed and spluttered over it.

"Commodore Shatrak," he said sternly. "I hope that you will take severe disciplinary action; this is the most outrageous. . . ."

"I'll do nothing of the sort," Shatrak retorted. "The colonel is to be commended; did the best thing he could, under the circumstances. What are you going to do when slavery is abolished here, Colonel?"

"Oh, tell them that they have been given their freedom as a special reward for meritorious service, and then sign them up for a five year enlistment."

"That might work. Again, it might not."

"I think, Colonel, that before you do that, you had better disarm them again. You might possibly have some trouble, otherwise."

Ravney looked at him sharply. "They might not want to be free? I'd thought of that."

"Nonsense!" Erskyll declared. "Who ever heard of slaves rebelling against freedom?"

Freedom was a Good Thing. It was a Good Thing for everybody, everywhere and all the time. Count Erskyll knew it, because freedom was a Good Thing for him.

He thought, suddenly, of an old tomcat belonging to a lady of his acquaintance at Paris-on-Baldur, a most affectionate cat, who insisted on catching mice and bringing them as presents to all his human friends. To this cat's mind, it was inconceivable that anybody would not be most happy to receive a nice fresh-killed mouse.

"Too bad we have to set any of them free," Vann Shatrak said. "Too bad we can't just issue everybody new servile gorgets marked, *Personal Property of his Imperial Majesty* and let it go at that. But I guess we can't."

"Commodore Shatrak, you are joking," Erskyll began.

"I hope I am," Shatrak replied grimly.

The top landing-stage of the Citadel grew and filled the forward viewscreen of the ship's launch. It was only when he realized that the tiny specks were people, and the larger, birdseed-sized, specks vehicles, that the real size of the thing was apparent. Obray of Erskyll, beside him, had been silent. He had been looking at the crescent-shaped industrial city, like a servile gorget around Zeggensburg's neck.

"The way they've been crowded together!" he said. "And the buildings; no space between. And all that smoke! They must be using fossil-fuel!"

"It's probably too hard to process fissionables in large quantities, with what they have."

"You were right, last evening. These people have deliberately halted progress, even retrogressed, rather than give up slavery."

Halting progress, to say nothing of retrogression, was an unthinkable crime to him. Like freedom, progress was a Good Thing, anywhere, at all times, and without regard to direction.

Colonel Ravney met them when they left the launch. The top landing-stage was swarming with Imperial troops.

"Convocation Chamber's three stages down," he said. "About two thousand of them there now; been coming in all morning. We have everything set up." He laughed. "They tell me slaves are never permitted to enter it. Maybe, but they have the place bugged to the ceiling all around."

"Bugged? What with?" Shatrak asked, and Erskyll was wanting to know what he meant. No doubt he thought Ravney was talking about things crawling out of the woodwork.

"Screen pickups, radio pickups, wired microphones; you name it and it's there. I'll bet every slave in the Citadel knows everything that happens in there while it's happening."

Shatrak wanted to know if he had done anything about them. Ravney shook his head.

"If that's how they want to run a government, that's how they have a right to run it. Commander Douvrin put in a few of our own, a little better camouflaged than theirs."

There were more troops on the third stage down. They formed a procession down a long empty hallway, a few scared-looking slaves peeping from doorways at them. There were more troops where the corridor ended in great double doors, emblazoned with a straight broadsword diagonally across an eight-pointed star. Emblematology of planets conquered by the Space Vikings always included swords and stars. An officer gave a signal; the doors started to slide apart, and within, from a screen-speaker, came a fanfare of trumpets.

At first, all he could see was the projection-screen, far ahead, and the tessellated aisle stretching toward it. The trumpets stopped, and they advanced, and then he saw the Lords-Master.

They were massed, standing among benches on either side, and if anything Pyairr Ravney had understated their numbers. They all wore black, trimmed with gold; he wondered if the coincidence that these were also the Imperial colors might be useful. Queer garments, tightly fitted tunics at the top which became flowing robes below the waist, deeply scalloped at the edges. The sleeves were exaggeratedly wide; a knife or a pistol, and not necessarily a small one, could be concealed in every one. He was sure that thought had entered Vann Shatrak's mind. They were armed, not with dress-daggers, but with swords; long, straight cross-hilted broadswords. They were the first actual swords he had ever seen, except in museums or on the stage.

There was a bench of gold and onyx at the front, where, normally the seven-man Presidium sat, and in front of it were thronelike seats for the Chiefs of Managements, equivalent to the Imperial Council of Ministers. Because of the projection screen that had been installed, they had all been moved to an improvised daïs on the left. There was another daïs on the right, under a canopy of black and gold velvet, emblazoned with the gold sun and superimposed black cogwheel of the Empire. There were three thrones, for himself, Shatrak, and Erskyll, and a number of lesser but still imposing chairs for their staffs.

They took their seats. He slipped the earplug of his memophone into his left ear and pressed the stud in the middle of his Grand Star of the Order of Odin. The memophone began giving him the names of the Presidium and of the Chiefs of Managements. He wondered how many upper-slaves had been gunbutted to produce them.

"Lords and Gentlemen," he said, after he had greeted them and introduced himself and the others, "I speak to you in the name of his Imperial Majesty, Rodrik III. His Majesty will now greet you in his own voice, by recording."

He pressed a button on the arm of his chair. The screen lighted, flickered, and steadied, and the trumpets blared again. When the fanfare ended, a voice thundered:

"The Emperor speaks!"

Rodrik III compromised on the beard question with a small mustache. He wore the stern but kindly expression the best theatrical directors in Asgard had taught him; Public Face Number Three. He inclined his head slightly and stiffly, as a man wearing a seven-pound crown must.

"We greet our subjects of Aditya to the fellowship of the Empire. We have long had good reports of you, and we are happy now to speak to you. Deserve well of us, and prosper under the Sun and Cogwheel."

Another fanfare, as the image vanished. Before any of the Lords-Master could find voice, he was speaking to them:

"Well, Lords and Gentlemen, you have been welcomed into the Empire by his Majesty. I know, there hasn't been a ship in or out of this system for five centuries, and I suppose you have a great many questions to ask about the Galactic Empire. Members of the Presidium and Chiefs of Managements may address me directly; others will please address the chairman."

Olvir Nikkolon, the owner of Tchall Hozhet, was on his feet at once. He had a loose-lipped mouth and a not entirely straight nose and pale eyes that were never entirely still.

"What I want to know is; why did you people have to come here to take our planet away from us? Isn't the rest of the Galaxy big enough for you?"

"No, Lord Nikkolon. The Galaxy is not big enough for any competition of sovereignty. There must be one and only one completely sovereign power. The Terran Federation was once such a power. It failed, and vanished; you know what followed. Darkness and anarchy. We are clawing our way up out of that darkness. We will not fail. We will create a peaceful and unified Galaxy."

He talked to them, about the collapse of the old Federation, about the interstellar wars, about the Neobarbarians, about the long night. He told them how the Empire had risen on a few planets five thousand light-years away, and how it had spread.

"We will not repeat the mistakes of the Terran Federation. We will not attempt to force every planetary government into a common pattern, or dictate the ways in which they govern themselves. We will foster in every way peaceful trade and communication. But we will not again permit the plague of competing sovereignties, the condition under which war is inevitable. The first attempt to set up such a sovereignty in competition with the Empire will be crushed mercilessly, and no planet inhabited by any sapient race will be permitted to remain outside the Empire.

"Lords and Gentlemen, permit me to show you a little of what we have already accomplished, in the past three hundred years."

He pressed another button. The screen flickered, and the show started. It lasted for almost two hours; he used a handphone to interject comments and explanations. He showed them planet after planet – Marduk, where the Empire had begun, Baldur, Vishnu, Belphegor, Morglay, whence their ancestors had come, Amaterasu, Irminsul, Fafnir, finally Odin, the Imperial Planet. He showed towering cities swarming with aircars; spaceports where the huge globes of interstellar ships landed and lifted out; farms and industries; vast crowds at public celebrations; troop-reviews and naval bases and fleet-maneuvers; historical views of the battles that had created Imperial power.

"That, Lords and Gentlemen, is what you have an opportunity to bring your planet into. If you accept, you will continue to rule Aditya under the Empire. If you refuse, you will only put us to the inconvenience of replacing you with a new planetary government, which will be annoying for us and, probably, fatal for you."

Nobody said anything for a few minutes. Then Rovard Javasan, the Chief of Administration and the owner of the mountainous Khreggor Chmidd, rose.

"Lords and Gentlemen, we cannot resist anything like this," he said. "We cannot even resist the force they have here; that was tried yesterday, and you all saw what happened. Now, Prince Trevannion; just to what extent will the Mastership retain its sovereignty under the Empire?"

"To practically the same extent as at present. You will, of course, acknowledge the Emperor as your supreme ruler, and will govern subject to the Imperial Constitution. Have you any colonies on any of the other planets of this system?"

"We had a shipyard and docks on the inner moon, and we had mines on the fourth planet of this system, but it is almost airless and the colony was limited to a couple of dome-cities. Both were abandoned years ago."

"Both will be reopened before long, I daresay. We'd better make the limits of your sovereignty the orbit of the outer planet of this system. You may have your own normal-space ships, but the Empire will control all hyperdrive craft, and all nuclear weapons. I take it you are the sole government on this planet? Then no other will be permitted to compete with you."

"Well, what are they taking away from us, then?" somebody in the rear asked.

"I assume that you are agreed to accept the sovereignty of his Imperial Majesty? Good. As a matter of form, Lord Nikkolon, will you take a vote? His Imperial Majesty would be most gratified if it were unanimous."

Somebody insisted that the question would have to be debated, which meant that everybody would have to make a speech, all two thousand of them. He informed them that there was nothing to debate; they were confronted with an accomplished fact which they must accept. So Nikkolon made a speech, telling them at what a great moment in Adityan history they stood, and concluded by saying:

"I take it that it is the unanimous will of this Convocation that the sovereignty of the Galactic Emperor be acknowledged, and that we, the 'Mastership of Aditya' do here proclaim our loyal allegiance to his Imperial Majesty, Rodrik the Third. Any dissent? Then it is ordered so recorded."

Then he had to make another speech, to inform the representatives of his new sovereign of the fact. Prince Trevannion, in the name of the Emperor, delivered the well-worn words of welcome, and Lanze Degbrend got the coronet out of the black velvet bag under his arm and the Imperial Proconsul, Obray, Count Erskyll, was crowned. Erskyll's chargé d'affaires, Sharll Ernanday, produced the scroll of the Imperial Constitution, and Erskyll began to read.

Section One: The universality of the Empire. The absolute powers of the Emperor. The rules of succession. The Emperor also to be Planetary King of Odin.

Section Two: Every planetary government to be sovereign in its own internal affairs. . . . Only one sovereign government upon any planet, or within normal-space travel distance. . . . All hyperspace ships, and all nuclear weapons. . . . No planetary government shall make war . . . enter into any alliance . . . tax, regulate or restrain interstellar trade or communication. . . . Every sapient being shall be equally protected. . . .

Then he came to Article Six. He cleared his throat, raised his voice, and read:

"There shall be no chattel-slavery or serfdom anywhere in the Empire; no sapient being, of any race whatsoever, shall be the property of any being but himself."

The Convocation Chamber was silent, like a bomb with a defective fuse, for all of thirty seconds. Then it blew up with a roar. Out of the corner of his eye, he saw the doors slide apart and an airjeep, bristling with machine guns, float in and rise to the ceiling. The first inarticulate roar was followed by a Babel of voices, like a tropical cloudburst on a prefab hut. Olvir Nikkolon's mouth was working as he shouted unheard.

He pressed another of the row of buttons on the arm of his chair. Out of the screen-speaker a voice, as loud, by actual sound-meter test, as an anti-vehicle gun, thundered:

"SILENCE!"

Into the shocked stillness which it produced, he spoke, like a schoolmaster who has returned to find his room in an uproar:

"Lord Nikkolon; what is this nonsense? You are Chairman of the Presidium; is this how you keep order here? What is this, a planetary parliament or a spaceport saloon?"

"You tricked us!" Nikkolon accused. "You didn't tell us about that article when we voted. Why, our whole society is based on slavery!"

Other voices joined in:

"That's all right for you people, you have robots. . . ."

"Maybe you don't know it, but there are twenty million slaves on this planet. . . ."

"Look, you can't free slaves! That's ridiculous. A slave's a *slave!*"

"Who'll do the work? And who would they belong to? They'd have to belong to somebody!"

"What I want to know," Rovard Javasan made himself heard, is, *"how* are you going to free them?"

There was an ancient word, originating in one of the lost languages of Pre-Atomic Terra – *sixtifor.* It meant, the basic, fundamental, question. Rovard Javasan, he suspected, had just asked the sixtifor. Of course, Obray, Count Erskyll, Planetary Proconsul of Aditya, didn't realize that. He didn't even know what Javasan meant. Just free them. Commodore Vann Shatrak couldn't see much of a problem, either. He would have answered, Just free them, and then shoot down the first two or three thousand who took it seriously. Jurgen, Prince Trevannion, had no intention whatever of attempting to answer the sixtifor.

"My dear Lord Javasan, that is the problem of the Adityan Mastership. They are your slaves; we have neither the intention nor the right to free them. But let me remind you that slavery is specifically prohibited by the Imperial Constitution; if you do not abolish it immediately, the Empire will be forced to intervene. I believe, toward the last of those audio-visuals, you saw some examples of Imperial intervention."

They had. A few looked apprehensively at the ceiling, as though expecting the hellburners and planet-busters and nega-matter-bombs at any moment. Then one of the members among the benches rose.

"We don't know how we are going to do it, Prince Trevannion," he said. "We will do it, since this is the Empire law, but you will have to tell us how."

"Well, the first thing will have to be an Act of Convocation, outlawing the ownership of one being by another. Set some definite date on which the slaves must all be freed; that need not be too immediate. Then, I would suggest that you set up some agency to handle all the details. And, as soon as you have enacted the abolition of slavery, which should be this afternoon, appoint a committee, say a dozen of you, to confer with Count Erskyll and myself. Say you have your committee aboard the *Empress Eulalie* in six hours. We'll have transportation arranged by then. And let me point out, I hope for the last time, that we discuss matters directly, without intermediaries. We don't want anymore slaves, pardon, freedmen, coming aboard to talk for you, as happened yesterday."

Obray, Count Erskyll, was unhappy about it. He did not think that the Lords-Master were to be trusted to abolish slavery; he said so, on the launch, returning to the ship. Jurgen, Prince Trevannion was inclined to agree. He doubted if any of the Lords-Master he had seen were to be trusted, unassisted, to fix a broken mouse-trap.

Line-Commodore Vann Shatrak was also worried. He was wondering how long it would take for Pyairr Ravney to make useful troops out of the newly-surrendered slave soldiers, and where he was going to find contragravity to shift them expeditiously from trouble-spot to trouble-spot. Erskyll thought he was anticipating resistance on the part of the Masters, and for once he approved the use of force. Ordinarily, force was a Bad Thing, but this was a Good Cause, which justified any means.

They entertained the committee from the Convocation for dinner, that evening. They came aboard stiffly hostile – most understandably so, under the circumstances – and Prince Trevannion exerted all his copious charm to thaw them out, beginning with the pre-dinner cocktails and continuing through the meal. By the time they retired for coffee and brandy to the parlor where the conference was to be held, the Lords-ex-Masters were almost friendly.

"We've enacted the Emancipation Act," Olvir Nikkolon, who was ex officio chairman of the committee, reported. "Every slave on the planet must be free before the opening of the next Midyear Feasts."

"And when will that be?"

Aditya, he knew, had a three hundred and fifty-eight day year; even if the Midyear Feasts were just past, they were giving themselves very little time. In about a hundred and fifty days, Nikkolon said.

"Good heavens!" Erskyll began, indignantly.

"I should say so, myself," he put in, cutting off anything else the new Proconsul might have said. "You gentlemen are allowing yourselves dangerously little time. A hundred and fifty days will pass quite rapidly, and you have twenty million slaves to deal with. If you start at this moment and work continuously, you'll have a little under a second apiece for each slave."

The Lords-Master looked dismayed. So, he was happy to observe, did Count Erskyll.

"I assume you have some system of slave registration?" he continued.

That was safe. They had a bureaucracy, and bureaucracies tend to have registrations of practically everything.

"Oh, yes, of course," Rovard Javasan assured him. "That's your Management, isn't it, Sesar; Servile Affairs?"

"Yes, we have complete data on every slave on the planet," Sesar Martwynn, the Chief of Servile Management, said. "Of course, I'd have to ask Zhorzh about the details. . . ."

Zhorzh was Zhorzh Khouzhik, Martwynn's chief-slave in office.

"At least, he was my chief-slave; now you people have taken him away from me. I don't know what I'm going to do without him. For that matter, I don't know what poor Zhorzh will do, either."

"Have you gentlemen informed your chief-slaves that they are free, yet?"

Nikkolon and Javasan looked at each other. Sesar Martwynn laughed.

"They know," Javasan said. "I must say they are much disturbed."

"Well, reassure them, as soon as you're back at the Citadel," he told them. "Tell them that while they are now free, they need not leave you unless they so desire; that you will provide for them as before."

"You mean, we can keep our chief-slaves?" somebody cried.

"Yes, of course – chief-freedmen, you'll have to call them, now. You'll have to pay them a salary. . . ."

"You mean, give them money?" Ranal Valdry, the Lord Provost-Marshal demanded, incredulously. "Pay our own slaves?"

"You idiot," somebody told him, "they aren't our slaves anymore. That's the whole point of this discussion."

"But . . . but how can we pay slaves?" one of the committeemen-at-large asked. "Freedmen, I mean?"

"With money. You do have money, haven't you?"

"Of course we have. What do you think we are, savages?"

"What kind of money?"

Why, money; what did he think? The unit was the star-piece, the stelly. When he asked to see some of it, they were indignant. Nobody carried money; wasn't Masterly. A Master never even touched the stuff; that was what slaves were for. He wanted to know how it was secured, and they didn't know what he meant, and when he tried to explain their incomprehension deepened. It seemed that the Mastership issued money to finance itself, and individual Masters issued money on their personal credit, and it was handled through the Mastership Banks.

"That's Fedrig Daffysan's Management; he isn't here," Rovard Javasan said. "I can't explain it, myself."

And without his chief-slave, Fedrig Daffysan probably would not be able to, either.

"Yes, gentlemen. I understand. You have money. Now, the first thing you will have to do is furnish us with a complete list of all the slave-owners on the planet, and a list of all the slaves held by each. This will be sent back to Odin, and will be the basis for the compensation to be paid for the destruction of your property-rights in these slaves. How much is a slave worth, by the way?"

Nobody knew. Slaves were never sold; it wasn't Masterly to sell one's slaves. It wasn't even heard of.

"Well, we'll arrive at some valuation. Now, as soon as you get back to the Citadel, talk at once to your former chief-slaves, and their immediate subordinates, and explain the situation to them. This can be passed down through administrative freedmen to the workers; you must see to it that it is clearly understood, at all levels, that as long as the freedmen remain at their work they will be provided for and paid, but that if they quit your service they will receive nothing. Do you think you can do that?"

"You mean, give them everything we've been giving them now, and then pay them money?" Ranal Valdry almost howled.

"Oh, no. You pay them a fixed wage. You charge them for everything you give them, and deduct that from their wages. It will mean considerable extra bookkeeping, but outside of that I believe you'll find that things will go along much as they always did."

The Masters had begun to relax, and by the time he was finished all of them were smiling in relief. Count Erskyll, on the other hand, was almost writhing in his chair. It must be horrible to be a brilliant young Proconsul of liberal tendencies and to have to sit mute while a cynical old Ministerial Secretary, vastly one's superior in the Imperial Establishment and a distant cousin of the Emperor to boot, calmly bartered away the sacred liberties of twenty million people.

"But would that be legal, under the Imperial Constitution?" Olvir Nikkolon asked.

"I shouldn't have suggested it if it hadn't been. The Constitution only forbids physical ownership of one sapient being by another; it emphatically does not guarantee anyone an unearned livelihood."

The Convocation committee returned to Zeggensburg to start preparing the servile population for freedom, or reasonable facsimile. The chief-slaves would take care of that; each one seemed to have a list of other chief-slaves, and the word would spread from them on an each-one-call-five system. The public announcement would be postponed until the word could be passed out to the upper servile levels. A meeting with the chief-slaves in office of the various Managements was scheduled for the next afternoon.

Count Erskyll chatted with forced affability while the departing committeemen were being seen to the launch that would take them down. When the airlock closed behind them, he drew Prince Trevannion aside out of earshot of their subordinates.

"You know what you're doing?" he raged, in a hoarse whisper. "You're simply substituting peonage for outright slavery!"

"I'd call that something of a step." He motioned Erskyll into one of the small hall-cars, climbed in beside him, and lifted it, starting toward the living-area. "The Convocation has acknowledged the principle that sapient beings should not be property. That's a great deal, for one day."

"But the people will remain in servitude, you know that. The Masters will keep them in debt, and they'll be treated just as brutally. . . ."

"Oh, there will be abuses; that's to be expected. This Freedmen's Management, née Servile Management, will have to take care of that. Better make a memo to talk with this chief-freedman of Martwynn's, what's his name? Zhorzh Khouzhik; that's right, let Zhorzh do it. Employment Practices Code, investigation agency, enforcement. If he can't do the job, that's not our fault. The Empire does not guarantee every planet an honest, intelligent and efficient government; just a single one."

"But. . . ."

"It will take two or three generations. At first, the freedmen will be exploited just as they always have been, but in time there will be protests, and disorders, and each time, there will be some small improvement. A society must evolve, Obray. Let these people earn their freedom. Then they will be worthy of it."

"They should have their freedom now."

"This present generation? What do you think freedom means to them? *We don't have to work, anymore.* So down tools and let everything stop at once. *We can do anything we want to.* Let's kill the overseer. And: *Anything that belongs to the Masters belongs to us; we're Masters too, now.* No, I think it's better, for the present, to tell them that this freedom business is just a lot of Masterly funny-talk, and that things aren't really being changed at all. It will effect a considerable saving of his Imperial Majesty's ammunition, for one thing."

He dropped Erskyll at his apartment and sent the hall-car back from his own. Lanze Degbrend was waiting for him when he entered.

"Ravney's having trouble. That is the word he used," Degbrend said. In Pyairr Ravney's lexicon, trouble meant shooting. "The news of the Emancipation Act is leaking all over the place. Some of the troops in the north who haven't been disarmed yet are mutinying, and there are slave insurrections in a number of places."

"They think the Masters have forsaken them, and it's every slave for himself." He hadn't expected that to start so soon. "The announcement had better go out as quickly as possible. And I think we're going to have some trouble. You have information-taps into Count Erskyll's numerous staff? Use them as much as you can."

"You think he's going to try to sabotage this employment program of yours, sir?"

"Oh, he won't think of it in those terms. He'll be preventing me from sabotaging the Emancipation. He doesn't want to wait three generations; he wants to free them at once. Everything has to be at once for six-month-old puppies, six-year-old children, and reformers of any age."

The announcement did not go out until nearly noon the next day. In terms comprehensible to any low-grade submoron, it was emphasized that all this meant was that slaves should henceforth be called freedmen, that they could have money just like Lords-Master, and that if they worked faithfully and obeyed orders they would be given everything they were now receiving. Ravney had been shuttling troops about, dealing with the sporadic outbreaks of disorder here and there: many of these had been put down, and the rest died out after the telecast explaining the situation.

In addition, some of Commander Douvrin's intelligence people had discovered that the only source of fissionables and radioactives for the planet was a complex of uranite mines, separation plants, refineries and reaction-plants on the smaller of Aditya's two continents, Austragonia. In spite of other urgent calls on his resources, Ravney landed troops to seize these, and a party of engineers followed them down from the *Empress Eulalie* to make an inspection.

At lunch, Count Erskyll was slightly less intransigent on the subject of the wage-employment proposals. No doubt some of his advisors had been telling him what would happen if any appreciable number of Aditya's labor-force stopped work suddenly, and the wave of uprisings that had broken out before any public announcement had been made puzzled him. He was also concerned about finding a suitable building for a proconsular palace; the business of the Empire on Aditya could not be conducted long from shipboard.

Going down to the Citadel that afternoon, they found the chief-freedmen of the non-functional Chiefs of Management assembled in a large room on the fifth level down. There was a cluster of big tables and communication-screens and wired telephones in the middle, with smaller tables around them, at which freedmen in variously colored gowns sat. The ones at the central tables, a dozen and a half, all wore chief-slaves' white gowns.

Trevannion and Erskyll and Patrique Morvill and Lanze Degbrend joined these; subordinates guided the rest of the party – a couple of Ravney's officers and Erskyll's numerous staff of advisors and specialists – to distribute themselves with their opposite numbers in the Mastership. Everybody on the Adityan side seemed uneasy with these strange hermaphrodite creatures who were neither slaves nor Lords-Master.

"Well, gentlemen," Count Erskyll began, "I suppose you have been informed by your former Lords-Master of how relations between them and you will be in the future?"

"Oh, yes, Lord Proconsul," Khreggor Chmidd replied happily. "Everything will be just as before, except that the Lords-Master will be called Lords-Employer, and the slaves will be called freedmen, and anytime they want to starve to death, they can leave their Employers if they wish."

Count Erskyll frowned. That wasn't just exactly what he had hoped Emancipation would mean to these people.

"Nobody seems to understand about this money thing, though," Zhorzh Khouzhik, Sesar Martwynn's chief-freedman said. "My Lord-Master –" He slapped himself across the mouth and said, "Lord-Employer!" five times, rapidly. "My Lord-*Employer* tried to explain it to me, but I don't think he understands very clearly, himself."

"None of them do."

The speaker was a small man with pale eyes and a mouth like a rat-trap; Yakoop Zhannar, chief-freedman to Ranal Valdry, the Provost-Marshal.

"Its really your idea, Prince Trevannion," Erskyll said. "Perhaps you can explain it."

"Oh, it's very simple. You see. . . ."

At least, it had seemed simple when he started. Labor was a commodity, which the worker sold and the employer purchased; a "fair wage" was one which enabled both to operate at a profit. Everybody knew that – except here on Aditya. On Aditya, a slave worked because he was a slave, and a Master provided for him because he was a Master, and that was all there was to it. But now, it seemed, there weren't anymore Masters, and there weren't anymore slaves.

"That's exactly it," he replied, when somebody said as much. "So now, if the slaves, I mean, freedmen, want to eat, they have to work to earn money to buy food, and if the Employers want work done, they have to pay people to do it."

"Then why go to all the trouble about the money?" That was an elderly chief-freedman, Mykhyl Eschkhaffar, whose Lord-Employer, Oraze Borztall, was Manager of Public Works. "Before your ships came, the slaves worked for the Masters, and the Masters took care of the slaves, and everybody was content. Why not leave it like that?"

"Because the Galactic Emperor, who is the Lord-Master of these people, says that there must be no more slaves. Don't ask me why," Tchall Hozhet snapped at him. "I don't know, either. But they are here with ships and guns and soldiers; what can we do?"

"That's very close to it," he admitted. "But there is one thing you haven't considered. A slave only gets what his master gives him. But a free worker for pay gets money which he can spend for whatever he wants, and he can save money, and if he finds that he can make more money working for somebody else, he can quit his employer and get a better job."

"We hadn't thought of that," Khreggor Chmidd said. "A slave, even a chief-slave, was never allowed to have money of his own, and if he got hold of any, he couldn't spend it. But now. . . ." A glorious vista seemed to open in front of him. "And he can accumulate money. I don't suppose a common worker could, but an upper slave. . . . Especially a chief-slave. . . ." He slapped his mouth, and said, "Freedman!" five times.

"Yes, Khreggor." That was Ridgerd Schferts (Fedrig Daffysan; Fiscal Management). "I am sure we could all make quite a lot of money, now that we are freedmen."

Some of them were briefly puzzled; gradually, comprehension dawned. Obray, Count Erskyll, looked distressed; he seemed to be hoping, vainly, that they weren't thinking of what he suspected they were.

"How about the Mastership freedmen?" another asked. "We, here, will be paid by our Lords-Mas –. . . Lords-Employer. But everybody from the green robes down were provided for by the Mastership. Who will pay them, now?"

"Why, the Mastership, of course," Ridgerd Schferts said. "My Management – my Lord-Employer's, I mean – will issue the money to pay them."

"You may need a new printing-press," Lanze Degbrend said. "And an awful lot of paper."

"This planet will need currency acceptable in interstellar trade," Erskyll said.

Everybody looked blankly at him. He changed the subject:

"Mr. Chmidd, could you or Mr. Hozhet tell me what kind of a constitution the Mastership has?"

"You mean, like the paper you read in the Convocation?" Hozhet asked. "Oh, there is nothing at all like that. The former Lords-Master simply ruled."

No. They reigned. This servile *tammanihal* – another ancient Terran word, of uncertain origin – ruled.

"Well, how is the Mastership organized, then?" Erskyll persisted. "How did the Lord Nikkolon get to be Chairman of the Presidium, and the Lord Javasan to be Chief of Administration?"

That was very simple. The Convocation, consisting of the heads of all the Masterly families, actually small clans, numbered about twenty-five hundred. They elected the seven members of the Presidium, who drew lots for the Chairmanship. They served for life. Vacancies were filled by election on nomination of the surviving members. The Presidium appointed the Chiefs of Managements, who also served for life.

At least, it had stability. It was self-perpetuating.

"Does the Convocation make the laws?" Erskyll asked.

Hozhet was perplexed. "*Make* laws, Lord Proconsul? Oh, no. We have laws."

There were planets, here and there through the Empire, where an attitude like that would have been distinctly beneficial; planets with elective parliaments, every member of which felt himself obligated to get as many laws enacted during his term of office as possible.

"But this is dreadful; you *must* have a constitution!" Obray of Erskyll was shocked. "We will have to get one drawn up and adopted."

"We don't know anything about that at all," Khreggor Chmidd admitted. "This is something new. You will have to help us."

"I certainly will, Mr. Chmidd. Suppose you form a committee – yourself, and Mr. Hozhet, and three or four others; select them among yourselves – and we can get together and talk over what will be needed. And another thing. We'll have to stop calling this the Mastership. There are no more Masters."

"The Employership?" Lanze Degbrend dead-panned.

Erskyll looked at him angrily. "This is something," he told the chief-freedmen, "that should not belong to the Employers alone. It should belong to everybody. Let us call it the Commonwealth. That means something everybody owns in common."

"Something everybody owns, nobody owns," Mykhyl Eschkhaffar objected.

"Oh, no, Mykhyl; it will belong to everybody," Khreggor Chmidd told him earnestly. "But somebody will have to take care of it for everybody. That," he added complacently, "will be you and me and the rest of us here."

"I believe," Yakoop Zhannar said, almost smiling, "that this freedom is going to be a wonderful thing. For us."

"I don't like it!" Mykhyl Eschkhaffar said stubbornly. "Too many new things, and too much changing names. We have to call slaves freedmen; we have to call Lords Master Lords-Employer; we have to call the Management of Servile Affairs the Management for Freedmen. Now we have to call the Mastership this new name, Commonwealth. And all these new things, for which we have no routine procedures and no directives. I wish these people had never heard of this planet."

"That makes at least two of us," Patrique Morvill said, *sotto voce.*

"Well, the planetary constitution can wait just a bit," Prince Trevannion suggested. "We have a great many items on the agenda which must be taken care of immediately. For instance, there's this thing about finding a proconsular palace. . . ."

A surprising amount of work had been done at the small tables where Erskyll's staff of political and economic and technological experts had been conferring with the subordinate upper-freedmen. It began coming out during the pre-dinner cocktails aboard the *Empress Eulalie,* continued through the meal, and was fully detailed during the formal debriefing session afterward.

Finding a suitable building for the Proconsular Palace would present difficulties. Real estate was not sold on Aditya, anymore than slaves were. It was not only un-Masterly but illegal; estates were all entailed and the inalienable property of Masterly families. What was wanted was one of the isolated residential towers in Zeggensburg, far enough from the Citadel to avoid an appearance of too close supervision. The last thing anybody wanted was to establish the Proconsul in the Citadel itself. The Management of Business of the Mastership, however, had promised to do something about it. That would mean, no doubt, that the *Empress Eulalie* would be hanging over Zeggensburg, serving as Proconsular Palace, for the next year or so.

The Servile Management, rechristened Freedmen's Management, would undertake to safeguard the rights of the newly emancipated slaves. There would be an Employment Code – Count Erskyll was invited to draw that up – and a force of investigators, and an enforcement agency, under Zhorzh Khouzhik.

One of Commander Douvrin's men, who had been at the Austragonia nuclear-industries establishment, was present and reported:

"Great Ghu, you ought to see that place! They've people working in places I wouldn't send an unshielded robot, and the hospital there is bulging with radiation-sickness cases. The equipment must have been brought here by the Space Vikings. What's left of it is the damnedest mess of goldbergery I ever saw. The whole thing ought to be shut down and completely rebuilt."

Erskyll wanted to know who owned it. The Mastership, he was told.

"That's right," one of his economics men agreed. "Management of Public Works." That would be Mykhyl Eschkhaffar, who had so bitterly objected to the new nomenclature. "If anybody needs fissionables for a power-reactor or radioactives for nuclear-electric conversion, his chief business slave gets what's needed. Furthermore, doesn't even have to sign for it."

"Don't they sell it for revenue?"

"Nifflheim, no! This government doesn't need revenue. This government supports itself by counterfeiting. When the Mastership needs money, they just have Ridgerd Schferts print up another batch. Like everybody else."

"Then the money simply isn't worth anything!" Erskyll was horrified, which was rapidly becoming his normal state.

"Who cares about money, Obray," he said. "Didn't you hear them, last evening? It's un-Masterly to bother about things like money. Of course, everybody owes everybody for everything, but it's all in the family."

"Well, something will have to be done about that!"

That was at least the tenth time he had said that, this evening.

It came practically as a thunderbolt when Khreggor Chmidd screened the ship the next afternoon to report that a Proconsular Palace had been found, and would be ready for occupancy in a day or so. The chief-freedmen of the Management of Business of the Mastership and of the Lord Chief Justiciar had found one, the Elegry Palace, which had been unoccupied except for what he described as a small caretaking staff for years, while two Masterly families disputed inheritance rights and slave lawyers quibbled endlessly before a slave judge. The chief freedman of the Lord Chief Justiciar had simply summoned judge and lawyers into his office and ordered them to settle the suit at once. The settlement had consisted of paying both litigants the full value of the building; this came to fifty million stellies apiece. Arbitrarily, the stelly was assigned a value in Imperial crowns of a hundred for one. A million crowns was about what the building would be worth, with contents, on Odin. It would be paid for with a draft on the Imperial Exchequer.

"Well, you have some hard currency on the planet, now," he told Count Erskyll, while they were having a pre-dinner drink together that evening. "I hope it doesn't touch off an inflation, if the term is permissible when applied to Adityan currency."

Erskyll snapped his fingers. "Yes! And there's the money we've been spending for supplies. And when we start compensation payments. . . . Excuse me for a moment."

He dashed off, his drink in his hand. After a long interval, he was back, carrying a fresh one he had gotten from a bartending robot en route.

"Well, that's taken care of," he said. "My fiscal man's getting in touch with Ridgerd Schferts; the Elegry heirs will be paid in Adityan stellies, and the Imperial crowns will be held in the Commonwealth Bank, or, better, banked in Asgard, to give Aditya some off-planet credit. And we'll do the same with our other expenditures, and with the slave-compensation. This is going to be wonderful; this planet needs everything in the way of industrial equipment; this is how they're going to get it."

"But, Obray; the compensations are owing to the individual Masters. They should be paid in crowns. You know as well as I do that this hundred-for-one rate is purely a local fiction. On the interstellar exchange, these stellies have a crown value of precisely zero-point-zero."

"You know what would happen if these ci-devant Masters got hold of Imperial crowns," Erskyll said. "They'd only squander them back again for useless imported luxuries. This planet needs a complete modernization, and this is the only way the money to pay for it can be gotten." He was gesturing excitedly with the almost-full glass in his hand; Prince Trevannion stepped back out of the way of the splash he anticipated. "I have no sympathy for these ci-devant Masters. They own every stick and stone and pinch of dust on this planet, as it is. Is that fair?"

"Possibly not. But neither is what you're proposing to do."

Obray, Count Erskyll, couldn't see that. He was proposing to secure the Greatest Good for the Greatest Number, and to Nifflheim with any minorities who happened to be in the way.

The Navy took over the Elegry Palace the next morning, ran up the Imperial Sun and Cogwheel flag, and began transmitting views of its interior up to the *Empress Eulalie.* It was considerably smaller than the

Imperial Palace at Asgard on Odin, but room for room the furnishings were rather more ornate and expensive. By the next afternoon, the counter-espionage team that had gone down reported the Masterly living quarters clear of pickups, microphones, and other apparatus of servile snooping, of which they had found many. The *Canopus* was recalled from her station over the northern end of the continent and began sending down the proconsulate furnishings stowed aboard, including several hundred domestic robots.

The skeleton caretaking staff Chmidd had mentioned proved to number five hundred.

"What are we going to do about them?" Erskyll wanted to know. "There's a limit to the upkeep allowance for a proconsulate, and we can't pay five hundred useless servants. The chief-freedman, and about a dozen assistants, and a few to operate the robots, when we train them, but five hundred. . .!"

"Let Zhorzh do it," Prince Trevannion suggested. "Isn't that what this Freedmen's Management is for; to find employment for emancipated slaves? Just emancipate them and turn them over to Khouzhik."

Khouzhik promptly placed all of them on the payroll of his Management. Khouzhik was having his hands full. He had all his top mathematical experts, some of whom even understood the use of the slide-rule, trying to work up a scale of wages. Erskyll loaned him a few of his staff. None of the ideas any of them developed proved workable. Khouzhik had also organized a corps of investigators, and he was beginning to annex the private guard-companies of the Lords-ex-Master, whom he was organizing into a police force.

The nuclear works on Austragonia were closed down. Mykhyl Eschkhaffar ordered a program of rationing and priorities to conserve the stock of plutonium and radioactive isotopes on hand, and he decided that henceforth nuclear-energy materials would be sold instead of furnished freely. He simply found out what the market quotations on Odin were, translated that into stellies, and adopted it. This was just a base price; there would have to be bribes for priority allocations, rakeoffs for the under-freedmen, and graft for the business-freedmen of the Lords-ex-Masters who bought the stuff. The latter were completely unconcerned; none of them even knew about it.

The Convocation adjourned until the next regular session, at the Midyear Feasts, an eight-day intercalary period which permitted dividing the 358-day Adityan year into ten months of thirty-five days each. Count Erskyll was satisfied to see them go. He was working on a constitution for the Commonwealth of Aditya, and was making very little progress with it.

"It's one of these elaborate check-and-balance things," Lanze Degbrend reported. "To begin with, it was the constitution of Aton, with an elective president substituted for a hereditary king. Of course, there are a lot of added gadgets; Atonian Radical Democrat stuff. Chmidd and Hozhet and the other chief-slaves don't like it, either."

"Slap your mouth and say, 'Freedmen,' five times."

"Nuts," his subordinate retorted insubordinately. "I know a slave when I see one. A slave is a slave, with or without a gorget; if he doesn't wear it around his neck, he has it tattooed on his soul. It takes at least three generations to rub it off."

"I could wish that Count Erskyll. . . ." he began. "What else is our Proconsul doing?"

"Well, I'm afraid he's trying to set up some kind of a scheme for the complete nationalization of all farms, factories, transport facilities, and other means of production and distribution," Degbrend said.

"He's not going to try to do that himself, is he?" He was, he discovered, speaking sharply, and modified his tone. "He won't do it with Imperial authority, or with Imperial troops. Not as long as I'm here. And when we go back to Odin, I'll see to it that Vann Shatrak understands that."

"Oh, no. The Commonwealth of Aditya will do that," Degbrend said. "Chmidd and Hozhet and Yakoop Zhannar and Zhorzh Khouzhik and the rest of them, that is. He wants it done legitimately and legally. That means, he'll have to wait till the Midyear Feasts, when the Convocation assembles, and he can get his constitution enacted. If he can get it written by then."

Vann Shatrak sent two of the destroyers off to explore the moons of Aditya, of which there were two. The outer moon, Aditya-*Ba'*, was an irregular chunk of rock fifty miles in diameter, barely visible to the naked eye. The inner, Aditya-*Alif*, however, was an eight-hundred-mile sphere; it had once been the planetary ship-station and shipyard-base. It seemed to have been abandoned when the Adityan technology and economy had begun sagging under the weight of the slave system. Most of the installations remained, badly run down but repairable. Shatrak transferred as many of his technicians as he could spare to the *Mizar* and sent her to recondition the shipyard and render the underground city inhabitable again so that the satellite could be used as a base for his ships. He decided, then, to send the *Irma* back to Odin with reports of the annexation of Aditya, a proposal that Aditya-*Alif* be made a permanent Imperial naval-base, and a request for more troops.

Prince Trevannion taped up his own reports, describing the general situation on the newly annexed planet, and doing nothing to minimize the problems facing its Proconsul.

"Count Erskyll" he finished, "is doing the best possible under circumstances from which I myself would feel inclined to shrink. If not carried to excess, perhaps youthful idealism is not without value in Empire statecraft. I understand that Commodore Shatrak, who is also coping with some very trying problems, is requesting troop reinforcements. I believe this request amply justified, and would recommend that they be gotten here as speedily as possible.

"I understand that he is also recommending a permanent naval base on the larger of this planet's two satellites. This I also endorse unreservedly. It would have a most salutary effect on the local government. I would further recommend that Commodore Shatrak be placed in command of it, with suitable promotion, which he has long ago earned."

Erskyll was surprised that he was not himself returning to Odin on the destroyer, and evidently disturbed. He mentioned it during pre-dinner cocktails that evening.

"I know, my own work here is finished; was the moment the Convocation voted acknowledgment of Imperial rule." Prince Trevannion replied. "I would like to stay on for the Midyear Feasts, though. The Convocation will vote on your constitution, and I would like to be able to report their action to the Prime Minister. How is it progressing, by the way?"

"Well, we have a rough draft. I don't care much for it, myself, but Citizen Hozhet and Citizen Chmidd and Citizen Zhannar and the others are most enthusiastic, and, after all, they are the ones who will have to operate under it."

The Masterly estates would be the representative units; from each, the freedmen would elect representatives to regional elective councils, and these in turn would elect representatives to a central electoral council which would elect a Supreme People's Legislative Council. This would not only function as the legislative body, but would also elect a Manager-in-Chief, who would appoint the Chiefs of Management, who, in turn, would appoint their own subordinates.

"I don't like it, myself," Erskyll said. "It's not democratic enough. There should be a direct vote by the people. Well," he grudged, "I suppose it will take a little time for them to learn democracy." This was the first time he had come out and admitted that. "There is to be a Constituent Convention in five years, to draw up a new constitution."

"How about the Convocation? You don't expect them to vote themselves out of existence, do you?"

"Oh, we're keeping the Convocation, in the present constitution, but they won't have any power. Five years from now, we'll be rid of them entirely. Look here; you're not going to work against this, are you? You won't advise these ci-devant Lords-Master to vote against it, when it comes up?"

"Certainly not. I think your constitution – Khreggor Chmidd's and Tchall Hozhet's, to be exact – will be nothing short of a political disaster, but it will insure some political stability, which is all that matters from the Imperial point of view. An Empire statesman must always guard against sympathizing with local factions and interests, and I can think of no planet on which I could be safer from any such temptation. If these Lords-Master want to vote their throats cut, and the slaves want to re-enslave themselves, they may all do so with my complete blessing."

If he had been at all given to dramatic gestures he would then have sent for water and washed his hands.

Metaphorically, he did so at that moment; thereafter his interest in Adityan affairs was that of a spectator at a boring and stupid show, watching only because there is nothing else to watch, and wishing that it had been possible to have returned to Odin on the *Irma.* The Prime Minister, however, was entitled to a full and impartial report, which he would scarcely get from Count Erskyll, on this new jewel in the Imperial Crown. To be able to furnish that, he would have to remain until the Midyear Feasts, when the Convocation would act on the new constitution. Whether the constitution was adopted or rejected was, in itself, unimportant; in either case, Aditya would have a government recognizable as such by the Empire, which was already recognizing some fairly unlikely-looking governments. In either case, too, Aditya would make nobody on any other planet any trouble. It wouldn't have, at least for a long time, even if it had been left unannexed, but no planet inhabited by Terro-humans could be trusted to remain permanently peaceful and isolated. There is a spark of aggressive ambition in every Terro-human people, no matter how debased, which may smolder for centuries or even millennia and then burst, fanned by some random wind, into flame. To shift the metaphor slightly, the Empire could afford to leave no unwatched pots around to boil over unexpectedly.

Occasionally, he did warn young Erskyll of the dangers of overwork and emotional overinvolvement. Each time, the Proconsul would pour out some tale of bickering and rivalry among the chief-freedmen of the Managements. Citizen Khouzhik and Citizen Eschkhaffar – they were all calling each other Citizen, now – were contesting overlapping jurisdictions. Khouzhik wanted to change the name of his Management – he no longer bothered mentioning Sesar Martwynn – to Labor and Industry. To this, Mykhyl Eschkhaffar objected vehemently; any Industry that was going to be managed would be managed by his – Oraze Borztall was similarly left unmentioned – management of Public Works. And they were also feuding about the robotic and remote-controlled equipment that had been sent down from the *Empress Eulalie* to the Austragonia nuclear-power works.

Khouzhik was also in controversy with Yakoop Zhannar, who was already calling himself People's Provost-Marshal. Khouzhik had taken over all the private armed-guards on the Masterly farms and in the factories, and assimilated them into something he was calling the People's Labor Police, ostensibly to enforce the new Code of Employment Practice. Zhannar insisted that they should be under his Management; when Chmidd and Hozhet supported Khouzhik, he began clamoring for the return of the regular army to his control.

Commodore Shatrak was more than glad to get rid of the Adityan army, and so was Pyairr Ravney, who was in immediate command of them. The Adityans didn't care one way or the other. Zhannar was delighted, and so were Chmidd and Hozhet. So, oddly, was Zhorzh Khouzhik. At the same time, the state of martial law proclaimed on the day of the landing was terminated.

The days slipped by. There were entertainments at the new Proconsular Palace for the Masterly residents of Zeggensburg, and Erskyll and his staff were entertained at Masterly palaces. The latter affairs pained Prince Trevannion excessively – hours on end of gorging uninspired cooking and guzzling too-sweet wine and watching ex-slave performers whose acts were either brutal or obscene and frequently both, and, more unforgivable, stupidly so. The Masterly conversation was simply stupid.

He borrowed a reconn-car from Ravney; he and Lanze Degbrend and, usually, one or another of Ravney's young officers, took long trips of exploration. They fished in mountain streams, and hunted the small deerlike game, and he found himself enjoying these excursions more than anything he had done in recent years; certainly anything since Aditya had come into the viewscreens of the *Empress Eulalie.* Once in a while, they claimed and received Masterly hospitality at some large farming estate. They were always greeted with fulsome cordiality, and there was always surprise that persons of their rank and consequence should travel unaccompanied by a retinue of servants.

He found things the same wherever he stopped. None of the farms were producing more than a quarter of the potential yield per acre, and all depleting the soil outrageously. Ten slaves – he didn't bother to think of them as freedmen – doing the work of one, and a hundred of them taking all day to do what one robot would have done before noon. White-gowned chief-slaves lording it over green and orange gowned supervisors and clerks; overseers still carrying and frequently using whips and knouts and sandbag flails.

Once or twice, when a Masterly back was turned, he caught a look of murderous hatred flickering into the eyes of some upper-slave. Once or twice, when a Master thought his was turned, he caught the same look in Masterly eyes, directed at him or at Lanze.

The Midyear Feasts approached; each time he returned to the city he found more excitement as preparations went on. Mykhyl Eschkhaffar's Management of Public Works was giving top priority to redecorating the Convocation Chamber and the lounges and dining rooms around it in which the Masters would relax during recesses. More and more Masterly families flocked in from outlying estates, with contragravity-flotillas and retinues of attendants, to be entertained at the city palaces. There were more and gaudier banquets and balls and entertainments. By the time the Feasts began, every Masterly man, woman and child would be in the city.

There were long columns of military contragravity coming in, too; troop-carriers and combat-vehicles. Yakoop Zhannar was bringing in all his newly recovered army, and Zhorzh Khouzhik his newly organized People's Labor Police. Vann Shatrak, who was now commanding his battle-line unit by screen from the Proconsular Palace, began fretting.

"I wish I hadn't been in such a hurry to terminate martial rule," he said, once. "And I wish Pyairr hadn't been so confoundedly efficient in retraining those troops. That may cost us a few extra casualties, before we're through."

Count Erskyll laughed at his worries.

"It's just this rivalry between Citizen Khouzhik and Citizen Zhannar," he said, "They're like a couple of ci-devant Lords-Master competing to give more extravagant feasts. Zhannar's going to hold a review of his troops, and of course, Khouzhik intends to hold a review of his police. That's all there is to it."

"Well, just the same, I wish some reinforcements would get here from Odin," Shatrak said.

Erskyll was busy, in the days before the Midyear Feasts, either conferring at the Citadel with the ex-slaves who were the functional heads of the Managements or at the Proconsular Palace with Hozhet and Chmidd and the chief-freedmen of the influential Convocation leaders and Presidium members. Everybody was extremely optimistic about the constitution.

He couldn't quite understand the optimism, himself.

"If I were one of these Lords-Master, I wouldn't even consider the thing," he told Erskyll. "I know, they're stupid, but I can't believe they're stupid enough to commit suicide, and that's what this amounts to."

"Yes, it does," Erskyll agreed, cheerfully. "As soon as they enact it, they'll be of no more consequence than the Assemblage of Peers on Aton; they'll have no voice in the operation of the Commonwealth, and none in the new constitution that will be drawn up five years from now. And that will be the end of them. All the big estates, and the factories and mines and contragravity-ship lines will be nationalized."

"And they'll have nothing at all, except a hamper-full of repudiated paper stellies," he finished. "That's what I mean. What makes you think they'll be willing to vote for that?"

"They don't know they're voting for it. They'll think they're voting to keep control of the Mastership. People like Olvir Nikkolon and Rovard Javasan and Ranal Valdry and Sesar Martwynn think they still own their chief-freedmen; they think Hozhet and Chmidd and Zhannar and Khouzhik will do exactly what they tell them. And they believe anything the Hozhets and Chmidds and Zhannars tell them. And every chief-freedman is telling his Lord-Employer that the only way they can keep control is by adopting the constitution; that they can control the elections on their estates, and hand-pick the People's Legislative Council. I tell you, Prince Trevannion, the constitution is as good as enacted."

Two days before the opening of the Convocation, the *Irma* came into radio-range, five light-hours away, and began transmitting in taped matter at sixty-speed. Erskyll's report and his own acknowledged; a routine "well done" for the successful annexation. Commendation for Shatrak's handling of the landing operation. Orders to take over Aditya-*Alif* and begin construction of a permanent naval base. Notification of promotion to base-admiral, and blank commission as line-commodore; that would be Patrique Morvill. And advice that one transport-cruiser, *Algol*, with an Army contragravity brigade aboard, and two engineering ships, would leave Odin for Aditya in fifteen days. The last two words erased much of the new base-admiral's pleasure.

"Fifteen days, great Ghu! And those tubs won't make near the speed of *Irma*, getting here. We'll be lucky to see them in twenty. And Beelzebub only knows what'll be going on here then."

Four times, the big screen failed to respond. They were all crowded into one of the executive conference-rooms at the Proconsular Palace, the batteries of communication and recording equipment incongruously functional among the gold-encrusted luxury of the original Masterly furnishings. Shatrak swore.

"Andrey, I thought your people had planted those pickups where they couldn't be found," he said to Commander Douvrin.

"There is no such place, sir," the intelligence officer replied. "Just places where things are hard to find."

"Did you mention our pickups to Chmidd or Hozhet or any of the rest of the shaveheads?" Shatrak asked Erskyll.

"No. I didn't even know where they were. And it was the freedmen who found them," Erskyll said. "I don't know why they wouldn't want us looking in."

Lanze Degbrend, at the screen, twisted the dial again, and this time the screen flickered and cleared, and they were looking into the Convocation Chamber from the extreme rear, above the double doors. Far away, in front, Olvir Nikkolon was rising behind the gold and onyx bench, and from the speaker the call bell tolled slowly, and the buzz of over two thousand whispering voices diminished. Nikkolon began to speak:

"Seven and a half centuries ago, our fathers went forth from Morglay to plant upon this planet a new banner. . . ."

It was evidently a set speech, one he had recited year after year, and every Lord Chairman of the Presidium before him. The splendid traditions. The glories of the Masterly race. The all-conquering Space Vikings. The proud heritage of the Sword-Worlds. Lanze was fiddling with the control knobs, stepping up magnification and focusing on the speaker's head and shoulders. Then everybody laughed; Nikkolon had a small plug in one ear, with a fine wire running down to vanish under his collar. Degbrend brought back the full view of the Convocation Chamber.

Nikkolon went on and on. Vann Shatrak summoned a robot to furnish him with a cold beer and another cigar. Erskyll was drumming an impatient devil's tattoo with his fingernails on the gold-encrusted table in front of him. Lanze Degbrend began interpolating sarcastic comments. And finally, Pyairr Ravney, who came from Lugaluru, reverted to the idiom of his planet's favorite sport:

"Come on, come on; turn out the bull! What's the matter, is the gate stuck?"

If so, it came quickly unstuck, and the bull emerged, pawing and snorting.

"This year, other conquerors have come to Aditya, here to plant another banner, the Sun and Cogwheel of the Galactic Empire, and I blush to say it, we are as helpless against these conquerors as were the miserable barbarians and their wretched serfs whom our fathers conquered seven hundred and sixty-two years ago, whose descendants, until this black day, had been our slaves."

He continued, his voice growing more impassioned and more belligerent. Count Erskyll fidgeted. This wasn't the way the Chmidd-Hozhet Constitution ought to be introduced.

"So, perforce, we accepted the sovereignty of this alien Empire. We are now the subjects of his Imperial Majesty, Rodrik III. We must govern Aditya subject to the Imperial Constitution." (Groans, boos; catcalls, if the Adityan equivalent of cats made noises like that.) "At one stroke, this Constitution has abolished our peculiar institution, upon which is based our entire social structure. This I know. But this same Imperial Constitution is a collapsium-strong shielding; let me call your attention to Article One, Section Two: *Every Empire planet shall be self-governed as to its own affairs, in the manner of its own choice and without interference.* Mark this well, for it is our guarantee that this government, of the Masters, by the Masters, and for the Masters, shall not perish from Aditya." (Prolonged cheering.)

"Now, these arrogant conquerors have overstepped their own supreme law. They have written for this Mastership a constitution, designed for the sole purpose of accomplishing the liquidation of the Masterly class and race. They have endeavored to force this planetary constitution upon us by threats of force, and by a shameful attempt to pervert the fidelity of our chief-slaves – I will not insult these loyal servitors with this disgusting new name, freedmen – so that we might, a second time, be tricked into voting assent to our own undoing. But in this, they have failed. Our chief-slaves have warned us of the trap concealed in this constitution written by the Proconsul, Count Erskyll. My faithful Tchall Hozhet has shown me all the pitfalls in this infamous document. . . ."

Obray, Count Erskyll, was staring in dismay at the screen. Then he began cursing blasphemously, the first time he had ever been heard to do so, and, as he was at least nominally a Pantheist, this meant blaspheming the entire infinite universe.

"The rats! The dirty treacherous rats! We came here to help them, and look; they've betrayed us. . .!" He lost his voice in a wheezing sob, and then asked: "Why did they do it? Do they want to go on being slaves?"

Perhaps they did. It wasn't for love of their Lords-Master; he was sure of that. Even from the beginning, they had found it impossible to disguise their contempt. . . .

Then he saw Olvir Nikkolon stop short and thrust out his arm, pointing directly below the pickup, and as he watched, something green-grey, a remote-control contragravity lorry, came floating into the field of the screen. One of the vehicles that had been sent down from the *Empress Eulalie* for use at the uranium mines. As it lifted and advanced toward the center of the room, the other Lords-Master were springing to their feet.

Vann Shatrak also sprang to his feet, reaching the controls of the screen and cutting the sound. He was just in time to save them from being, at least temporarily, deafened, for no sooner had he silenced the speaker than the lorry vanished in a flash that filled the entire room.

When the dazzle left their eyes, and the smoke and dust began to clear, they saw the Convocation Chamber in wreckage, showers of plaster and bits of plastiboard still falling from above. The gold and onyx bench was broken in a number of places; the Chiefs of Management in front of it, and the Presidium above, had vanished. Among the benches lay black-clad bodies, a few still moving. Smoke rose from burning clothing. Admiral Shatrak put on the sound again; from the screen came screams and cries of pain and fright.

Then the doors on the two long sides opened, and red-brown uniforms appeared. The soldiers advanced into the Chamber, unslinging rifles and submachine guns. Unheeding the still falling plaster, they moved forward, firing as they came. A few of them slung their firearms and picked up Masterly dress swords, using them to finish the wounded among the benches. The screams grew fewer, and then stopped.

Count Erskyll sat frozen, staring white-faced and horror-sick into the screen. Some of the others had begun to recover and were babbling excitedly. Vann Shatrak was at a communication-screen, talking to Commodore Patrique Morvill, aboard the *Empress Eulalie*:

"All the Landing-Troops, and all the crewmen you can spare and arm. And every vehicle you have. This is only the start of it; there'll be a general massacre of Masters next. I don't doubt it's started already."

At another screen, Pyairr Ravney was saying, to the officer of the day of the Palace Guard: "No, there's no telling what they'll do next. Whatever it is, be ready for it ten minutes ago."

He stubbed out his cigarette and rose, and as he did, Erskyll came out of his daze and onto his feet.

"Commodore Shatrak! I mean, Admiral," he corrected himself. "We must re-impose martial rule. I wish I'd never talked you into terminating it. Look at that!" He pointed at the screen; big dump-lorries were already coming in the doors under the pickup, with a mob of gowned civil-service people crowding in under them. They and the soldiers began dragging bodies out from among the seats to be loaded and hauled away. "There's the planetary government, murdered to the last man!"

"I'm afraid we can't do anything like that," he said. "This seems to be a simple transfer of power by *coup-d'état*; rather more extreme than usual, but normal political practice on this sort of planet. The Empire has no right to interfere."

Erskyll turned on him indignantly. "But it's mass murder!"

"It's an accomplished fact. Whoever ordered this, Citizen Chmidd and Citizen Hozhet and Citizen Zhannar and the rest of your good democratic citizens, are now the planetary government of Aditya. As long as they don't attack us, or repudiate the sovereignty of the Emperor, you'll have to recognize them as such."

"A bloody-handed gang of murderers; recognize them?"

"All governments have a little blood here and there on their hands; you've seen this by screen instead of reading about it in a history book, but that shouldn't make any difference. And you've said, yourself, that the Masters would have to be eliminated. You've told Chmidd and Hozhet and the others that, repeatedly. Of course, you meant legally, by constitutional and democratic means, but that seemed just a bit too tedious to them. They had them all together in one room, where they could be eliminated easily, and . . . Lanze; see if you can get anything on the Citadel telecast."

Degbrend put on another communication-screen and fiddled for a moment. What came on was a view, from another angle, of the Convocation Chamber. A voice was saying:

". . . not one left alive. The People's Labor Police, acting on orders of People's Manager of Labor Zhorzh Khouzhik and People's Provost-Marshal Yakoop Zhannar, are now eliminating the rest of the ci-devant Masterly class, all of whom are here in Zeggensburg. The people are directed to cooperate; kill them all, men, women and children. We must allow none of these foul exploiters of the people live to see today's sun go down. . . ."

"You mean, we sit here while those animals butcher women and children?" Shatrak demanded, looking from the Proconsul to the Ministerial Secretary. "Well, by Ghu, I won't! If I have to face a court for it, all well and good, but. . . ."

"You won't, Admiral. I seem to recall, some years ago, a Commodore Hastings, who got a baronetcy for stopping a pogrom on Anath. . . ."

"And broadcast an announcement that any of the Masterly class may find asylum here at the Proconsular Palace. They're political fugitives; scores of precedents for that," Erskyll added.

Shatrak was back at the screen to the *Empress Eulalie.*

"Patrique, get a jam-beam focused on that telecast station at the Citadel; get it off the air. Then broadcast on the same wavelength; announce that anybody claiming sanctuary at the Proconsular Palace will be taken in and protected. And start getting troops down, and all the spacemen you can spare."

At the same time, Ravney was saying, into his own screen:

"Plan Four. Variation H-3; this is a rescue operation. This is not, repeat, underscore, *not* an intervention in planetary government. You are to protect members of the Masterly class in danger from mob violence. That's anybody with hair on his head. Stay away from the Citadel; the ones there are all dead. Start with the four buildings closest to us, and get them cleared out. If the shaveheads give you any trouble, don't argue with them, just shoot them. . . ."

Erskyll, after his brief moment of decisiveness, was staring at the screen to the Convocation Chamber, where bodies were still being heaved into the lorries like black sacks of grain. Lanze Degbrend summoned a robot, had it pour a highball, and gave it to the Proconsul.

"Go ahead, Count Erskyll; drink it down. Medicinal," he was saying. "Believe me you certainly need it."

Erskyll gulped it down. "I think I could use another, if you please," he said, handing the glass back to Lanze. "And a cigarette." After he had tasted his second drink and puffed on the cigarette, he said: "I was so proud. I thought they were learning democracy."

"We don't, any of us, have too much to be proud about," Degbrend told him. "They must have been planning and preparing this for a couple of months, and we never caught a whisper of it."

That was correct. They had deluded Erskyll into thinking that they were going to let the Masters vote themselves out of power and set up a representative government. They had deluded the Masters into believing that they were in favor of the *status quo,* and opposed to Erkyll's democratization and socialization. There must be only a few of them in the conspiracy. Chmidd and Hozhet and Zhannar and Khouzhik and Schferts and the rest of the Citadel chief-slave clique. Among them, they controlled all the armed force. The bickering and rivalries must have been part of the camouflage. He supposed that a few of the upper army commanders had been in on it, too.

A communication-screen began making noises. Somebody flipped the switch, and Khreggor Chmidd appeared in it. Erskyll swore softly, and went to face the screen-image of the elephantine ex-slave of the ex-Lord Master, the late Rovard Javasan.

"Citizen Proconsul; why is our telecast station, which is vitally needed to give information to the people, jammed off the air, and why are you broadcasting, on our wavelength, advice to the criminals of the ci-devant Masterly class to take refuge in your Proconsular Palace from the just vengeance of the outraged victims of their century-long exploitation?" he began. "This is a flagrant violation of the Imperial Constitution; our Emperor will not be pleased at this unjustified intervention in the affairs, and this interference with the planetary authority, of the People's Commonwealth of Aditya!"

Obray of Erskyll must have realized, for the first time, that he was still holding a highball glass in one hand and a cigarette in the other. He flung both of them away.

"If the Imperial troops we are sending into the city to rescue women and children in danger from your hoodlums meet with the least resistance, you won't be in a position to find out what his Majesty thinks about it, because Admiral Shatrak will have you and your accomplices shot in the Convocation Chamber, where you massacred the legitimate government of this planet," he barked.

So the real Obray, Count Erskyll, had at last emerged. All the liberalism and socialism and egalitarianism, all the Helping-Hand, Torch-of-Democracy, idealism, was merely a surface stucco applied at the university during the last six years. For twenty-four years before that, from the day of his birth, he had been taught, by his parents, his nurse, his governess, his tutors, what it meant to be an Erskyll of Aton and a grandson of Errol, Duke of Yorvoy. As he watched Khreggor Chmidd in the screen, he grew angrier, if possible.

"Do you know what you blood-thirsty imbeciles have done?" he demanded. "You have just murdered, along with two thousand men, some five billion crowns, the money needed to finance all these fine modernization and industrialization plans. Or are you crazy enough to think that the Empire is going to indemnify you for being emancipated and pay that money over to you?"

"But, Citizen Proconsul. . . ."

"And don't call me Citizen Proconsul! I am a noble of the Galactic Empire, and on this pigpen of a planet I represent his Imperial Majesty. You will respect, and address, me accordingly."

Khreggor Chmidd no longer wore the gorget of servility, but, as Lanze Degbrend had once remarked, it was still tattooed on his soul. He gulped.

"Y-yes, Lord-Master Proconsul!"

They were together again in the big conference-room, which Vann Shatrak had been using, through the day, as an extemporized Battle-Control. They slumped wearily in chairs; they smoked and drank coffee; they anxiously looked from viewscreen to viewscreen, wondering when, and how soon, the trouble would break out again. It was dark, outside, now. Floodlights threw a white dazzle from the top of the Proconsular Palace and from the tops of the four buildings around it that Imperial troops had cleared and occupied, and from contragravity vehicles above. There was light and activity at the Citadel, and in the Servile City to the southeast; the rest of Zeggensburg was dark and quiet.

"I don't think we'll have anymore trouble," Admiral Shatrak was saying. "They won't be fools enough to attack us here, and all the Masters are dead, except for the ones we're sheltering."

"How many did we save?" Count Erskyll asked.

Eight hundred odd, Shatrak told him. Erskyll caught his breath.

"So few! Why, there were almost twelve thousand of them in the city this morning."

"I'm surprised we saved so many," Lanze Degbrend said. He still wore combat coveralls, and a pistol-belt lay beside his chair. "Most of them were killed in the first hour."

And that had been before the landing-craft from the ships had gotten down, and there had only been seven hundred men and forty vehicles available. He had gone out with them, himself; it had been the first time he had worn battle-dress and helmet or carried a weapon except for sport in almost thirty years. It had been an ugly, bloody, business; one he wanted to forget as speedily as possible. There had been times, after seeing the mutilated bodies of Masterly women and children, when he had been forced to remind himself that he had come out to prevent, not to participate in, a massacre. Some of Ravney's men hadn't even tried. Atrocity has a horrible facility for begetting atrocity.

"What'll we do with them?" Erskyll asked. "We can't turn them loose; they'd all be murdered in a matter of hours, and in any case, they'd have nowhere to go. The Commonwealth," – he pronounced the name he had himself selected as though it were an obscenity – "has nationalized all the Masterly property."

That had been announced almost as soon as the Citadel telecast-station had been unjammed, and shortly thereafter they had begun encountering bodies of Yakoop Zhannar's soldiers and Zhorzh Khouzhik's police who had been sent out to stop looting and vandalism and occupy the Masterly palaces. There had been considerable shooting in the Servile City; evidently the ex-slaves had to be convinced that they must not pillage or destroy their places of employment.

"Evacuate them off-planet," Shatrak said. "As soon as *Algol* gets here, we'll load the lot of them onto *Mizar* or *Canopus* and haul them somewhere. Ghu only knows how they'll live, but. . . ."

"Oh, they won't be paupers, or public charges, Admiral," he said. "You know, there's an estimated five billion crowns in slave-compensation, and when I return to Odin I shall represent most strongly that these survivors be paid the whole sum. But I shall emphatically not recommend that they be resettled on Odin. They won't be at all grateful to us for today's business, and on Odin they could easily stir up some very adverse public sentiment."

"My resignation will answer any criticism of the Establishment the public may make," Erskyll began.

"Oh, rubbish; don't talk about resigning, Obray. You made a few mistakes here, though I can't think of a better planet in the Galaxy on which you could have made them. But no matter what you did or did not do, this would have happened eventually."

"You really think so?" Obray, Count Erskyll, was desperately anxious to be assured of that. "Perhaps if I hadn't been so insistent on this constitution. . . ."

"That wouldn't have made a particle of difference. We all made this inevitable simply by coming here. Before we came, it would have been impossible. No slave would have been able even to imagine a society without Lords-Master; you heard Chmidd and Hozhet, the first day, aboard the *Empress Eulalie.* A slave had to have a Master; he simply couldn't belong to nobody at all. And until you started talking socialization, nobody could have imagined property without a Masterly property-owning class. And a massacre like this would have been impossible to organize or execute. For one thing, it required an elaborate conspiratorial organization, and until we emancipated them, no slave would have dared trust any other slave; every one would have betrayed any other to curry favor with his Lord-Master. We taught them that they didn't need Lords-Master, or Masterly favor, anymore. And we presented them with a situation their established routines didn't cover, and forced them into doing some original thinking, which must have hurt like Nifflheim at first. And we retrained the army and handed it over to Yakoop Zhannar, and inspired Zhorzh Khouzhik to organize the Labor Police, and fundamentally, no government is anything but armed force. Really, Obray, I can't see that you can be blamed for anything but speeding up an inevitable process slightly."

"You think they'll see it that way at Asgard?"

"You mean the Prime Minister and His Majesty? That will be the way I shall present it to them. That was another reason I wanted to stay on here. I anticipated that you might want a credible witness to what was going to happen," he said. "Now, you'll be here for not more than five years before you're promoted elsewhere. Nobody remains longer than that on a first Proconsular appointment. Just keep your eyes and ears and, especially, your mind, open while you are here. You will learn many things undreamed-of by the political-science faculty at the University of Nefertiti."

"You said I made mistakes," Erskyll mentioned, ready to start learning immediately.

"Yes. I pointed one of them out to you some time ago: emotional involvement with local groups. You began sympathizing with the servile class here almost immediately. I don't think either of us learned anything about them that the other didn't, yet I found them despicable, one and all. Why did you think them worthy of your sympathy?"

"Why, because. . . ." For a moment, that was as far as he could get. His motivation had been thalamic rather than cortical and he was having trouble externalizing it verbally. "They were *slaves.* They were being exploited and oppressed. . . ."

"And, of course, their exploiters were a lot of heartless villains, so that made the slaves good and virtuous innocents. That was your real, fundamental, mistake. You know, Obray, the downtrodden and long-suffering proletariat aren't at all good or innocent or virtuous. They are just incompetent; they lack the abilities necessary for overt villainy. You saw, this afternoon, what they were capable of doing when they were given an opportunity. You know, it's quite all right to give the underdog a hand, but only one hand. Keep the other hand on your pistol – or he'll try to eat the one you gave him! As you may have noticed, today, when underdogs get up, they tend to turn out to be wolves."

"What do you think this Commonwealth will develop into, under Chmidd and Hozhet and Khouzhik and the rest?" Lanze Degbrend asked, to keep the lecture going.

"Oh, a slave-state, of course; look who's running it, and whom it will govern. Not the kind of a slave-state we can do anything about," he hastened to add. "The Commonwealth will be very definite about recognizing that sapient beings cannot be property. But all the rest of the property will belong to the Commonwealth. Remember that remark of Chmidd's: 'It will belong to everybody, but somebody will have to take care of it for everybody. That will be you and me.'"

Erskyll frowned. "I remember that. I didn't like it, at the time. It sounded. . . ."

Out of character, for a good and virtuous proletarian; almost Masterly, in fact. He continued:

"The Commonwealth will be sole employer as well as sole property-owner, and anybody who wants to eat will have to work for the Commonwealth on the Commonwealth's terms. Chmidd's and Hozhet's and

Khouzhik's, that is. If that isn't substitution of peonage for chattel slavery, I don't know what the word peonage means. But you'll do nothing to interfere. You will see to it that Aditya stays in the empire and adheres to the Constitution and makes no trouble for anybody off-planet. I fancy you won't find that too difficult. They'll be good, as long as you deny them the means to be anything else. And make sure that they continue to call you Lord-Master Proconsul."

Lecturing, he found, was dry work. He summoned a bartending robot:

"Ho, slave! Attend your Lord-Master!"

Then he had to use his ultraviolet pencil-light to bring it to him, and dial for the brandy-and-soda he wanted. As long as that was necessary, there really wasn't anything to worry about. But some of these days, they'd build robots that would anticipate orders, and robots to operate robots, and robots to supervise them, and. . . .

No. It wouldn't quite come to that. A slave is a slave, but a robot is only a robot. As long as they stuck to robots, they were reasonably safe.

Oomphel in the Sky

Miles Gilbert watched the landscape slide away below him, its quilt of rounded treetops mottled red and orange in the double sunlight and, in shaded places, with the natural yellow of the vegetation of Kwannon. The aircar began a slow swing to the left, and Gettler Alpha came into view, a monstrous smear of red incandescence with an optical diameter of two feet at arm's length, slightly flattened on the bottom by the western horizon. In another couple of hours it would be completely set, but by that time Beta, the planet's G-class primary, would be at its midafternoon hottest. He glanced at his watch. It was 1005, but that was Galactic Standard Time, and had no relevance to anything that was happening in the local sky. It did mean, though, that it was five minutes short of two hours to 'cast-time.

He snapped on the communication screen in front of him, and Harry Walsh, the news editor, looked out of it at him from the office in Bluelake, halfway across the continent. He wanted to know how things were going.

"Just about finished. I'm going to look in at a couple more native villages, and then I'm going to Sanders' plantation to see Gonzales. I hope I'll have a personal statement from him, and the final situation-progress map, in time for the 'cast. I take it Maith's still agreeable to releasing the story at twelve-hundred?"

"Sure; he was always agreeable. The Army wants publicity; it was Government House that wanted to sit on it, and they've given that up now. The story's all over the place here, native city and all."

"What's the situation in town, now?"

"Oh, it's still going on. Some disorders, mostly just unrest. Lot of street meetings that could have turned into frenzies if the police hadn't broken them up in time. A couple of shootings, some sleep-gassing, and a lot of arrests. Nothing to worry about – at least, not immediately."

That was about what he thought. "Maybe it's not bad to have a little trouble in Bluelake," he considered. "What happens out here in the plantation country the Government House crowd can't see, and it doesn't worry them. Well, I'll call you from Sanders'."

He blanked the screen. In the seat in front, the native pilot said: "Some contragravity up ahead, boss." It sounded like two voices speaking in unison, which was just what it was. "I'll have a look."

The pilot's hand, long and thin, like a squirrel's, reached up and pulled down the fifty-power binoculars on their swinging arm. Miles looked at the screen-map and saw a native village just ahead of the dot of light that marked the position of the aircar. He spoke the native name of the village aloud, and added:

"Let down there, Heshto. I'll see what's going on."

The native, still looking through the glasses, said, "Right, boss." Then he turned.

His skin was blue-grey and looked like sponge rubber. He was humanoid, to the extent of being an upright biped, with two arms, a head on top of shoulders, and a torso that housed, among other oddities, four lungs. His face wasn't even vaguely human. He had two eyes in front, close enough for stereoscopic vision, but that was a common characteristic of sapient life forms everywhere. His mouth was strictly for eating; he breathed through separate intakes and outlets, one of each on either side of his neck; he talked through the outlets and had his scent and hearing organs in the intakes. The car was air-conditioned, which was a mercy; an overheated Kwann exhaled through his skin, and surrounded himself with stenches like an organic chemistry lab. But then, Kwanns didn't come any closer to him than they could help when he was hot and sweated, which, lately, had been most of the time.

"A V and a half of air cavalry, circling around," Heshto said. "Making sure nobody got away. And a combat car at a couple of hundred feet and another one just at treetop level."

He rose and went to the seat next to the pilot, pulling down the binoculars that were focused for his own eyes. With them, he could see the air cavalry – egg-shaped things just big enough for a seated man, with jets and contragravity field generators below and a bristle of machine gun muzzles in front. A couple of them jetted up for a look at him and then went slanting down again, having recognized the Kwannon Planetwide News Service car.

The village was typical enough to have been an illustration in a sociography textbook – fields in a belt for a couple of hundred yards around it, dome-thatched mud-and-wattle huts inside a pole stockade with log storehouses built against it, their flat roofs high enough to provide platforms for defending archers, the open oval gathering-place in the middle. There was a big hut at one end of this, the khamdoo, the sanctum of the adult males, off limits for women and children. A small crowd was gathered in front of it; fifteen or twenty Terran air cavalrymen, a couple of enlisted men from the Second Kwannon Native Infantry, a Terran second lieutenant, and half a dozen natives. The rest of the village population, about two hundred, of both sexes and all ages, were lined up on the shadier side of the gathering-place, most of them looking up apprehensively at the two combat cars which were covering them with their guns.

Miles got to his feet as the car lurched off contragravity and the springs of the landing-feet took up the weight. A blast of furnacelike air struck him when he opened the door; he got out quickly and closed it behind him. The second lieutenant had come over to meet him; he extended his hand.

"Good day, Mr. Gilbert. We all owe you our thanks for the warning. This would have been a real baddie if we hadn't caught it when we did."

He didn't even try to make any modest disclaimer; that was nothing more than the exact truth.

"Well, lieutenant, I see you have things in hand here." He glanced at the line-up along the side of the oval plaza, and then at the selected group in front of the khamdoo. The patriarchal village chieftain in a loose slashed shirt; the shoonoo, wearing a multiplicity of amulets and nothing else; four or five of the village elders. "I take it the word of the swarming didn't get this far?"

"No, this crowd still don't know what the flap's about, and I couldn't think of anything to tell them that wouldn't be worse than no explanation at all."

He had noticed hoes and spades flying in the fields, and the cylindrical plastic containers the natives bought from traders, dropped when the troops had surprised the women at work. And the shoonoo didn't have a fire-dance cloak or any other special regalia on. If he'd heard about the swarming, he'd have been dressed to make magic for it.

"What time did you get here, lieutenant?"

"Oh-nine-forty. I just called in and reported the village occupied, and they told me I was the last one in, so the operation's finished."

That had been smart work. He got the lieutenant's name and unit and mentioned it into his memophone. That had been a little under five hours since he had convinced General Maith, in Bluelake, that the mass labor-desertion from the Sanders plantation had been the beginning of a swarming. Some division commanders wouldn't have been able to get a brigade off the ground in that time, let alone landed on objective. He said as much to the young officer.

"The way the Army responded, today, can make the people of the Colony feel a lot more comfortable for the future."

"Why, thank you, Mr. Gilbert." The Army, on Kwannon, was rather more used to obloquy than praise. "How did you spot what was going on so quickly?"

This was the hundredth time, at least, that he had been asked that today.

"Well, Paul Sanders' labor all comes from neighboring villages. If they'd just wanted to go home and spend the end of the world with their families, they'd have been dribbling away in small batches for the last couple of hundred hours. Instead, they all bugged out in a bunch, they took all the food they could carry and nothing else, and they didn't make any trouble before they left. Then, Sanders said they'd been building fires out in the fallow ground and moaning and chanting around them for a couple of days, and idling on the job. Saving their strength for the trek. And he said they had a shoonoo among them. He's probably the lad who started it. Had a dream from the Gone Ones, I suppose."

"You mean, like this fellow here?" the lieutenant asked. "What are they, Mr. Gilbert; priests?"

He looked quickly at the lieutenant's collar-badges. Yellow trefoil for Third Fleet-Army Force, Roman IV for Fourth Army, 907 for his regiment, with C under it for cavalry. That outfit had only been on Kwannon for the last two thousand hours, but somebody should have briefed him better than that.

He shook his head. "No, they're magicians. Everything these Kwanns do involves magic, and the shoonoon are the professionals. When a native runs into something serious, that his own do-it-yourself magic can't cope with, he goes to the shoonoo. And, of course, the shoonoo works all the magic for the community as a whole – rain-magic, protective magic for the village and the fields, that sort of thing."

The lieutenant mopped his face on a bedraggled handkerchief. "They'll have to struggle along somehow for a while; we have orders to round up all the shoonoon and send them in to Bluelake."

"Yes." That hadn't been General Maith's idea; the governor had insisted on that. "I hope it doesn't make more trouble than it prevents."

The lieutenant was still mopping his face and looking across the gathering-place toward Alpha, glaring above the huts.

"How much worse do you think this is going to get?" he asked.

"The heat, or the native troubles?"

"I was thinking about the heat, but both."

"Well, it'll get hotter. Not much hotter, but some. We can expect storms, too, within twelve to fifteen hundred hours. Nobody has any idea how bad they'll be. The last periastron was ninety years ago, and we've only been here for sixty-odd; all we have is verbal accounts from memory from the natives, probably garbled and exaggerated. We had pretty bad storms right after transit a year ago; they'll be much worse this time. Thermal convections; air starts to cool when it gets dark, and then heats up again in double-sun daylight."

It was beginning, even now; starting to blow a little after Alpha-rise.

"How about the natives?" the lieutenant asked. "If they can get any crazier than they are now –"

"They can, and they probably will. They think this is the end of the world. The Last Hot Time." He used the native expression, and then translated it into Lingua Terra. "The Sky Fire – that's Alpha – will burn up the whole world."

"But this happens every ninety years. Mean they always acted this way at periastron?"

He shook his head. "Race would have exterminated itself long ago if they had. No, this is something special. The coming of the Terrans was a sign. The Terrans came and brought oomphel to the world; this a sign that the Last Hot Time is at hand."

"What the devil *is* oomphel?" The lieutenant was mopping the back of his neck with one hand, now, and trying to pull his sticky tunic loose from his body with the other. "I hear that word all the time."

"Well, most Terrans, including the old Kwannon hands, use it to mean trade-goods. To the natives, it means any product of Terran technology, from paper-clips to spaceships. They think it's . . . well, not exactly supernatural; extranatural would be closer to expressing their idea. Terrans are natural; they're just a different kind of people. But oomphel isn't; it isn't subject to any of the laws of nature at all. They're all positive that we don't make it. Some of them even think it makes us."

When he got back in the car, the native pilot, Heshto, was lolling in his seat and staring at the crowd of natives along the side of the gathering-place with undisguised disdain. Heshto had been educated at one of the Native Welfare Commission schools, and post-graded with Kwannon Planetwide News. He could speak, read and write Lingua Terra. He was a mathematician as far as long division and decimal fractions. He knew that Kwannon was the second planet of the Gettler Beta system, 23,000 miles in circumference, rotating on its axis once in 22.8 Galactic Standard hours and making an orbital circuit around Gettler Beta once in 372.06 axial days, and that Alpha was an M-class pulsating variable with an average period of four hundred days, and that Beta orbited around it in a long elipse every ninety years. He didn't believe there was going to be a Last Hot Time. He was an intellectual, he was.

He started the contragravity-field generator as soon as Miles was in his seat. "Where now, boss?" he asked.

"Qualpha's Village. We won't let down; just circle low over it. I want some views of the ruins. Then to Sanders' plantation."

"O.K., boss; hold tight."

He had the car up to ten thousand feet. Aiming it in the map direction of Qualpha's Village, he let go with everything he had – hot jets, rocket-booster and all. The forest landscape came hurtling out of the horizon toward them.

Qualpha's was where the trouble had first broken out, after the bug-out from Sanders; the troops hadn't been able to get there in time, and it had been burned. Another village, about the same distance south of the plantation, had also gone up in flames, and at a dozen more they had found the natives working themselves into frenzies and had had to sleep-gas them or stun them with concussion-bombs. Those had been the villages to which the deserters from Sanders' had themselves gone; from every one, runners had gone out to neighboring villages – "The Gone Ones are returning; all the People go to greet them at the Deesha-Phoo. Burn your villages; send on the word. Hasten; the Gone Ones return!"

Saving some of those villages had been touch-and-go, too; the runners, with hours lead-time, had gotten there ahead of the troops, and there had been shooting at a couple of them. Then the Army contragravity began landing at villages that couldn't have been reached in hours by foot messengers. It had been stopped – at least for the time, and in this area. When and where another would break out was anybody's guess.

The car was slowing and losing altitude, and ahead he could see thin smoke rising above the trees. He moved forward beside the pilot and pulled down his glasses; with them he could distinguish the ruins of the village. He called Bluelake, and then put his face to the view-finder and began transmitting in the view.

It had been a village like the one he had just visited, mud-and-wattle huts around an oval gathering-place, stockade, and fields beyond. Heshto brought the car down to a few hundred feet and came coasting in on momentum helped by an occasional spurt of the cold-jets. A few sections of the stockade still stood, and one side of the khamdoo hadn't fallen, but the rest of the structures were flat. There wasn't a soul, human or parahuman, in sight; the only living thing was a small black-and-grey quadruped investigating some bundles that had been dropped in the fields, in hope of finding something tasty. He got a view of that – everybody liked animal pictures on a newscast – and then he was swinging the pickup over the still-burning ruins. In the ashes of every hut he could see the remains of something like a viewscreen or a nuclear-electric stove or a refrigerator or a sewing machine. He knew how dearly the Kwanns cherished such possessions. That they had destroyed them grieved him. But the Last Hot Time was at hand; the whole world would be destroyed by fire, and then the Gone Ones would return.

So there were uprisings on the plantations. Paul Sanders had been lucky; his Kwanns had just picked up and left. But he had always gotten along well with the natives, and his plantation house was literally a castle and he had plenty of armament. There had been other planters who had made the double mistake of incurring the enmity of their native labor and of living in unfortified houses. A lot of them weren't around, anymore, and their plantations were gutted ruins.

And there were plantations on which the natives had destroyed the klooba plants and smashed the crystal which lived symbiotically upon them. They thought the Terrans were using the living crystals to make magic. Not too far off, at that; the properties of Kwannon biocrystals had opened a major breakthrough in subnucleonic physics and initiated half a dozen technologies. New kinds of oomphel. And down in the south, where the spongy and resinous trees were drying in the heat, they were starting forest fires and perishing in them in hecatombs. And to the north, they were swarming into the mountains; building great fires there, too, and attacking the Terran radar and radio beacons.

Fire was a factor common to all these frenzies. Nothing could happen without magical assistance; the way to bring on the Last Hot Time was People.

Maybe the ones who died in the frenzies and the swarmings were the lucky ones at that. They wouldn't live to be crushed by disappointment when the Sky Fire receded as Beta went into the long swing toward apastron. The surviving shoonoon wouldn't be the lucky ones, that was for sure. The magician-in-public-practice needs only to make one really bad mistake before he is done to some unpleasantly ingenious death by his clientry, and this was going to turn out to be the biggest magico-prophetic blooper in all the long unrecorded history of Kwannon.

A few minutes after the car turned south from the ruined village, he could see contragravity-vehicles in the air ahead, and then the fields and buildings of the Sanders plantation. A lot more contragravity was grounded in the fallow fields, and there were rows of pneumatic balloon-tents, and field-kitchens, and a whole park of engineering equipment. Work was going on in the klooba-fields, too; about three hundred natives were cutting open the six-foot leafy balls and getting out the biocrystals. Three of the plantation airjeeps, each with a pair of machine guns, were guarding them, but they didn't seem to be having any trouble. He saw Sanders in another jeep, and had Heshto put the car alongside.

"How's it going, Paul?" he asked over his radio. "I see you have some help, now."

"Everybody's from Qualpha's, and from Darshat's," Sanders replied. "The Army had no place to put them, after they burned themselves out." He laughed happily. "Miles, I'm going to save my whole crop! I thought I was wiped out, this morning."

He would have been, if Gonzales hadn't brought those Kwanns in. The klooba was beginning to wither; if left unharvested, the biocrystals would die along with their hosts and crack into worthlessness. Like all the other planters, Sanders had started no new crystals since the hot weather, and would start none until the worst of the heat was over. He'd need every crystal he could sell to tide him over.

"The Welfarers'll make a big forced-labor scandal out of this," he predicted.

"Why, such an idea." Sanders was scandalized. "I'm not forcing them to eat."

"The Welfarers don't think anybody ought to have to work to eat. They think everybody ought to be fed whether they do anything to earn it or not, and if you try to make people earn their food, you're guilty of economic coercion. And if you're in business for yourself and want them to work for you, you're an exploiter and you ought to be eliminated as a class. Haven't you been trying to run a plantation on this planet, under this Colonial Government, long enough to have found that out, Paul?"

Brigadier General Ramón Gonzales had taken over the first – counting down from the landing-stage – floor of the plantation house for his headquarters. His headquarters company had pulled out removable partitions and turned four rooms into one, and moved in enough screens and teleprinters and photoprint machines and computers to have outfitted the main newsroom of *Planetwide News.* The place had the feel of a newsroom – a newsroom after a big story has broken and the 'cast has gone on the air and everybody – in this case about twenty Terran officers and non-coms, half women – standing about watching screens and smoking and thinking about getting a follow-up ready.

Gonzales himself was relaxing in Sanders' business-room, with his belt off and his tunic open. He had black eyes and black hair and mustache, and a slightly equine face that went well with his Old Terran Spanish name. There was another officer with him, considerably younger – Captain Foxx Travis, Major General Maith's aide.

"Well, is there anything we can do for you, Miles?" Gonzales asked, after they had exchanged greetings and sat down.

"Why, could I have your final situation-progress map? And would you be willing to make a statement on audio-visual." He looked at his watch. "We have about twenty minutes before the 'cast."

"You have a map," Gonzales said, as though he were walking tiptoe from one word to another. "It accurately represents the situation as of the moment, but I'm afraid some minor unavoidable inaccuracies may have crept in while marking the positions and times for the earlier phases of the operation. I teleprinted a copy to *Planetwide* along with the one I sent to Division Headquarters."

He understood about that and nodded. Gonzales was zipping up his tunic and putting on his belt and sidearm. That told him, before the brigadier general spoke again, that he was agreeable to the audio-visual appearance and statement. He called the recording studio at *Planetwide* while Gonzales was inspecting himself in the mirror and told them to get set for a recording. It only ran a few minutes; Gonzales, speaking without notes, gave a brief description of the operation.

"At present," he concluded, "we have every native village and every plantation and trading-post within two hundred miles of the Sanders plantation occupied. We feel that this swarming has been definitely stopped, but we will continue the occupation for at least the next hundred to two hundred hours. In the meantime, the natives in the occupied villages are being put to work building shelters for themselves against the anticipated storms."

"I hadn't heard about that," Miles said, as the general returned to his chair and picked up his drink again.

"Yes. They'll need something better than these thatched huts when the storms start, and working on them will keep them out of mischief. Standard megaton-kilometer field shelters, earth and log construction. I think they'll be adequate for anything that happens at periastron."

Anything designed to resist the heat, blast and radiation effects of a megaton thermonuclear bomb at a kilometer ought to stand up under what was coming. At least, the periastron effects; there was another angle to it.

"The Native Welfare Commission isn't going to take kindly to that. That's supposed to be their job."

"Then why the devil haven't they done it?" Gonzales demanded angrily. "I've viewed every native village in this area by screen, and I haven't seen one that's equipped with anything better than those log storage-bins against the stockades."

"There was a project to provide shelters for the periastron storms set up ten years ago. They spent one year arguing about how the natives survived storms prior to the Terrans' arrival here. According to the older natives, they got into those log storage-houses you were mentioning; only about one out of three in any village survived. I could have told them that. Did tell them, repeatedly, on the air. Then, after they decided that shelters were needed, they spent another year hassling over who would be responsible for designing them. Your predecessor here, General Nokami, offered the services of his engineer officers. He was frostily informed that this was a humanitarian and not a military project."

Ramón Gonzales began swearing, then apologized for the interruption. "Then what?" he asked.

"Apology unnecessary. Then they did get a shelter designed, and started teaching some of the students at the native schools how to build them, and then the meteorologists told them it was no good. It was a dugout shelter; the weathermen said there'd be rainfall measured in meters instead of inches and anybody who got caught in one of those dugouts would be drowned like a rat."

"Ha, I thought of that one." Gonzales said. "My shelters are going to be mounded up eight feet above the ground."

"What did they do then?" Foxx Travis wanted to know.

"There the matter rested. As far as I know, nothing has been done on it since."

"And you think, with a disgraceful record of non-accomplishment like that, that they'll protest General Gonzales' action on purely jurisdictional grounds?" Travis demanded.

"Not jurisdictional grounds, Foxx. The general's going at this the wrong way. He actually knows what has to be done and how to do it, and he's going right ahead and doing it, without holding a dozen conferences and round-table discussions and giving everybody a fair and equal chance to foul things up for him. You know as well as I do that that's undemocratic. And what's worse, he's making the natives build them themselves, whether they want to or not, and that's forced labor. That reminds me; has anybody started raising the devil about those Kwanns from Qualpha's and Darshat's you brought here and Paul put to work?"

Gonzales looked at Travis and then said: "Not with me. Not yet, anyhow."

"They've been at General Maith," Travis said shortly. After a moment, he added: "General Maith supports General Gonzales completely; that's for publication. I'm authorized to say so. What else was there to do? They'd burned their villages and all their food stores. They had to be placed somewhere. And why in the name of reason should they sit around in the shade eating Government native-type rations while Paul Sanders has fifty to a hundred thousand sols' worth of crystals dying on him?"

"Yes; that's another thing they'll scream about. Paul's making a profit out of it."

"Of course he's making a profit," Gonzales said. "Why else is he running a plantation? If planters didn't make profits, who'd grow biocrystals?"

"The Colonial Government. The same way they built those storm-shelters. But that would be in the public interest, and if the Kwanns weren't public-spirited enough to do the work, they'd be made to – at about half what planters like Sanders are paying them now. But don't you realize that profit is sordid and dishonest and selfish? Not at all like drawing a salary-cum-expense-account from the Government."

"You're right, it isn't," Gonzales agreed. "People like Paul Sanders have ability. If they don't, they don't stay in business. You have ability and people who don't never forgive you for it. Your very existence is a constant reproach to them."

"That's right. And they can't admit your ability without admitting their own inferiority, so it isn't ability at all. It's just dirty underhanded trickery and selfish ruthlessness." He thought for a moment. "How did Government House find out about these Kwanns here?"

"The Welfare Commission had people out while I was still setting up headquarters," Gonzales said. "That was about oh-seven-hundred."

"This isn't for publication?" Travis asked. "Well, they know, but they can't prove, that our given reason for moving in here in force is false. Of course, we can't change our story now; that's why the situation-progress map that was prepared for publication is incorrect as to the earlier phases. They do not know that it was you who gave us our first warning; they ascribe that to Sanders. And they are claiming that there never was any swarming; according to them, Sanders' natives are striking for better pay and conditions, and Sanders got General Maith to use troops to break the strike. I wish we could give you credit for putting us onto this, but it's too late now."

He nodded. The story was that a battalion of infantry had been sent in to rescue a small detail under attack by natives, and that more troops had been sent in to re-enforce them, until the whole of Gonzales' brigade had been committed.

"That wasted an hour, at the start," Gonzales said. "We lost two native villages burned, and about two dozen casualties, because we couldn't get our full strength in soon enough."

"You'd have lost more than that if Maith had told the governor general the truth and requested orders to act. There'd be a hundred villages and a dozen plantations and trading posts burning, now, and Lord knows how many dead, and the governor general would still be arguing about whether he was justified in ordering troop-action." He mentioned several other occasions when something like that had happened. "You can't tell that kind of people the truth. They won't believe it. It doesn't agree with their preconceptions."

Foxx Travis nodded. "I take it we are still talking for nonpublication?" When Miles nodded, he continued: "This whole situation is baffling, Miles. It seems that the government here knew all about the weather conditions they could expect at periastron, and had made plans for them. Some of them excellent plans, too, but all based on the presumption that the natives would co-operate or at least not obstruct. You see what the situation actually is. It should be obvious to everybody that the behavior of these natives is nullifying everything the civil government is trying to do to ensure the survival of the Terran colonists, the production of Terran-type food without which we would all starve, the biocrystal plantations without which the Colony would perish, and even the natives themselves. Yet the Civil Government will not act to stop these native frenzies and swarmings which endanger everything and everybody here, and when the Army attempts to act, we must use every sort of shabby subterfuge and deceit or the Civil Government will prevent us. What ails these people?"

"You have the whole history of the Colony against you, Foxx," he said. "You know, there never was any Chartered Kwannon Company set up to exploit the resources of the planet. At first, nobody realized that there were any resources worth exploiting. This planet was just a scientific curiosity; it was and is still the only planet of a binary system with a native population of sapient beings. The first people who came here were scientists, mostly sociographers and para-anthropologists. And most of them came from the University of Adelaide."

Travis nodded. Adelaide had a Federation-wide reputation for left-wing neo-Marxist "liberalism."

"Well, that established the political and social orientation of the Colonial Government, right at the start, when study of the natives was the only business of the Colony. You know how these ideological cliques form in a government – or any other organization. Subordinates are always chosen for their agreement with the views of their superiors, and the extremists always get to the top and shove the moderates under or out. Well, the Native Affairs Administration became the tail that wagged the Government dog, and the Native Welfare Commission is the big muscle in the tail."

His parents hadn't been of the left-wing Adelaide clique. His mother had been a biochemist; his father a roving news correspondent who had drifted into trading with the natives and made a fortune in keffa-gum before the chemists on Terra had found out how to synthesize hopkinsine.

"When the biocrystals were discovered and the plantations started, the Government attitude was set. Biocrystal culture is just sordid money grubbing. The real business of the Colony is to promote the betterment of the natives, as defined in University of Adelaide terms. That's to say, convert them into ersatz Terrans. You know why General Maith ordered these shoonoon rounded up?"

Travis made a face. "Governor general Kovac insisted on it; General Maith thought that a few minor concessions would help him on his main objective, which was keeping a swarming from starting out here."

"Yes. The Commissioner of Native Welfare wanted that done, mainly at the urging of the Director of Economic, Educational and Technical Assistance. The EETA crowd don't like shoonoon. They have been trying, ever since their agency was set up, to undermine and destroy their influence with the natives. This looked like a good chance to get rid of some of them."

Travis nodded. "Yes. And as soon as the disturbances in Bluelake started, the Constabulary started rounding them up there, too, and at the evacuee cantonments. They got about fifty of them, mostly from the cantonments east of the city – the natives brought in from the flooded tidewater area. They just dumped the lot of them onto us. We have them penned up in a lorry-hangar on the military reservation now." He turned to Gonzales. "How many do you think you'll gather up out here, general?" he asked.

"I'd say about a hundred and fifty, when we have them all."

Travis groaned. "We can't keep all of them in that hangar, and we don't have anywhere else –"

Sometimes a new idea sneaked up on Miles, rubbing against him and purring like a cat. Sometimes one hit him like a sledgehammer. This one just seemed to grow inside him.

"Foxx, you know I have the top three floors of the Suzikami Building; about five hundred hours ago, I leased the fourth and fifth floors, directly below. I haven't done anything with them, yet; they're just as they were when Trans-Space Imports moved out. There are ample water, light, power, air-conditioning and toilet facilities, and they can be sealed off completely from the rest of the building. If General Maith's agreeable, I'll take his shoonoon off his hands."

"What in blazes will you do with them?"

"Try a little experiment in psychological warfare. At minimum, we may get a little better insight into why these natives think the Last Hot Time is coming. At best, we may be able to stop the whole thing and get them quieted down again."

"Even the minimum's worth trying for," Travis said. "What do you have in mind, Miles? I mean, what procedure?"

"Well, I'm not quite sure, yet." That was a lie; he was very sure. He didn't think it was quite time to be specific, though. "I'll have to size up my material a little, before I decide on what to do with it. Whatever happens, it won't hurt the shoonoon, and it won't make anymore trouble than arresting them has made already. I'm sure we can learn something from them, at least."

Travis nodded. "General Maith is very much impressed with your grasp of native psychology," he said. "What happened out here this morning was exactly as you predicted. Whatever my recommendation's worth, you have it. Can you trust your native driver to take your car back to Bluelake alone?"

"Yes, of course."

"Then suppose you ride in with me in my car. We'll talk about it on the way in, and go see General Maith at once."

Bluelake was peaceful as they flew in over it, but it was an uneasy peace. They began running into military contragravity twenty miles beyond the open farmlands – they were the chlorophyll green of Terran vegetation – and the natives at work in the fields were being watched by more military and police vehicles. The carniculture plants, where Terran-type animal tissue was grown in nutrient-vats, were even more heavily guarded, and the native city was being patrolled from above and the streets were empty, even of the hordes of native children who usually played in them.

The Terran city had no streets. Its dwellers moved about on contragravity, and tall buildings rose, singly or in clumps, among the landing-staged residences and the green transplanted trees. There was a triple wire fence around it, the inner one masked by vines and the middle one electrified, with warning lights on. Even a government dedicated to the betterment of the natives and unwilling to order military action against them was, it appeared, unwilling to take too many chances.

Major General Denis Maith, the Federation Army commander on Kwannon, was considerably more than willing to find a temporary home for his witch doctors, now numbering close to two hundred. He did insist that they be kept under military guard, and on assigning his aide, Captain Travis, to co-operate on the project. Beyond that, he gave Miles a free hand.

Miles and Travis got very little rest in the next ten hours. A half-company of engineer troops was also kept busy, as were a number of Kwannon Planetwide News technicians and some Terran and native mechanics borrowed from different private business concerns in the city. Even the most guarded hints of what he had in mind were enough to get this last cooperation; he had been running a news-service in Bluelake long enough to have the confidence of the business people.

He tried, as far as possible, to keep any intimation of what was going on from Government House. That, unfortunately, hadn't been far enough. He found that out when General Maith was on his screen, in the middle of the work on the fourth and fifth floors of the Suzikami Building.

"The governor general just screened me," Maith said. "He's in a tizzy about our shoonoon. Claims that keeping them in the Suzikami Building will endanger the whole Terran city."

"Is that the best he can do? Well, that's rubbish, and he knows it. There are less than two hundred of them, I have them on the fifth floor, twenty stories above the ground, and the floor's completely sealed off from the floor below. They can't get out, and I have tanks of sleep-gas all over the place which can be opened either individually or all together from a switch on the fourth floor, where your sepoys are quartered."

"I know, Mr. Gilbert; I screen-viewed the whole installation. I've seen regular maximum-security prisons that would be easier to get out of."

"Governor general Kovac is not objecting personally. He has been pressured into it by this Native Welfare government-within-the-Government. They don't know what I'm doing with those shoonoon, but whatever it is, they're afraid of it."

"Well, for the present," Maith said, "I think I'm holding them off. The Civil Government doesn't want the responsibility of keeping them in custody, I refused to assume responsibility for them if they were kept anywhere else, and Kovac simply won't consider releasing them, so that leaves things as they are. I did have to make one compromise, though." That didn't sound good. It sounded less so when Maith continued: "They insisted on having one of their people at the Suzikami Building as an observer. I had to grant that."

"That's going to mean trouble."

"Oh, I shouldn't think so. This observer will observe, and nothing else. She will take no part in anything you're doing, will voice no objections, and will not interrupt anything you are saying to the shoonoon. I was quite firm on that, and the governor general agreed completely."

"She?"

"Yes. A Miss Edith Shaw; do you know anything about her?"

"I've met her a few times; cocktail parties and so on." She was young enough, and new enough to Kwannon, not to have a completely indurated mind. On the other hand, she was EETA which was bad, and had a master's in sociography from Adelaide, which was worse. "When can I look for her?"

"Well, the governor general's going to screen me and find out when you'll have the shoonoon on hand."

Doesn't want to talk to me at all, Miles thought. Afraid he might say something and get quoted.

"For your information, they'll be here inside an hour. They will have to eat, and they're all tired and sleepy. I should say 'bout oh-eight-hundred. Oh, and will you tell the governor general to tell Miss Shaw to bring an overnight kit with her. She's going to need it."

He was up at 0400, just a little after Beta-rise. He might be a civilian big-wheel in an Army psychological warfare project, but he still had four newscasts a day to produce. He spent a couple of hours checking the 0600 'cast and briefing Harry Walsh for the indeterminate period in which he would be acting chief editor and producer. At 0700, Foxx Travis put in an appearance. They went down to the fourth floor, to the little room they had fitted out as command-post, control room and office for Operation Shoonoo.

There was a rectangular black traveling-case, initialed E. S., beside the open office door. Travis nodded at it, and they grinned at one another; she'd come early, possibly hoping to catch them hiding something they didn't want her to see. Entering the office quietly, they found her seated facing the big viewscreen, smoking and watching a couple of enlisted men of the First Kwannon Native Infantry at work in another room where the pickup was. There were close to a dozen lipstick-tinted cigarette butts in the ashtray beside her. Her private face wasn't particularly happy. Maybe she was being earnest and concerned about the betterment of the underpriviledged, or the satanic maneuvers of the selfish planters.

Then she realized that somebody had entered; with a slight start, she turned, then rose. She was about the height of Foxx Travis, a few inches shorter than Miles, and slender. Light blond; green suit costume. She ditched her private face and got on her public one, a pleasant and deferential smile, with a trace of uncertainty behind it. Miles introduced Travis, and they sat down again facing the screen.

It gave a view, from one of the long sides and near the ceiling, of a big room. In the center, a number of seats – the drum-shaped cushions the natives had adopted in place of the seats carved from sections of tree trunk that they had been using when the Terrans had come to Kwannon – were arranged in a semicircle, one in the middle slightly in advance of the others. Facing them were three armchairs, a remote-control box beside one and another Kwann cushion behind and between the other two. There was a large globe of Kwannon, and on the wall behind the chairs an array of viewscreens.

"There'll be an interpreter, a native Army sergeant, between you and Captain Travis," he said. "I don't know how good you are with native languages, Miss Shaw; the captain is not very fluent."

"Cushions for them, I see, and chairs for the lordly Terrans," she commented. "Never miss a chance to rub our superiority in, do you?"

"I never deliberately force them to adopt our ways," he replied. "Our chairs are as uncomfortable for them as their low seats are for us.

Difference, you know, doesn't mean inferiority or superiority. It just means difference."

"Well, what are you trying to do, here?"

"I'm trying to find out a little more about the psychology back of these frenzies and swarmings."

"It hasn't occurred to you to look for them in the economic wrongs these people are suffering at the hands of the planters and traders, I suppose."

"So they're committing suicide, and that's all you can call these swarmings, and the fire-frenzies in the south, from economic motives," Travis said. "How does one better oneself economically by dying?"

She ignored the question, which was easier than trying to answer it.

"And why are you bothering to talk to these witch doctors? They aren't representative of the native people. They're a lot of cynical charlatans, with a vested interest in ignorance and superstition –"

"Miss Shaw, for the past eight centuries, earnest souls have been bewailing the fact that progress in the social sciences has always lagged behind progress in the physical sciences. I would suggest that the explanation might be in difference of approach. The physical scientist works *with* physical forces, even when he is trying, as in the case of contragravity, to nullify them. The social scientist works *against* social forces."

"And the result's usually a miserable failure, even on the physical-accomplishment level," Foxx Travis added. "This storm shelter project that was set up ten years ago and got nowhere, for instance. Ramón Gonzales set up a shelter project of his own seventy-five hours ago, and he's half through with it now."

"Yes, by forced labor!"

"Field surgery's brutal, too, especially when the anaesthetics run out. It's better than letting your wounded die, though."

"Well, we were talking about these shoonoon. They are a force among the natives; that can't be denied. So, since we want to influence the natives, why not use them?"

"Mr. Gilbert, these shoonoon are blocking everything we are trying to do for the natives. If you use them for propaganda work in the villages, you will only increase their prestige and make it that much harder for us to better the natives' condition, both economically and culturally –"

"That's it, Miles," Travis said. "She isn't interested in facts about specific humanoid people on Kwannon. She has a lot of high-order abstractions she got in a classroom at Adelaide on Terra."

"No. Her idea of bettering the natives' condition is to rope in a lot of young Kwanns, put them in Government schools, overload them with information they aren't prepared to digest, teach them to despise their own people, and then send them out to the villages, where they behave with such insufferable arrogance that the wonder is that so few of them stop an arrow or a charge of buckshot, instead of so many. And when that happens, as it does occasionally, Welfare says they're murdered at the instigation of the shoonoon."

"You know, Miss Shaw, this isn't just the roughneck's scorn for the egghead," Travis said. "Miles went to school on Terra, and majored in extraterrestrial sociography, and got a master's, just like you did. At Montevideo," he added. "And he spent two more years traveling on a Paula von Schlicten Fellowship."

Edith Shaw didn't say anything. She even tried desperately not to look impressed. It occurred to him that he'd never mentioned that fellowship to Travis. Army Intelligence must have a pretty good *dossier* on him. Before anybody could say anything further, a Terran captain and a native sergeant of the First K.N.I. came in. In the screen, the four sepoys who had been fussing around straightening things picked up auto-carbines and posted themselves two on either side of a door across from the pickup, taking positions that would permit them to fire into whatever came through without hitting each other.

What came through was one hundred and eighty-four shoonoon. Some wore robes of loose gauze strips, and some wore fire-dance cloaks of red and yellow and orange ribbons. Many were almost completely naked, but they were all amulet-ed to the teeth. There must have been a couple of miles of brass and bright-alloy wire among them, and half a ton of bright scrap-metal, and the skulls, bones, claws, teeth, tails and other components of most of the native fauna. They debouched into the big room, stopped, and stood looking around them. A native sergeant and a couple more sepoys followed. They got the shoonoon over to the semicircle of cushions, having to chase a couple of them away from the single seat at front and center, and induced them to sit down.

The native sergeant in the little room said something under his breath; the captain laughed. Edith Shaw gaped for an instant and said, *"Muggawsh!"* Travis simply remarked that he'd be damned.

"They do look kind of unusual, don't they?" Miles said. "I wouldn't doubt that this is the biggest assemblage of shoonoon in history. They aren't exactly a gregarious lot."

"Maybe this is the beginning of a new era. First meeting of the Kwannon Thaumaturgical Society."

A couple more K.N.I. privates came in with serving-tables on contragravity floats and began passing bowls of a frozen native-food delicacy of which all Kwanns had become passionately fond since its introduction by the Terrans. He let them finish, and then, after they had been relieved of the empty bowls, he nodded to the K.N.I. sergeant, who opened a door on the left. They all went through into the room they had been seeing in the screen. There was a stir when the shoonoon saw him, and he heard his name, in its usual native mispronunciation, repeated back and forth.

"You all know me," he said, after they were seated. "Have I ever been an enemy to you or to the People?"

"No," one of them said. "He speaks for us to the other Terrans. When we are wronged, he tries to get the wrongs righted. In times of famine he has spoken of our troubles, and gifts of food have come while the Government argued about what to do."

He wished he could see Edith Shaw's face.

"There was a sickness in our village, and my magic could not cure it," another said. "Mailsh Heelbare gave me oomphel to cure it, and told me how to use it. He did this privately, so that I would not be made to look small to the people of the village."

And that had infuriated EETA; it was a question whether unofficial help to the natives or support of the prestige of a shoonoo had angered them more.

"His father was a trader; he gave good oomphel, and did not cheat. Mailsh Heelbare grew up among us; he took the Manhood Test with the boys of the village," another oldster said. "He listened with respect to the grandfather-stories. No, Mailsh Heelbare is not our enemy. He is our friend."

"And so I will prove myself now," he told them. "The Government is angry with the People, but I will try to take their anger away, and in the meantime I am permitted to come here and talk with you. Here is a chief of soldiers, and one of the Government people, and your words will be heard by the oomphel machine that remembers and repeats, for the Governor and the Great Soldier Chief."

They all brightened. To make a voice recording was a wonderful honor. Then one of them said:

"But what good will that do now? The Last Hot Time is here. Let us be permitted to return to our villages, where our people need us."

"It is of that that I wish to speak. But first of all, I must hear your words, and know what is in your minds. Who is the eldest among you? Let him come forth and sit in the front, where I may speak with him."

Then he relaxed while they argued in respectfully subdued voices. Finally one decrepit oldster, wearing a cloak of yellow ribbons and carrying a highly obscene and ineffably sacred wooden image, was brought forward and installed on the front-and-center cushion. He'd come from some village to the west that hadn't gotten the word of the swarming; Gonzales' men had snagged him while he was making crop-fertility magic.

Miles showed him the respect due his advanced age and obviously great magical powers, displaying, as he did, an understanding of the regalia.

"I have indeed lived long," the old shoonoo replied. "I saw the Hot Time before; I was a child of so high." He measured about two and a half feet off the floor; that would make him ninety-five or thereabouts. "I remember it."

"Speak to us, then. Tell us of the Gone Ones, and of the Sky Fire, and of the Last Hot Time. Speak as though you alone knew these things, and as though you were teaching me."

Delighted, the oldster whooshed a couple of times to clear his outlets and began:

"In the long-ago time, there was only the Great Spirit. The Great Spirit made the World, and he made the People. In that time, there were no more People in the World than would be in one village, now. The Gone Ones dwelt among them, and spoke to them as I speak to you. Then, as more People were born, and died and went to join the Gone Ones, the Gone Ones became many, and they went away and build a place for themselves, and built the Sky Fire around it, and in the Place of the Gone Ones, at the middle of the Sky Fire, it is cool. From their place in the Sky Fire, the Gone Ones send wisdom to the people in dreams.

"The Sky Fire passes across the sky, from east to west, as the Always-Same does, but it is farther away than the Always-Same, because sometimes the Always Same passes in front of it, but the Sky Fire never passes in front of the Always-Same. None of the grandfather-stories, not even the oldest, tell of a time when this happened.

"Sometimes the Sky Fire is big and bright; that is when the Gone Ones feast and dance. Sometimes it is smaller and dimmer; then the Gone Ones rest and sleep. Sometimes it is close, and there is a Hot Time; sometimes it goes far away, and then there is a Cool Time.

"Now, the Last Hot Time has come. The Sky Fire will come closer and closer, and it will pass the Always-Same, and then it will burn up the World. Then will be a new World, and the Gone Ones will return, and the People will be given new bodies. When this happens, the Sky Fire will go out, and the Gone Ones will live in the World again with the People; the Gone Ones will make great magic and teach wisdom as I teach to you, and will no longer have to send dreams. In that time the crops will grow without planting or tending or the work of women; in that time, the game will come into the villages to be killed in the gathering-places. There will be no more hunger and no more hard work, and no more of the People will die or be slain. And that time is now here," he finished. "All the People know this."

"Tell me, Grandfather; how is this known? There have been many Hot Times before. Why should this one be the Last Hot Time?"

"The Terrans have come, and brought oomphel into the World," the old shoonoo said. "It is a sign."

"It was not prophesied beforetime. None of the People had prophesies of the coming of the Terrans. I ask you, who were the father of children and the grandfather of children's children when the Terrans came; was there any such prophesy?"

The old shoonoo was silent, turning his pornographic icon in his hands and looked at it.

"No," he admitted, at length. "Before the Terrans came, there were no prophesies among the People of their coming. Afterward, of course, there were many such prophesies, but there were none before."

"That is strange. When a happening is a sign of something to come, it is prophesied beforetime." He left that seed of doubt alone to grow, and continued: "Now, Grandfather, speak to us about what the People believe concerning the Terrans."

"The Terrans came to the World when my eldest daughter bore her first child," the old shoonoo said. "They came in great round ships, such as come often now, but which had never before been seen. They said that they came from another world like the World of People, but so far away that even the Sky Fire could not be seen from it. They still say this, and many of the People believe it, but it is not real.

"At first, it was thought that the Terrans were great shoonoon who made powerful magic, but this is not real either. The Terrans have no magic and no wisdom of their own. All they have is the oomphel, and the oomphel works magic for them and teaches them their wisdom. Even in the schools which the Terrans have made for the People, it is the oomphel which teaches." He went on to describe, not too incorrectly, the reading-screens and viewscreens and audio-visual equipment. "Nor do the Terrans make the oomphel, as they say. The oomphel makes more oomphel for them."

"Then where did the Terrans get the first oomphel?"

"They stole it from the Gone Ones," the old shoonoo replied. "The Gone Ones make it in their place in the middle of the Sky Fire, for themselves and to give to the People when they return. The Terrans stole it from them. For this reason, there is much hatred of the Terrans among the People. The Terrans live in the Dark Place, under the World, where the Sky Fire and the Always-Same go when they are not in the sky. It is there that the Terrans get the oomphel from the Gone Ones, and now they have come to the World, and they are using oomphel to hold back the Sky-Fire and keep it beyond the Always-Same so that the Last Hot Time will not come and the Gone Ones will not return. For this reason, too, there is much hatred of the Terrans among the People."

"Grandfather, if this were real there would be good reason for such hatred, and I would be ashamed for what my people had done and were doing. But it is not real." He had to rise and hold up his hands to quell the indignant outcry "Have any of you known me to tell not-real things and try to make the People act as though they were real? Then trust me in this. I will show you real things, which you will all see, and I will give you great secrets, which it is now time for you to have and use for the good of the People. Even the greatest secret," he added.

There was a pause of a few seconds. Then they burst out, in a hundred and eighty-four – no, three hundred and sixty eight – voices:

"The Oomphel Secret, Mailsh Heelbare?"

He nodded slowly. "Yes. The Oomphel Secret will be given."

He leaned back and relaxed again while they were getting over the excitement. Foxx Travis looked at him apprehensively.

"Rushing things, aren't you? What are you going to tell them?"

"Oh, a big pack of lies, I suppose," Edith Shaw said scornfully.

Behind her and Travis, the native noncom interpreter was muttering something in his own language that translated roughly as: "This better be good!"

The shoonoon had quieted, now, and were waiting breathlessly.

"But if the Oomphel Secret is given, what will become of the shoonoon?" he asked. "You, yourselves, say that we Terrans have no need for magic, because the oomphel works magic for us. This is real. If the People get the Oomphel Secret, how much need will they have for you shoonoon?"

Evidently that hadn't occurred to them before. There was a brief flurry of whispered – whooshed, rather – conversation, and then they were silent again. The eldest shoonoo said:

"We trust you, Mailsh Heelbare. You will do what is best for the People, and you will not let us be thrown out like broken pots, either."

"No, I will not," he promised. "The Oomphel Secret will be given to you shoonoon." He thought for a moment of Foxx Travis' joking remark about the Kwannon Thaumaturgical Society. "You have been jealous of one another, each keeping his own secrets," he said. "This must be put away. You will all receive the Oomphel Secret equally, for the good of all the People. You must all swear brotherhood, one with another, and later if any other shoonoo comes to you for the secret, you must swear brotherhood with him and teach it to him. Do you agree to this?"

The eldest shoonoo rose to his feet, begged leave, and then led the others to the rear of the room, where they went into a huddle. They didn't stay huddled long; inside of ten minutes they came back and took their seats.

"We are agreed, Mailsh Heelbare," the spokesman said.

Edith Shaw was impressed, more than by anything else she had seen. "Well, that was a quick decision!" she whispered.

"You have done well, Grandfathers. You will not be thrown out by the People like broken pots; you will be greater among them than ever. I will show you how this will be.

"But first, I must speak around the Oomphel Secret." He groped briefly for a comprehensible analogy, and thought of a native vegetable, layered like an onion, with a hard kernel in the middle. "The Oomphel Secret is like a fooshkoot. There are many lesser secrets around it, each of which must be peeled off like the skins of a fooshkoot and eaten. Then you will find the nut in the middle."

"But the nut of the fooshkoot is bitter," somebody said.

He nodded, slowly and solemnly. "The nut of the fooshkoot is bitter," he agreed.

They looked at one another, disquieted by his words. Before anybody could comment, he was continuing:

"Before this secret is given, there are things to be learned. You would not understand it if I gave it to you now. You believe many not-real things which must be chased out of your minds, otherwise they would spoil your understanding."

That was verbatim what they told adolescents before giving them the Manhood Secret. Some of them huffed a little; most of them laughed. Then one called out: "Speak on, Grandfather of Grandfathers," and they all laughed. That was fine, it had been about time for teacher to crack his little joke. Now he became serious again.

"The first of these not-real things you must chase from your mind is this which you believe about the home of the Terrans. It is not real that they come from the Dark Place under the World. There is no Dark Place under the World."

Bedlam for a few seconds; that was a pretty stiff jolt. No Dark Place; who ever heard of such a thing? The eldest shoonoo rose, cradling his graven image in his arms, and the noise quieted.

"Mailsh Heelbare, if there is no Dark Place where do the Sky Fire and the Always-Same go when they are not in the sky?"

"They never leave the sky; the World is round, and there is sky everywhere around it."

They knew that, or had at least heard it, since the Terrans had come. They just couldn't believe it. It was against common sense. The oldest shoonoo said as much, and more:

"These young ones who have gone to the Terran schools have come to the villages with such tales, but who listens to them? They show disrespect for the chiefs and the elders, and even for the shoonoon. They mock at the Grandfather-stories. They say men should do women's work and women do no work at all. They break taboos, and cause trouble. They are fools."

"Am I a fool, Grandfather? Do I mock at the old stories, or show disrespect to elders and shoonoon? Yet I, Mailsh Heelbare, tell you this. The World is indeed round, and I will show you."

The shoonoo looked contemptuously at the globe. "I have seen those things," he said. "That is not the World; that is only a makelike." He held up his phallic wood-carving. "I could say that this is a makelike of the World, but that would not make it so."

"I will show you for real. We will all go in a ship." He looked at his watch. "The Sky Fire is about to set. We will follow it all around the world to the west, and come back here from the east, and the Sky Fire will still be setting when we return. If I show you that, will you believe me?"

"If you show us for real, and it is not a trick, we will have to believe you."

When they emerged from the escalators, Alpha was just touching the western horizon, and Beta was a little past zenith. The ship was moored on contragravity beside the landing stage, her gangplank run out. The shoonoon, who had gone up ahead, had all stopped short and were staring at her; then they began gabbling among themselves, overcome by the wonder of being about to board such a monster and ride on her. She was the biggest ship any of them had ever seen. Maybe a few of them had been on small freighters; many of them had never been off the ground. They didn't look or act like cynical charlatans or implacable enemies of progress and enlightenment. They were more like a lot of schoolboys whose teacher is taking them on a surprise outing.

"Bet this'll be the biggest day in their lives," Travis said.

"Oh, sure. This'll be a grandfather-story ten generations from now."

"I can't get over the way they made up their minds, down there," Edith Shaw was saying. "Why, they just went and talked for a few minutes and came back with a decision."

They hadn't any organization, or anyplace to maintain on an organizational pecking-order. Nobody was obliged to attack anybody else's proposition in order to keep up his own status. He thought of the Colonial Government taking ten years not to build those storm-shelters.

Foxx Travis was commenting on the ship, now:

"I never saw that ship before; didn't know there was anything like that on the planet. Why, you could lift a whole regiment, with supplies and equipment –"

"She's been laid up for the last five years, since the heat and the native troubles stopped the tourist business here. She's the old *Hesperus.* Excursion craft. This sun-chasing trip we're going to make used to be a must for tourists here."

"I thought she was something like that, with all the glassed observation deck forward. Who's the owner?"

"Kwannon Air Transport, Ltd. I told them what I needed her for, and they made her available and furnished officers and crew and provisions for the trip. They were working to put her in commission while we were fitting up the fourth and fifth floors, downstairs."

"You just asked for that ship, and they just let you have it?" Edith Shaw was incredulous and shocked. They wouldn't have done that for the Government.

"They want to see these native troubles stopped, too. Bad for business. You know; selfish profit-move. That's another social force it's a good idea to work with instead of against."

The shoonoon were getting aboard, now, shepherded by the K.N.I. officer and a couple of his men and some of the ship's crew. A couple of sepoys were lugging the big globe that had been brought up from below after them. Everybody assembled on the forward top observation deck, and Miles called for attention and, finally, got it. He pointed out the three viewscreens mounted below the bridge, amidships. One on the left, was tuned to a pickup on the top of the Air Terminal tower, where the Terran city, the military reservation and the spaceport met. It showed the view to the west, with Alpha on the horizon. The one on the right, from the same point, gave a view in the opposite direction, to the east. The middle screen presented a magnified view of the navigational globe on the bridge.

Viewscreens were no novelty to the shoonoon. They were a very familiar type of oomphel. He didn't even need to do more than tell them that the little spot of light on the globe would show the position of the ship. When he was sure that they understood that they could see what was happening in Bluelake while they were away, he called the bridge and ordered Up Ship, telling the officer on duty to hold her at five thousand feet.

The ship rose slowly, turning toward the setting M-giant. Somebody called attention that the views in the screens weren't changing. Somebody else said:

"Of course not. What we see for real changes because the ship is moving. What we see in the screens is what the oomphel on the big building sees, and it does not move. That is for real as the oomphel sees it."

"Nice going," Edith said. "Your class has just discovered relativity." Travis was looking at the eastward viewscreen. He stepped over beside Miles and lowered his voice.

"Trouble over there to the east of town. Big swarm of combat contragravity working on something on the ground. And something's on fire, too."

"I see it."

"That's where those evacuees are camped. Why in blazes they had to bring them here to Bluelake –"

That had been EETA, too. When the solar tides had gotten high enough to flood the coastal area, the natives who had been evacuated from the district had been brought here because the Native Education people wanted them exposed to urban influences. About half of the shoonoon who had been rounded up locally had come in from the tide-inundated area.

"Parked right in the middle of the Terran-type food production area," Travis was continuing.

That was worrying him. Maybe he wasn't used to planets where the biochemistry wasn't Terra-type and a Terran would be poisoned or, at best, starve to death, on the local food; maybe, as a soldier he knew how fragile even the best logistics system can be. It was something to worry about. Travis excused himself and went off in the direction of the bridge. Going to call HQ and find out what was happening.

Excitement among the shoonoon; they had spotted the ship on which they were riding in the westward screen. They watched it until it had vanished from "sight of the seeing-oomphel," and by then were over the upland forests from whence they had been brought to Bluelake. Now and then one of them would identify his own village, and that would start more excitement.

Three infantry troop-carriers and a squadron of air cavalry were rushing past the eastward pickup in the right hand screen; another fire had started in the trouble area.

The crowd that had gathered around the globe that had been brought aboard began calling for Mailsh Heelbare to show them how they would go around the world and what countries they would pass over. Edith accompanied him and listened while he talked to them. She was bubbling with happy excitement, now. It had just dawned on her that shoonoon were fun.

None of them had ever seen the mountains along the western side of the continent except from a great distance. Now they were passing over them; the ship had to gain altitude and even then make a detour around one snow-capped peak. The whole hundred and eighty-four rushed to the starboard side to watch it as they passed. The ocean, half an hour later, started a rush forward. The score or so of them from the Tidewater knew what an ocean was, but none of them had known that there was another one to the west. Miles' view of the education program of the EETA, never bright at best, became even dimmer. *The young men who have gone to the Terran schools . . . who listens to them? They are fools.*

There were a few islands off the coast; the shoonoon identified them on the screen globe, and on the one on deck. Some of them wanted to know why there wasn't a spot of light on this globe, too. It didn't have the oomphel inside to do that; that was a satisfactory explanation. Edith started to explain about the orbital beacon-stations off-planet and the radio beams, and then stopped.

"I'm sorry; I'm not supposed to say anything to them," she apologized.

"Oh, that's all right. I wouldn't go into all that, though. We don't want to overload them."

She asked permission, a little later, to explain why the triangle tip of the arctic continent, which had begun to edge into sight on the screen globe, couldn't be seen from the ship. When he told her to go ahead, she got a platinum half-sol piece from her purse, held it on the globe from the classroom and explained about the curvature and told them they could see nothing farther away than the circle the coin covered. It was beginning to look as though the psychological-warfare experiment might show another, unexpected, success.

There was nothing, after the islands passed, but a lot of empty water. The shoonoon were getting hungry, but they refused to go below to eat. They were afraid they might miss something. So their dinner was brought up on deck for them. Miles and Travis and Edith went to the officers' dining room back of the bridge. Edith, by now, was even more excited than the shoonoon.

"They're so anxious to learn!" She was having trouble adjusting to that; that was dead against EETA doctrine. "But why wouldn't they listen to the teachers we sent to the villages?"

"You heard old Shatresh – the fellow with the pornographic sculpture and the yellow robe. These young twerps act like fools, and sensible people don't pay any attention to fools. What's more, they've been sent out indoctrinated with the idea that shoonoon are a lot of lying old fakes, and the shoonoon resent that. You know, they're not lying old fakes. Within their limitations, they are honest and ethical professional people."

"Oh, come, now! I know, I think they're sort of wonderful, but let's don't give them too much credit."

"I'm not. You're doing that."

"Huh?" She looked at him in amazement. "Me?"

"Yes, you. You know better than to believe in magic, so you expect them to know better, too. Well, they don't. You know that under the macroscopic world-of-the senses there exists a complex of biological, chemical and physical phenomena down to the subnucleonic level. They realize that there must be something beyond what they can see and handle, but they think it's magic. Well, as a race, so did we until only a few centuries pre-atomic. These people are still lower Neolithic, a hunting people who have just learned agriculture. Where we were twenty thousand years ago.

"You think any glib-talking Kwann can hang a lot of rags, bones and old iron onto himself, go through some impromptu mummery, and set up as shoonoo? Well, he can't. The shoonoon are a hereditary caste. A shoonoo father will begin teaching his son as soon as he can walk and talk, and he keeps on teaching him till he's the age-equivalent of a graduate M.D. or a science Ph. D."

"Well, what all is there to learn – ?"

"The theoretical basis and practical applications of sympathetic magic. Action-at-a-distance by one object upon another. Homeopathic magic: the principle that things which resemble one another will interact. For instance, there's an animal the natives call a shynph. It has an excrescence of horn on its brow like an arrowhead, and it arches its back like a bow when it jumps. Therefore, a shynph is equal to a bow and arrow, and for that reason the Kwanns made their bowstrings out of shynph-gut. Now they use tensilon because it won't break as easily or get wet and stretch. So they have to turn the tensilon into shynph-gut. They used to do that by drawing a picture of a shynph on the spool, and then the traders began labeling the spools with pictures of shynph. I think my father was one of the first to do that.

"Then, there's contagious magic. Anything that's been part of anything else or come in contact with it will interact permanently with it. I wish I had a sol for every time I've seen a Kwann pull the wad out of a shot-shell, pick up a pinch of dirt from the footprint of some animal he's tracking, put it in among the buckshot, and then crimp the wad in again.

"Everything a Kwann does has some sort of magical implications. It's the shoonoo's business to know all this; to be able to tell just what magical influences have to be produced, and what influences must be avoided. And there are circumstances in which magic simply will not work, even in theory. The reason is that there is some powerful counter-influence at work. He has to know when he can't use magic, and he has to be able to explain why. And when he's theoretically able to do something by magic, he has to have a plausible explanation why it won't produce results – just as any highly civilized and ethical Terran M.D. has to be able to explain his failures to the satisfaction of his late patient's relatives. Only a shoonoo doesn't get sued for malpractice; he gets a spear stuck in him. Under those circumstances, a caste of hereditary magicians is literally bred for quick thinking. These old gaffers we have aboard are the intellectual top crust among the natives. Any of them can think rings around your Government school products. As for preying on the ignorance and credulity of the other natives, they're only infinitesimally less ignorant and credulous themselves. But they want to learn – from anybody who can gain their respect by respecting them."

Edith Shaw didn't say anything in reply. She was thoughtful during the rest of the meal, and when they were back on the observation deck he noticed that she seemed to be looking at the shoonoon with new eyes.

In the screen-views of Bluelake, Beta had already set, and the sky was fading; stars had begun to twinkle. There were more fires – one, close to the city in the east, a regular conflagration – and fighting had broken out in the native city itself. He was wishing now, that he hadn't thought it necessary to use those screens. The shoonoon were noticing what was going on in them, and talking among themselves. Travis, after one look at the situation, hurried back to the bridge to make a screen-call. After a while, he returned, almost crackling with suppressed excitement.

"Well, it's finally happened! Maith's forced Kovac to declare martial rule!" he said in an exultant undertone.

"Forced him?" Edith was puzzled. "The Army can't force the Civil Government –"

"He threatened to do it himself. Intervene and suspend civil rule."

"But I thought only the Navy could do that."

"Any planetary commander of Armed Forces can, in a state of extreme emergency. I think you'll both agree that this emergency is about as extreme as they come. Kovac knew that Maith was unwilling to do it – he'd have to stand court-martial to justify his action – but he also knew that a governor general who has his Colony taken away from him by the Armed Forces never gets it back; he's finished. So it was just a case of the weaker man in the weaker position yielding."

"Where does this put us?"

"We are a civilian scientific project. You are under orders of General Maith. I am under your orders. I don't know about Edith."

"Can I draft her, or do I have to get you to get General Maith to do it?"

"Listen, don't do that," Edith protested. "I still have to work for Government House, and this martial rule won't last forever. They'll all be prejudiced against me –"

"You can shove your Government job on the air lock," Miles told her. "You'll have a better one with Planetwide News, at half again as much pay. And after the shakeup at Government House, about a year from now, you may be going back as director of EETA. When they find out on Terra just how badly this Government has been mismanaging things there'll be a lot of vacancies."

The shoonoon had been watching the fighting in the viewscreens. Then somebody noticed that the spot of light on the navigational globe was approaching a coastline, and they all rushed forward for a look.

Travis and Edith slept for a while; when they returned to relieve him, Alpha was rising to the east of Bluelake, and the fighting in the city was still going on. The shoonoon were still wakeful and interested; Kwanns could go without sleep for much longer periods than Terrans. The lack of any fixed cycle of daylight and darkness on their planet had left them unconditioned to any regular sleeping-and-waking rhythm.

"I just called in," Travis said. "Things aren't good, at all. Most of the natives in the evacuee cantonments have gotten into the native city, now, and they've gotten hold of a lot of firearms somehow. And they're getting nasty in the west, beyond where Gonzales is occupying, and in the northeast, and we only have about half enough troops to cope with everything. The general wants to know how you're making out with the shoonoon."

"I'll call him before I get in the sack."

He went up on the bridge and made the call. General Maith looked as sleepy as he felt; they both yawned as they greeted each other. There wasn't much he could tell the general, and it sounded like the glib reassurances one gets from a hospital about a friend's condition.

"We'll check in with you as soon as we get back and get our shoonoon put away. We understand what's motivating these frenzies, now, and in about twenty-five to thirty hours we'll be able to start doing something about it."

The general, in the screen, grimaced.

"That's a long time, Mr. Gilbert. Longer than we can afford to take, I'm afraid. You're not cruising at full speed now, are you?"

"Oh, no, general. We're just trying to keep Alpha level on the horizon." He thought for a moment. "We don't need to keep down to that. It may make an even bigger impression if we speed up."

He went back to the observation deck, picked up the PA-phone, and called for attention.

"You have seen, now, that we can travel around the world, so fast that we keep up with the Sky Fire and it is not seen to set. Now we will travel even faster, and I will show you a new wonder. I will show you the Sky Fire rising in the west; it and the Always-Same will seem to go backward in the sky. This will not be for real; it will only be seen so because we will be traveling faster. Watch, now, and see." He called the bridge for full speed, and then told them to look at the Sky-Fire and then see in the screens where it stood over Bluelake.

That was even better; now they were racing with the Sky-Fire and catching up to it. After half an hour he left them still excited and whooping gleefully over the steady gain. Five hours later, when he came back after a nap and a hasty breakfast, they were still whooping. Edith Shaw was excited, too; the shoonoon were trying to estimate how soon they would be back to Bluelake by comparing the position of the Sky Fire with its position in the screen.

General Maith received them in his private office at Army HQ; Foxx Travis mixed drinks for the four of them while the general checked the microphones to make sure they had privacy.

"I blame myself for not having forced martial rule on them hundreds of hours ago," he said. "I have three brigades; the one General Gonzales had here originally, and the two I brought with me when I took over here. We have to keep at least half a brigade in the south, to keep the tribes there from starting anymore forest fires. I can't hold Bluelake with anything less than half a brigade. Gonzales has his hands full in his area. He had a nasty business while you were off on that world cruise – natives in one village caught the men stationed there off guard and wiped them out, and then started another frenzy. It spread to two other villages before he got it stopped. And we need the Third Brigade in the northeast; there are three quarters of a million natives up there, inhabiting close to a million square miles. And if anything really breaks loose here, and what's been going on in the last few days is nothing even approaching what a real outbreak could be like, we'll have to pull in troops from everywhere. We must save the Terran-type crops and the carniculture plants. If we don't, we all starve."

Miles nodded. There wasn't anything he could think of saying to that.

"How soon can you begin to show results with those shoonoon, Mr. Gilbert?" the general asked. "You said from twenty-five to thirty hours. Can you cut that any? In twenty-five hours, all hell could be loose all over the continent."

Miles shook his head. "So far, I haven't accomplished anything positive," he said. "All I did with this trip around the world was convince them that I was telling the truth when I told them there was no Dark Place under the World, where Alpha and Beta go at night." He hastened, as the general began swearing, to add: "I know, that doesn't sound like much. But it was necessary. I have to convince them that there will be no Last Hot Time, and then –"

The shoonoon, on their drum-shaped cushions, stared at him in silence, aghast. All the happiness over the wonderful trip in the ship, when they had chased the Sky Fire around the World and caught it over Bluelake, and even their pleasure in the frozen delicacies they had just eaten, was gone.

"No – Last – Hot – Time?"

"Mailsh Heelbare, this is not real! It cannot be!"

"The Gone Ones –"

"The Always-Cool Time, when there will be no more hunger or hard work or death; it cannot be real that this will never come!"

He rose, holding up his hands; his action stopped the clamor.

"Why should the Gone Ones want to return to this poor world that they have gladly left?" he asked. "Have they not a better place in the middle of the Sky Fire, where it is always cool? And why should you want them to come back to this world? Will not each one of you pass, sooner or later, to the middle of the Sky Fire; will you not there be given new bodies and join the Gone Ones? There is the Always-Cool; there the crops grow without planting and without the work of women; there the game come into the villages to be killed in the gathering-places, without hunting. There you will talk with the other Gone Ones, your fathers and your fathers' fathers, as I talk with you. Why do you think this must come to the World of People? Can you not wait to join the Gone Ones in the Sky Fire?"

Then he sat down and folded his arms. They were looking at him in amazement; evidently they all saw the logic, but none of them had ever thought of it before. Now they would have to turn it over in their minds and accustom themselves to the new viewpoint. They began whooshing among themselves. At length, old Shatresh, who had seen the Hot Time before, spoke:

"Mailsh Heelbare, we trust you," he said. "You have told us of wonders, and you have shown us that they were real. But do you know this for real?"

"Do you tell me that you do not?" he demanded in surprise. "You have had fathers, and fathers' fathers. They have gone to join the Gone Ones. Why should you not, also? And why should the Gone Ones come back and destroy the World of People? Then your children will have no more children, and your children's children will never be. It is in the World of People that the People are born; it is in the World that they grow and gain wisdom to fit themselves to live in the Place of the Gone Ones when they are through with the bodies they use in the World. You should be happy that there will be no Last Hot Time, and that the line of your begettings will go on and not be cut short."

There were murmurs of agreement with this. Most of them were beginning to be relieved that there wouldn't be a Last Hot Time, after all. Then one of the class asked:

"Do the Terrans also go to the Place of the Gone Ones, or have they a place of their own?"

He was silent for a long time, looking down at the floor. Then he raised his head.

"I had hoped that I would not have to speak of this," he said. "But, since you have asked, it is right that I should tell you." He hesitated again, until the Kwanns in front of him had begun to fidget. Then he asked old Shatresh: "Speak of the beliefs of the People about how the World was made."

"The great Spirit made the world." He held up his carven obscenity. "He made the World out of himself. This is a makelike to show it."

"The Great Spirit made many worlds. The stars which you see in dark-time are all worlds, each with many smaller worlds around it. The Great Spirit made them all at one time, and made people on many of them. The Great Spirit made the World of People, and made the Always-Same and the Sky Fire, and inside the Sky Fire he made the Place of the Gone Ones. And when he made the Place of the Gone Ones, he put an Oomphel-Mother inside it, to bring forth oomphel."

This created a brief sensation. An Oomphel-Mother was something they had never thought of before, but now they were wondering why they hadn't. Of course there'd be an Oomphel-Mother; how else would there be oomphel?

"The World of the Terrans is far away from the World of People, as we have always told you. When the Great Spirit made it He gave it only an Always-Same, and no Sky Fire. Since there was no Sky Fire, there was no place to put a Place of the Gone Ones, so the Great Spirit made the Terrans so that they would not die, but live forever in their own bodies. The Oomphel-Mother for the World of the Terrans the Great Spirit hid in a cave under a great mountain.

"The Terrans whom the Great Spirit made lived for a long time, and then, one day, a man and a woman found a crack in a rock, and went inside, and they found the cave of the Oomphel-Mother, and the Oomphel-Mother in it. So they called all the other Terrans, and they brought the Oomphel-Mother out, and the Oomphel-Mother began to bring forth Oomphel. The Oomphel-Mother brought forth metal, and cloth, and glass, and plastic; knives, and axes and guns and clothing –" He went on, cataloguing the products of human technology, the shoonoon staring more and more wide-eyed at him. "And oomphel to make oomphel, and oomphel to teach wisdom," he finished. "They became very wise and very rich.

"Then the Great Spirit saw what the Terrans had done, and became angry, for it was not meant for the Terrans to do this, and the Great Spirit cursed the Terrans with a curse of death. It was not death as you know it. Because the Terrans had sinned by laying hands on the Oomphel-Mother, not only their bodies must die, but their spirits also. A Terran has a short life in the body, after that no life."

"This, then, is the Oomphel Secret. The last skin of the fooshkoot has been peeled away; behold the bitter nut, upon which we Terrans have chewed for more time than anybody can count. Happy people! When you die or are slain, you go to the Place of the Gone Ones, to join your fathers and your fathers' fathers and to await your children and children's children. When we die or are slain, that is the end of us."

"But you have brought your oomphel into this world; have you not brought the curse with it?" somebody asked, frightened.

"No. The People did not sin against the Great Spirit; they have not laid hands on an Oomphel-Mother as we did. The oomphel we bring you will do no harm; do you think we would be so wicked as to bring the curse upon you? It will be good for you to learn about oomphel here; in your Place of the Gone Ones there is much oomphel."

"Why did your people come to this world, Mailsh Heelbare?" old Shatresh asked. "Was it to try to hide from the curse?"

"There is no hiding from the curse of the Great Spirit, but we Terrans are not a people who submit without strife to any fate. From the time of the Curse of Death on, we have been trying to make spirits for ourselves."

"But how can you do that?"

"We do not know. The oomphel will not teach us that, though it teaches everything else. We have only learned many ways in which it cannot be done. It cannot be done with oomphel, or with anything that is in our own world. But the Oomphel-Mother made us ships to go to other worlds, and we have gone to many of them, this one among them, seeking things from which we try to make spirits. We are trying to make spirits for ourselves from the crystals that grow in the klooba plants; we may fail with them, too. But I say this; I may die, and all the other Terrans now living may die, and be as though they had never been, but someday we will not fail. Someday our children, or our children's children, will make spirits for themselves and live forever, as you do."

"Why were we not told this before, Mailsh Heelbare?"

"We were ashamed to have you know it. We are ashamed to be people without spirits."

"Can we help you and your people? Maybe our magic might help."

"It well might. It would be worth trying. But first, you must help yourselves. You and your people are sinning against the Great Spirit as grievously as did the Terrans of old. Be warned in time, lest you answer it as grievously."

"What do you mean, Mailsh Heelbare?" Old Shatresh was frightened.

"You are making magic to bring the Sky Fire to the World. Do you know what will happen? The World of People will pass whole into the place of the Gone Ones, and both will be destroyed. The World of People is a world of death; everything that lives on it must die. The Place of the Gone Ones is a world of life; everything in it lives forever. The two will strive against each other, and will destroy one another, and there will be nothing in the Sky Fire or the World but fire. This is wisdom which our oomphel teaches us. We know this secret, and with it we make weapons of great destruction." He looked over the seated shoonoon, picking out those who wore the flame-colored cloaks of the fire-dance. "You – and you – and you," he said. "You have been making this dreadful magic, and leading your people in it. And which among the rest of you have not been guilty?"

"We did not know," one of them said. "Mailsh Heelbare, have we yet time to keep this from happening?"

"Yes. There is only a little time, but there is time. You have until the Always-Same passes across the face of the Sky-Fire." That would be seven hundred and fifty hours. "If this happens, all is safe. If the Sky Fire blots Out the Always Same, we are all lost together. You must go among your people and tell them what madness they are doing, and command them to stop. You must command them to lay down their arms and cease fighting. And you must tell them of the awful curse that was put upon the Terrans in the long-ago time, for a lesser sin than they are now committing."

"If we say that Mailsh Heelbare told us this, the people may not believe us. He is not known to all, and some would take no Terran's word, not even his."

"Would anybody tell a secret of this sort, about his own people, if it were not real?"

"We had better say nothing about Mailsh Heelbare. We will say that the Gone Ones told us in dreams."

"Let us say that the Great Spirit sent a dream of warning to each of us," another shoonoo said. "There has been too much talk about dreams from the Gone Ones already."

"But the Great Spirit has never sent a dream –"

"Nothing like this has ever happened before, either."

He rose, and they were silent. "Go to your living-place, now," he told them. "Talk of how best you may warn your people." He pointed to the clock. "You have an oomphel like that in your living-place; when the shorter spear has moved three places, I will speak with you again, and then you will be sent in air cars to your people to speak to them."

They went up the escalator and down the hall to Miles' office on the third floor without talking. Foxx Travis was singing softly, almost inaudibly:

"You will eeeeat . . . in the sweeeet . . . bye-and-bye,
You'll get oooom . . . phel in the sky . . . when you die!"

Inside, Edith Shaw slumped dispiritedly in a chair. Foxx Travis went to the coffee-maker and started it. Miles snapped on the communication screen and punched the combination of General Maith's headquarters. As soon as the uniformed girl who appeared in it saw him, her hands moved quickly; the screen flickered, and the general appeared in it.

"We have it made, general. They're sold; we're ready to start them out in three hours."

Maith's thin, weary face suddenly lighted. "You mean they are going to co-operate?"

He shook his head. "They think they're saving the world; they think we're co-operating with them."

The general laughed. "That's even better! How do you want them sent out?"

"The ones in the Bluelake area first. Better have some picked K.N.I. in native costume, with pistols, to go with them. They'll need protection, till they're able to get a hearing for themselves. After they're all out, the ones from Gonzales' area can be started." He thought for a moment. "I'll want four or five of them left here to help me when you start bringing more shoonoon in from other areas. How soon do you think you'll have another class for me?"

"Two or three days, if everything goes all right. We have the villages and plantations in the south under pretty tight control now; we can start gathering them up right away. As soon as we get things stabilized here, we can send reinforcements to the north. We'll have transport for you in three hours."

The general blanked out. He turned from the screen. Travis was laughing happily.

"Miles, did anybody ever tell you you were a genius?" he asked. "That last jolt you gave them was perfect. Why didn't you tell us about it in advance?"

"I didn't know about it in advance; I didn't think of it till I'd started talking to them. No cream or sugar for me."

"Cream," Edith said, lifelessly. "Why did you do it? Why didn't you just tell them the truth?"

Travis asked her to define the term. She started to say something bitter about Jesting Pilate. Miles interrupted.

"In spite of Lord Beacon, Pilate wasn't jesting," he said. "And he didn't stay for an answer because he knew he'd die of old age waiting for one. What kind of truth should I have told them?"

"Why, what you started to tell them. That Beta moves in a fixed orbit and can't get any closer to Alpha –"

"There's been some work done on the question since Pilate's time," Travis said. "My semantics prof at Command College had the start of an answer. He defined truth as a statement having a practical correspondence with reality on the physical levels of structure and observation and the verbal order of abstraction under consideration."

"He defined truth as a statement. A statement exists only in the mind of the person making it, and the mind of the person to whom it is made. If the person to whom it is made can't understand or accept it, it isn't the truth."

"They understood when you showed them that the planet is round, and they understood that tri-dimensional model of the system. Why didn't you let it go at that?"

"They accepted it intellectually. But when I told them that there wasn't any chance of Kwannon getting any closer to Alpha, they rebelled emotionally. It doesn't matter how conclusively you prove anything, if the person to whom you prove it can't accept your proof emotionally, it's still false. Not-real."

"They had all their emotional capital invested in this Always-Cool Time," Travis told her. "They couldn't let Miles wipe that out for them. So he shifted it from this world to the next, and convinced them that they were getting a better deal that way. You saw how quickly they picked it up. And he didn't have the sin of telling children there is no Easter Bunny on his conscience, either."

"But why did you tell them that story about the Oomphel Mother?" she insisted. "Now they'll go out and tell all the other natives, and they'll believe it."

"Would they have believed it if I'd told them about Terran scientific technology? Your people have been doing that for close to half a century. You see what impression it's made."

"But you told them – You told them that Terrans have no souls!"

"Can you prove that was a lie?" Travis asked. "Let's see yours. Draw – *soul!* Inspection – *soul!*"

Naturally. Foxx Travis would expect a soul to be carried in a holster.

"But they'll look down on us, now. They'll say we're just like animals," Edith almost wailed.

"Now it comes out," Travis said. "We won't be the lordly Terrans, anymore, helping the poor benighted Kwanns out of the goodness of our hearts, scattering largess, bearing the Terran's Burden – new model, a give-away instead of a gun. Now *they'll* pity *us*; they'll think *we're* inferior beings."

"I don't think the natives are inferior beings!" She was almost in tears.

"If you don't, why did you come all the way to Kwannon to try to make them more like Terrans?"

"Knock it off, Foxx; stop heckling her." Travis looked faintly surprised. Maybe he hadn't realized, before, that a boss newsman learns to talk like a commanding officer. "You remember what Ramón Gonzales was saying, out at Sanders', about the inferior's hatred for the superior as superior? It's no wonder these Kwanns resent us. They have a right to; we've done them all an unforgivable injury. We've let them see us doing things they can't do. Of course they resent us. But now I've given them something to feel superior about. When they die, they'll go to the

Place of the Gone Ones, and have oomphel in the sky, and they will live forever in new bodies, but when we die, we just die, period. So they'll pity us and politely try to hide their condescension toward us.

"And because they feel superior to us, they'll want to help us. They'll work hard on the plantations, so that we can have plenty of biocrystals, and their shoonoon will work magic for us, to help us poor benighted Terrans to grow souls for ourselves, so that we can almost be like them. Of course, they'll have a chance to exploit us, and get oomphel from us, too, but the important thing will be to help the poor Terrans. Maybe they'll even organize a Spiritual and Magical Assistance Agency."

Omnilingual

Martha Dane paused, looking up at the purple-tinged copper sky. The wind had shifted since noon, while she had been inside, and the dust storm that was sweeping the high deserts to the east was now blowing out over Syrtis. The sun, magnified by the haze, was a gorgeous magenta ball, as large as the sun of Terra, at which she could look directly. Tonight, some of that dust would come sifting down from the upper atmosphere to add another film to what had been burying the city for the last fifty thousand years.

The red loess lay over everything, covering the streets and the open spaces of park and plaza, hiding the small houses that had been crushed and pressed flat under it and the rubble that had come down from the tall buildings when roofs had caved in and walls had toppled outward. Here, where she stood, the ancient streets were a hundred to a hundred and fifty feet below the surface; the breach they had made in the wall of the building behind her had opened into the sixth story. She could look down on the cluster of prefabricated huts and sheds, on the brush-grown flat that had been the waterfront when this place had been a seaport on the ocean that was now Syrtis Depression; already, the bright metal was thinly coated with red dust. She thought, again, of what clearing this city would mean, in terms of time and labor, of people and supplies and equipment brought across fifty million miles of space. They'd have to use machinery; there was no other way it could be done. Bulldozers and power shovels and draglines; they were fast, but they were rough and indiscriminate. She remembered the digs around Harappa and Mohenjo-Daro, in the Indus Valley, and the careful, patient native laborers – the painstaking foremen, the pickmen and spademen, the long files of basketmen carrying away the earth. Slow and primitive as the civilization whose ruins they were uncovering, yes, but she could count on the fingers of one hand the times one of her pickmen had damaged a valuable object in the ground. If it hadn't been for the underpaid and uncomplaining native laborer, archaeology would still be back where Wincklemann had found it. But on Mars there was no native labor; the last Martian had died five hundred centuries ago.

Something started banging like a machine gun, four or five hundred yards to her left. A solenoid jack-hammer; Tony Lattimer must have decided which building he wanted to break into next. She became conscious, then, of the awkward weight of her equipment, and began redistributing it, shifting the straps of her oxy-tank pack, slinging the camera from one shoulder and the board and drafting tools from the other, gathering the notebooks and sketchbooks under her left arm. She started walking down the road, over hillocks of buried rubble, around snags of wall jutting up out of the loess, past buildings still standing, some of them already breached and explored, and across the brush-grown flat to the huts.

There were ten people in the main office room of Hut One when she entered. As soon as she had disposed of her oxygen equipment, she lit a cigarette, her first since noon, then looked from one to another of them. Old Selim von Ohlmhorst, the Turco-German, one of her two fellow archaeologists, sitting at the end of the long table against the farther wall, smoking his big curved pipe and going through a loose-leaf notebook. The girl ordnance officer, Sachiko Koremitsu, between two droplights at the other end of the table, her head bent over her work. Colonel Hubert Penrose, the Space Force CO, and Captain Field, the intelligence officer, listening to the report of one of the airdyne pilots, returned from his afternoon survey flight. A couple of girl lieutenants from Signals, going over the script of the evening telecast, to be transmitted to the *Cyrano,* on orbit five thousand miles off planet and relayed from thence to Terra via Lunar. Sid Chamberlain, the Trans-Space News Service man, was with them. Like Selim and herself, he was a civilian; he was advertising the fact with a white shirt and a sleeveless blue sweater. And Major Lindemann, the engineer officer, and one of his assistants, arguing over some plans on a drafting board. She hoped, drawing a pint of hot water to wash her hands and sponge off her face, that they were doing something about the pipeline.

She started to carry the notebooks and sketchbooks over to where Selim von Ohlmhorst was sitting, and then, as she always did, she turned aside and stopped to watch Sachiko. The Japanese girl was restoring what had been a book, fifty thousand years ago; her eyes were masked by a binocular loupe, the black headband invisible against her glossy black hair, and she was picking delicately at the crumbled page with a hair-fine wire set in a handle of copper tubing. Finally, loosening a particle as tiny as a snowflake, she grasped it with tweezers, placed it on the sheet of transparent plastic on which she was reconstructing the page, and set it with a mist of fixative from a little spraygun. It was a sheer joy to watch her; every movement was as graceful and precise as though done to music after being rehearsed a hundred times.

"Hello, Martha. It isn't cocktail-time yet, is it?" The girl at the table spoke without raising her head, almost without moving her lips, as though she were afraid that the slightest breath would disturb the flaky stuff in front of her.

"No, it's only fifteen-thirty. I finished my work, over there. I didn't find anymore books, if that's good news for you."

Sachiko took off the loupe and leaned back in her chair, her palms cupped over her eyes.

"No, I like doing this. I call it micro-jigsaw puzzles. This book, here, really is a mess. Selim found it lying open, with some heavy stuff on top of it; the pages were simply crushed." She hesitated briefly. "If only it would mean something, after I did it."

There could be a faintly critical overtone to that. As she replied, Martha realized that she was being defensive.

"It will, some day. Look how long it took to read Egyptian hieroglyphics, even after they had the Rosetta Stone."

Sachiko smiled. "Yes. I know. But they did have the Rosetta Stone."

"And we don't. There is no Rosetta Stone, not anywhere on Mars. A whole race, a whole species, died while the first Cro-Magnon cave-artist was daubing pictures of reindeer and bison, and across fifty thousand years and fifty million miles there was no bridge of understanding.

"We'll find one. There must be something, somewhere, that will give us the meaning of a few words, and we'll use them to pry meaning out of more words, and so on. We may not live to learn this language, but we'll make a start, and some day somebody will."

Sachiko took her hands from her eyes, being careful not to look toward the unshaded light, and smiled again. This time Martha was sure that it was not the Japanese smile of politeness, but the universally human smile of friendship.

"I hope so, Martha: really I do. It would be wonderful for you to be the first to do it, and it would be wonderful for all of us to be able to read what these people wrote. It would really bring this dead city to life again." The smile faded slowly. "But it seems so hopeless."

"You haven't found anymore pictures?"

Sachiko shook her head. Not that it would have meant much if she had. They had found hundreds of pictures with captions; they had never been able to establish a positive relationship between any pictured object and any printed word. Neither of them said anything more, and after a moment Sachiko replaced the loupe and bent her head forward over the book.

Selim von Ohlmhorst looked up from his notebook, taking his pipe out of his mouth.

"Everything finished, over there?" he asked, releasing a puff of smoke.

"Such as it was." She laid the notebooks and sketches on the table. "Captain Gicquel's started airsealing the building from the fifth floor down, with an entrance on the sixth; he'll start putting in oxygen generators as soon as that's done. I have everything cleared up where he'll be working."

Colonel Penrose looked up quickly, as though making a mental note to attend to something later. Then he returned his attention to the pilot, who was pointing something out on a map.

Von Ohlmhorst nodded. "There wasn't much to it, at that," he agreed. "Do you know which building Tony has decided to enter next?"

"The tall one with the conical thing like a candle extinguisher on top, I think. I heard him drilling for the blasting shots over that way."

"Well, I hope it turns out to be one that was occupied up to the end."

The last one hadn't. It had been stripped of its contents and fittings, a piece of this and a bit of that, haphazardly, apparently over a long period of time, until it had been almost gutted. For centuries, as it had died, this city had been consuming itself by a process of auto-cannibalism. She said something to that effect.

"Yes. We always find that – except, of course, at places like Pompeii. Have you seen any of the other Roman cities in Italy?" he asked. "Minturnae, for instance? First the inhabitants tore down this to repair that, and then, after they had vacated the city, other people came along and tore down what was left, and burned the stones for lime, or crushed them to mend roads, till there was nothing left but the foundation traces. That's where we are fortunate; this is one of the places where the Martian race perished, and there were no barbarians to come later and destroy what they had left." He puffed slowly at his pipe. "Some of these days, Martha, we are going to break into one of these buildings and find that it was one in which the last of these people died. Then we will learn the story of the end of this civilization."

And if we learn to read their language, we'll learn the whole story, not just the obituary. She hesitated, not putting the thought into words.

"We'll find that, sometime, Selim," she said, then looked at her watch. "I'm going to get some more work done on my lists, before dinner."

For an instant, the old man's face stiffened in disapproval; he started to say something, thought better of it, and put his pipe back into his mouth. The brief wrinkling around his mouth and the twitch of his white mustache had been enough, however; she knew what he was thinking. She was wasting time and effort, he believed; time and effort belonging not to herself but to the expedition. He could be right, too, she realized. But he had to be wrong; there had to be a way to do it. She turned from him silently and went to her own packing-case seat, at the middle of the table.

Photographs, and photostats of restored pages of books, and transcripts of inscriptions, were piled in front of her, and the notebooks in which she was compiling her lists. She sat down, lighting a fresh cigarette, and reached over to a stack of unexamined material, taking off the top sheet. It was a photostat of what looked like the title page and contents of some sort of a periodical. She remembered it; she had found it herself, two days before, in a closet in the basement of the building she had just finished examining.

She sat for a moment, looking at it. It was readable, in the sense that she had set up a purely arbitrary but consistently pronounceable system of phonetic values for the letters. The long vertical symbols were vowels. There were only ten of them; not too many, allowing separate characters for long and short sounds. There were twenty of the short horizontal letters, which meant that sounds like -ng or -ch or -sh were single letters. The odds were millions to one against her system being anything like the original sound of the language, but she had listed several thousand Martian words, and she could pronounce all of them.

And that was as far as it went. She could pronounce between three and four thousand Martian words, and she couldn't assign a meaning to one of them. Selim von Ohlmhorst believed that she never would. So did Tony Lattimer, and he was a great deal less reticent about saying so. So, she was sure, did Sachiko Koremitsu. There were times, now and then, when she began to be afraid that they were right.

The letters on the page in front of her began squirming and dancing, slender vowels with fat little consonants. They did that, now, every night in her dreams. And there were other dreams, in which she read them as easily as English; waking, she would try desperately and vainly to remember. She blinked, and looked away from the photostatted page;

when she looked back, the letters were behaving themselves again. There were three words at the top of the page, over-and-underlined, which seemed to be the Martian method of capitalization. *Mastharnorvod Tadavas Sornhulva.* She pronounced them mentally, leafing through her notebooks to see if she had encountered them before, and in what contexts. All three were listed. In addition, *masthar* was a fairly common word, and so was *norvod,* and so was *nor,* but *-vod* was a suffix and nothing but a suffix. *Davas,* was a word, too, and *ta-* was a common prefix; *sorn* and *hulva* were both common words. This language, she had long ago decided, must be something like German; when the Martians had needed a new word, they had just pasted a couple of existing words together. It would probably turn out to be a grammatical horror. Well, they had published magazines, and one of them had been called *Mastharnorvod Tadavas Sornhulva.* She wondered if it had been something like the *Quarterly Archaeological Review,* or something more on the order of *Sexy Stories.*

A smaller line, under the title, was plainly the issue number and date; enough things had been found numbered in series to enable her to identify the numerals and determine that a decimal system of numeration had been used. This was the one thousand and seven hundred and fifty-fourth issue, for Doma, 14837; then Doma must be the name of one of the Martian months. The word had turned up several times before. She found herself puffing furiously on her cigarette as she leafed through notebooks and piles of already examined material.

Sachiko was speaking to somebody, and a chair scraped at the end of the table. She raised her head, to see a big man with red hair and a red face, in Space Force green, with the single star of a major on his shoulder, sitting down. Ivan Fitzgerald, the medic. He was lifting weights from a book similar to the one the girl ordnance officer was restoring.

"Haven't had time, lately," he was saying, in reply to Sachiko's question. "The Finchley girl's still down with whatever it is she has, and it's something I haven't been able to diagnose yet. And I've been checking on bacteria cultures, and in what spare time I have, I've been dissecting specimens for Bill Chandler. Bill's finally found a mammal. Looks like a lizard, and it's only four inches long, but it's a real warm-blooded, gamogenetic, placental, viviparous mammal. Burrows, and seems to live on what pass for insects here."

"Is there enough oxygen for anything like that?" Sachiko was asking.

"Seems to be, close to the ground." Fitzgerald got the headband of his loupe adjusted, and pulled it down over his eyes. "He found this thing in a ravine down on the sea bottom – Ha, this page seems to be intact; now, if I can get it out all in one piece –"

He went on talking inaudibly to himself, lifting the page a little at a time and sliding one of the transparent plastic sheets under it, working with minute delicacy. Not the delicacy of the Japanese girl's small hands, moving like the paws of a cat washing her face, but like a steam-hammer cracking a peanut. Field archaeology requires a certain delicacy of touch, too, but Martha watched the pair of them with envious admiration. Then she turned back to her own work, finishing the table of contents.

The next page was the beginning of the first article listed; many of the words were unfamiliar. She had the impression that this must be some kind of scientific or technical journal; that could be because such publications made up the bulk of her own periodical reading. She doubted if it were fiction; the paragraphs had a solid, factual look.

At length, Ivan Fitzgerald gave a short, explosive grunt.

"Ha! Got it!"

She looked up. He had detached the page and was cementing another plastic sheet onto it.

"Any pictures?" she asked.

"None on this side. Wait a moment." He turned the sheet. "None on this side, either." He sprayed another sheet of plastic to sandwich the page, then picked up his pipe and relighted it.

"I get fun out of this, and it's good practice for my hands, so don't think I'm complaining," he said, "but, Martha, do you honestly think anybody's ever going to get anything out of this?"

Sachiko held up a scrap of the silicone plastic the Martians had used for paper with her tweezers. It was almost an inch square.

"Look; three whole words on this piece," she crowed. "Ivan, you took the easy book."

Fitzgerald wasn't being sidetracked. "This stuff's absolutely meaningless," he continued. "It had a meaning fifty thousand years ago, when it was written, but it has none at all now."

She shook her head. "Meaning isn't something that evaporates with time," she argued. "It has just as much meaning now as it ever had. We just haven't learned how to decipher it."

"That seems like a pretty pointless distinction," Selim von Ohlmhorst joined the conversation. "There no longer exists a means of deciphering it."

"We'll find one." She was speaking, she realized, more in self-encouragement than in controversy.

"How? From pictures and captions? We've found captioned pictures, and what have they given us? A caption is intended to explain the picture, not the picture to explain the caption. Suppose some alien to our culture found a picture of a man with a white beard and mustache sawing a billet from a log. He would think the caption meant, 'Man Sawing Wood.' How would he know that it was really 'Wilhelm II in Exile at Doorn?'"

Sachiko had taken off her loupe and was lighting a cigarette.

"I can think of pictures intended to explain their captions," she said. "These picture language-books, the sort we use in the Service – little line drawings, with a word or phrase under them."

"Well, of course, if we found something like that," von Ohlmhorst began.

"Michael Ventris found something like that, back in the Fifties," Hubert Penrose's voice broke in from directly behind her.

She turned her head. The colonel was standing by the archaeologists' table; Captain Field and the airdyne pilot had gone out.

"He found a lot of Greek inventories of military stores," Penrose continued. "They were in Cretan Linear B script, and at the head of each list was a little picture, a sword or a helmet or a cooking tripod or a chariot wheel. That's what gave him the key to the script."

"Colonel's getting to be quite an archaeologist," Fitzgerald commented. "We're all learning each others' specialties, on this expedition."

"I heard about that long before this expedition was even contemplated." Penrose was tapping a cigarette on his gold case. "I heard about that back before the Thirty Days' War, at Intelligence School, when I was a lieutenant. As a feat of cryptanalysis, not an archaeological discovery."

"Yes, cryptanalysis," von Ohlmhorst pounced. "The reading of a known language in an unknown form of writing. Ventris' lists were in the known language, Greek. Neither he nor anybody else ever read a word of the Cretan language until the finding of the Greek-Cretan bilingual in 1963, because only with a bilingual text, one language already known, can an unknown ancient language be learned. And what hope, I ask you, have we of finding anything like that here? Martha, you've been working on these Martian texts ever since we landed here – for the last six months. Tell me, have you found a single word to which you can positively assign a meaning?"

"Yes, I think I have one." She was trying hard not to sound too exultant. "*Doma.* It's the name of one of the months of the Martian calendar."

"Where did you find that?" von Ohlmhorst asked. "And how did you establish – ?"

"Here." She picked up the photostat and handed it along the table to him. "I'd call this the title page of a magazine."

He was silent for a moment, looking at it. "Yes. I would say so, too. Have you any of the rest of it?"

"I'm working on the first page of the first article, listed there. Wait till I see; yes, here's all I found, together, here." She told him where she had gotten it. "I just gathered it up, at the time, and gave it to Geoffrey and Rosita to photostat; this is the first I've really examined it."

The old man got to his feet, brushing tobacco ashes from the front of his jacket, and came to where she was sitting, laying the title page on the table and leafing quickly through the stack of photostats.

"Yes, and here is the second article, on page eight, and here's the next one." He finished the pile of photostats. "A couple of pages missing at the end of the last article. This is remarkable; surprising that a thing like a magazine would have survived so long."

"Well, this silicone stuff the Martians used for paper is pretty durable," Hubert Penrose said. "There doesn't seem to have been any water or any other fluid in it originally, so it wouldn't dry out with time."

"Oh, it's not remarkable that the material would have survived. We've found a good many books and papers in excellent condition. But only a really vital culture, an organized culture, will publish magazines, and this civilization had been dying for hundreds of years before the end. It might have been a thousand years before the time they died out completely that such activities as publishing ended."

"Well, look where I found it; in a closet in a cellar. Tossed in there and forgotten, and then ignored when they were stripping the building. Things like that happen."

Penrose had picked up the title page and was looking at it.

"I don't think there's any doubt about this being a magazine, at all." He looked again at the title, his lips moving silently. "*Mastharnorvod Tadavas Sornhulva.* Wonder what it means. But you're right about the date – *Doma* seems to be the name of a month. Yes, you have a word, Dr. Dane."

Sid Chamberlain, seeing that something unusual was going on, had come over from the table at which he was working. After examining the title page and some of the inside pages, he began whispering into the stenophone he had taken from his belt.

"Don't try to blow this up to anything big, Sid," she cautioned. "All we have is the name of a month, and Lord only knows how long it'll be till we even find out which month it was."

"Well, it's a start, isn't it?" Penrose argued. "Grotefend only had the word for 'king' when he started reading Persian cuneiform."

"But I don't have the word for month; just the name of a month. Everybody knew the names of the Persian kings, long before Grotefend."

"That's not the story," Chamberlain said. "What the public back on Terra will be interested in is finding out that the Martians published magazines, just like we do. Something familiar; make the Martians seem more real. More human."

Three men had come in, and were removing their masks and helmets and oxy-tanks, and peeling out of their quilted coveralls. Two were Space Force lieutenants; the third was a youngish civilian with close-cropped blond hair, in a checked woolen shirt. Tony Lattimer and his helpers.

"Don't tell me Martha finally got something out of that stuff?" he asked, approaching the table. He might have been commenting on the antics of the village half-wit, from his tone.

"Yes; the name of one of the Martian months." Hubert Penrose went on to explain, showing the photostat.

Tony Lattimer took it, glanced at it, and dropped it on the table.

"Sounds plausible, of course, but just an assumption. That word may not be the name of a month, at all – could mean 'published' or 'authorized' or 'copyrighted' or anything like that. Fact is, I don't think it's more than a wild guess that that thing's anything like a periodical." He dismissed the subject and turned to Penrose. "I picked out the next building to enter; that tall one with the conical thing on top. It ought to be in pretty good shape inside; the conical top wouldn't allow dust to accumulate, and from the outside nothing seems to be caved in or crushed. Ground level's higher than the other one, about the seventh floor. I found a good place and drilled for the shots; tomorrow I'll blast a hole in it, and if you can spare some people to help, we can start exploring it right away."

"Yes, of course, Dr. Lattimer. I can spare about a dozen, and I suppose you can find a few civilian volunteers," Penrose told him. "What will you need in the way of equipment?"

"Oh, about six demolition-packets; they can all be shot together. And the usual thing in the way of lights, and breaking and digging tools, and climbing equipment in case we run into broken or doubtful stairways. We'll divide into two parties. Nothing ought to be entered for the first time without a qualified archaeologist along. Three parties, if Martha can tear herself away from this catalogue of systematized incomprehensibilities she's making long enough to do some real work."

She felt her chest tighten and her face become stiff. She was pressing her lips together to lock in a furious retort when Hubert Penrose answered for her.

"Dr. Dane's been doing as much work, and as important work, as you have," he said brusquely. "More important work, I'd be inclined to say."

Von Ohlmhorst was visibly distressed; he glanced once toward Sid Chamberlain, then looked hastily away from him. Afraid of a story of dissension among archaeologists getting out.

"Working out a system of pronunciation by which the Martian language could be transliterated was a most important contribution," he said. "And Martha did that almost unassisted."

"Unassisted by Dr. Lattimer, anyway," Penrose added. "Captain Field and Lieutenant Koremitsu did some work, and I helped out a little, but nine-tenths of it she did herself."

"Purely arbitrary," Lattimer disdained. "Why, we don't even know that the Martians could make the same kind of vocal sounds we do."

"Oh, yes, we do," Ivan Fitzgerald contradicted, safe on his own ground. "I haven't seen any actual Martian skulls – these people seem to have been very tidy about disposing of their dead – but from statues and busts and pictures I've seen. I'd say that their vocal organs were identical with our own."

"Well, grant that. And grant that it's going to be impressive to rattle off the names of Martian notables whose statues we find, and that if we're ever able to attribute any placenames, they'll sound a lot better than this horse-doctors' Latin the old astronomers splashed all over the map of Mars," Lattimer said. "What I object to is her wasting time on this stuff, of which nobody will ever be able to read a word if she fiddles around with those lists till there's another hundred feet of loess on this city, when there's so much real work to be done and we're as shorthanded as we are."

That was the first time that had come out in just so many words. She was glad Lattimer had said it and not Selim von Ohlmhorst.

"What you mean," she retorted, "is that it doesn't have the publicity value that digging up statues has."

For an instant, she could see that the shot had scored. Then Lattimer, with a side glance at Chamberlain, answered:

"What I mean is that you're trying to find something that any archaeologist, yourself included, should know doesn't exist. I don't object to your gambling your professional reputation and making a laughingstock of yourself; what I object to is that the blunders of one archaeologist discredit the whole subject in the eyes of the public."

That seemed to be what worried Lattimer most. She was framing a reply when the communication-outlet whistled shrilly, and then squawked: "Cocktail time! One hour to dinner; cocktails in the library, Hut Four!"

The library, which was also lounge, recreation room, and general gathering-place, was already crowded; most of the crowd was at the long table topped with sheets of glasslike plastic that had been wall panels out of one of the ruined buildings. She poured herself what passed, here, for a martini, and carried it over to where Selim von Ohlmhorst was sitting alone.

For a while, they talked about the building they had just finished exploring, then drifted into reminiscences of their work on Terra – von Ohlmhorst's in Asia Minor, with the Hittite Empire, and hers in Pakistan, excavating the cities of the Harappa Civilization. They finished their drinks – the ingredients were plentiful; alcohol and flavoring extracts synthesized from Martian vegetation – and von Ohlmhorst took the two glasses to the table for refills.

"You know, Martha," he said, when he returned, "Tony was right about one thing. You are gambling your professional standing and reputation. It's against all archaeological experience that a language so completely dead as this one could be deciphered. There was a continuity between all the other ancient languages – by knowing Greek, Champollion learned to read Egyptian; by knowing Egyptian, Hittite was learned. That's why you and your colleagues have never been able to translate the Harappa hieroglyphics; no such continuity exists there. If you insist that this utterly dead language can be read, your reputation will suffer for it."

"I heard Colonel Penrose say, once, that an officer who's afraid to risk his military reputation seldom makes much of a reputation. It's the same with us. If we really want to find things out, we have to risk making mistakes. And I'm a lot more interested in finding things out than I am in my reputation."

She glanced across the room, to where Tony Lattimer was sitting with Gloria Standish, talking earnestly, while Gloria sipped one of the counterfeit martinis and listened. Gloria was the leading contender for the title of Miss Mars, 1996, if you liked big bosomy blondes, but Tony would have been just as attentive to her if she'd looked like the Wicked Witch in "The Wizard of Oz." because Gloria was the Pan-Federation Telecast System commentator with the expedition.

"I know you are," the old Turco-German was saying. "That's why, when they asked me to name another archaeologist for this expedition, I named you."

He hadn't named Tony Lattimer; Lattimer had been pushed onto the expedition by his university. There'd been a lot of high-level string-pulling to that; she wished she knew the whole story. She'd managed to keep clear of universities and university politics; all her digs had been sponsored by non-academic foundations or art museums.

"You have an excellent standing: much better than my own, at your age. That's why it disturbs me to see you jeopardizing it by this insistence that the Martian language can be translated. I can't, really, see how you can hope to succeed."

She shrugged and drank some more of her cocktail, then lit another cigarette. It was getting tiresome to try to verbalize something she only felt.

"Neither do I, now, but I will. Maybe I'll find something like the picture books Sachiko was talking about. A child's primer, maybe; surely they had things like that. And if I don't. I'll find something else. We've only been here six months. I can wait the rest of my life, if I have to, but I'll do it sometime."

"I can't wait so long," von Ohlmhorst said. "The rest of my life will only be a few years, and when the *Schiaparelli* orbits in, I'll be going back to Terra on the *Cyrano.*"

"I wish you wouldn't. This is a whole new world of archaeology. Literally."

"Yes." He finished the cocktail and looked at his pipe as though wondering whether to re-light it so soon before dinner, then put it in his pocket. "A whole new world – but I've grown old, and it isn't for me. I've spent my life studying the Hittites. I can speak the Hittite language, though maybe King Muwatallis wouldn't be able to understand my modern Turkish accent. But the things I'd have to learn here – chemistry, physics, engineering, how to run analytic tests on steel girders and beryllo-silver alloys and plastics and silicones. I'm more at home with a civilization that rode in chariots and fought with swords and was just learning how to work iron. Mars is for young people. This expedition is a cadre of leadership – not only the Space Force people, who'll be the commanders of the main expedition, but us scientists, too.

And I'm just an old cavalry general who can't learn to command tanks and aircraft. You'll have time to learn about Mars. I won't."

His reputation as the dean of Hittitologists was solid and secure, too, she added mentally. Then she felt ashamed of the thought. He wasn't to be classed with Tony Lattimer.

"All I came for was to get the work started," he was continuing. "The Federation Government felt that an old hand should do that. Well, it's started, now; you and Tony and whoever come out on the *Schiaparelli* must carry it on. You said it, yourself; you have a whole new world. This is only one city, of the last Martian civilization. Behind this, you have the Late Upland Culture, and the Canal Builders, and all the civilizations and races and empires before them, clear back to the Martian Stone Age." He hesitated for a moment. "You have no idea what all you have to learn, Martha. This isn't the time to start specializing too narrowly."

They all got out of the truck and stretched their legs and looked up the road to the tall building with the queer conical cap askew on its top. The four little figures that had been busy against its wall climbed into the jeep and started back slowly, the smallest of them, Sachiko Koremitsu, paying out an electric cable behind. When it pulled up beside the truck, they climbed out; Sachiko attached the free end of the cable to a nuclear-electric battery. At once, dirty grey smoke and orange dust puffed out from the wall of the building, and, a second later, the multiple explosion banged.

She and Tony Lattimer and Major Lindemann climbed onto the truck, leaving the jeep stand by the road. When they reached the building, a satisfyingly wide breach had been blown in the wall. Lattimer had placed his shots between two of the windows; they were both blown out along with the wall between, and lay unbroken on the ground. Martha remembered the first building they had entered. A Space Force officer had picked up a stone and thrown it at one of the windows, thinking that would be all they'd need to do. It had bounced back. He had drawn his pistol – they'd all carried guns, then, on the principle that what they didn't know about Mars might easily hurt them – and fired four shots. The bullets had ricocheted, screaming thinly; there were four coppery smears of jacket-metal on the window, and a little surface spalling. Somebody tried a rifle; the 4000-f.s. bullet had cracked the glasslike pane without penetrating. An oxyacetylene torch had taken an hour to cut the window out; the lab crew, aboard the ship, were still trying to find out just what the stuff was.

Tony Lattimer had gone forward and was sweeping his flashlight back and forth, swearing petulantly, his voice harshened and amplified by his helmet-speaker.

"I thought I was blasting into a hallway; this lets us into a room. Careful; there's about a two-foot drop to the floor, and a lot of rubble from the blast just inside."

He stepped down through the breach; the others began dragging equipment out of the trucks – shovels and picks and crowbars and sledges, portable floodlights, cameras, sketching materials, an extension ladder, even Alpinists' ropes and crampons and pickaxes. Hubert Penrose was shouldering something that looked like a surrealist machine gun but which was really a nuclear-electric jack-hammer. Martha selected one of the spike-shod mountaineer's ice axes, with which she could dig or chop or poke or pry or help herself over rough footing.

The windows, grimed and crusted with fifty millennia of dust, filtered in a dim twilight; even the breach in the wall, in the morning shade, lighted only a small patch of floor. Somebody snapped on a floodlight, aiming it at the ceiling. The big room was empty and bare; dust lay thick on the floor and reddened the once-white walls. It could have been a large office, but there was nothing left in it to indicate its use.

"This one's been stripped up to the seventh floor!" Lattimer exclaimed. "Street level'll be cleaned out, completely."

"Do for living quarters and shops, then," Lindemann said. "Added to the others, this'll take care of everybody on the *Schiaparelli.*"

"Seem to have been a lot of electric or electronic apparatus over along this wall," one of the Space Force officers commented. "Ten or twelve electric outlets." He brushed the dusty wall with his glove, then scraped on the floor with his foot. "I can see where things were pried loose."

The door, one of the double sliding things the Martians had used, was closed. Selim von Ohlmhorst tried it, but it was stuck fast. The metal latch-parts had frozen together, molecule bonding itself to molecule, since the door had last been closed. Hubert Penrose came over with the jack-hammer, fitting a spear-point chisel into place. He set the chisel in the joint between the doors, braced the hammer against his hip, and squeezed the trigger-switch. The hammer banged briefly like the weapon it resembled, and the doors popped a few inches apart, then stuck. Enough dust had worked into the recesses into which it was supposed to slide to block it on both sides.

That was old stuff; they ran into that every time they had to force a door, and they were prepared for it. Somebody went outside and brought in a power-jack and finally one of the doors inched back to the door jamb. That was enough to get the lights and equipment through: they all passed from the room to the hallway beyond. About half the other doors were open; each had a number and a single word, *Darfhulva,* over it.

One of the civilian volunteers, a woman professor of natural ecology from Penn State University, was looking up and down the hall.

"You know," she said, "I feel at home here. I think this was a college of some sort, and these were classrooms. That word, up there; that was the subject taught, or the department. And those electronic devices, all where the class would face them; audio-visual teaching aids."

"A twenty-five-story university?" Lattimer scoffed. "Why, a building like this would handle thirty thousand students."

"Maybe there were that many. This was a big city, in its prime," Martha said, moved chiefly by a desire to oppose Lattimer.

"Yes, but think of the snafu in the halls, every time they changed classes. It'd take half an hour to get everybody back and forth from one floor to another." He turned to von Ohlmhorst. "I'm going up above this floor. This place has been looted clean up to here, but there's a chance there may be something above," he said.

"I'll stay on this floor, at present," the Turco-German replied. "There will be much coming and going, and dragging things in and out. We should get this completely examined and recorded first. Then Major Lindemann's people can do their worst, here."

"Well, if nobody else wants it, I'll take the downstairs," Martha said.

"I'll go along with you," Hubert Penrose told her. "If the lower floors have no archaeological value, we'll turn them into living quarters. I like this building: it'll give everybody room to keep out from under everybody else's feet." He looked down the hall. "We ought to find escalators at the middle."

The hallway, too, was thick underfoot with dust. Most of the open rooms were empty, but a few contained furniture, including small seat-desks. The original proponent of the university theory pointed these out as just what might be found in classrooms. There were escalators, up and down, on either side of the hall, and more on the intersecting passage to the right.

"That's how they handled the students, between classes," Martha commented. "And I'll bet there are more ahead, there."

They came to a stop where the hallway ended at a great square central hall. There were elevators, there, on two of the sides, and four escalators, still usable as stairways. But it was the walls, and the paintings on them, that brought them up short and staring.

They were clouded with dirt – she was trying to imagine what they must have looked like originally, and at the same time estimating the labor that would be involved in cleaning them – but they were still distinguishable, as was the word, *Darfhulva,* in golden letters above each of the four sides. It was a moment before she realized, from the murals, that she had at last found a meaningful Martian word. They were a vast historical panorama, clockwise around the room. A group of skin-clad savages squatting around a fire. Hunters with bows and spears, carrying a carcass of an animal slightly like a pig. Nomads riding long-legged, graceful mounts like hornless deer. Peasants sowing and reaping; mud-walled hut villages, and cities; processions of priests and warriors; battles with swords and bows, and with cannon and muskets; galleys, and ships with sails, and ships without visible means of propulsion, and aircraft. Changing costumes and weapons and machines and styles of architecture. A richly fertile landscape, gradually merging into barren deserts and bushlands – the time of the great planet-wide drought. The Canal Builders – men with machines recognizable as steam-shovels and derricks, digging and quarrying and driving across the empty plains with aqueducts. More cities – seaports on the shrinking oceans; dwindling, half-deserted cities; an abandoned city, with four tiny humanoid figures and a thing like a combat-car in the middle of a brush-grown plaza, they and their vehicle dwarfed by the huge lifeless buildings around them. She had not the least doubt; *Darfhulva* was History.

"Wonderful!" von Ohlmhorst was saying. "The entire history of this race. Why, if the painter depicted appropriate costumes and weapons and machines for each period, and got the architecture right, we can break the history of this planet into eras and periods and civilizations."

"You can assume they're authentic. The faculty of this university would insist on authenticity in the *Darfhulva* – History – Department," she said.

"Yes! *Darfhulva* – History! And your magazine was a journal of *Sornhulva!*" Penrose exclaimed. "You have a word, Martha!" It took her an instant to realize that he had called her by her first name, and not Dr. Dane. She wasn't sure if that weren't a bigger triumph than learning a word of the Martian language. Or a more auspicious start. "Alone, I suppose that *hulva* means something like science or knowledge, or study;

combined, it would be equivalent to our 'ology. And *darf* would mean something like past, or old times, or human events, or chronicles."

"That gives you three words, Martha!" Sachiko jubilated. "You did it."

"Let's don't go too fast," Lattimer said, for once not derisively. "I'll admit that *darfhulva* is the Martian word for history as a subject of study; I'll admit that *hulva* is the general word and *darf* modifies it and tells us which subject is meant. But as for assigning specific meanings, we can't do that because we don't know just how the Martians thought, scientifically or otherwise."

He stopped short, startled by the blue-white light that blazed as Sid Chamberlain's Kliegettes went on. When the whirring of the camera stopped, it was Chamberlain who was speaking:

"This is the biggest thing yet; the whole history of Mars, stone age to the end, all on four walls. I'm taking this with the fast shutter, but we'll telecast it in slow motion, from the beginning to the end. Tony, I want you to do the voice for it – running commentary, interpretation of each scene as it's shown. Would you do that?"

Would he do that! Martha thought. If he had a tail, he'd be wagging it at the very thought.

"Well, there ought to be more murals on the other floors," she said. "Who wants to come downstairs with us?"

Sachiko did; immediately. Ivan Fitzgerald volunteered. Sid decided to go upstairs with Tony Lattimer, and Gloria Standish decided to go upstairs, too. Most of the party would remain on the seventh floor, to help Selim von Ohlmhorst get it finished. After poking tentatively at the escalator with the spike of her ice axe, Martha led the way downward.

The sixth floor was *Darfhulva,* too; military and technological history, from the character of the murals. They looked around the central hall, and went down to the fifth; it was like the floors above except that the big quadrangle was stacked with dusty furniture and boxes. Ivan Fitzgerald, who was carrying the floodlight, swung it slowly around. Here the murals were of heroic-sized Martians, so human in appearance as to seem members of her own race, each holding some object – a book, or a test tube, or some bit of scientific apparatus, and behind them were scenes of laboratories and factories, flame and smoke, lightning-flashes. The word at the top of each of the four walls was one with which she was already familiar – *Sornhulva.*

"Hey, Martha; there's that word," Ivan Fitzgerald exclaimed. "The one in the title of your magazine." He looked at the paintings. "Chemistry, or physics."

"Both." Hubert Penrose considered. "I don't think the Martians made any sharp distinction between them. See, the old fellow with the scraggly whiskers must be the inventor of the spectroscope; he has one in his hands, and he has a rainbow behind him. And the woman in the blue smock, beside him, worked in organic chemistry; see the diagrams of long-chain molecules behind her. What word would convey the idea of chemistry and physics taken as one subject?"

"Sornhulva," Sachiko suggested. "If *hulva's* something like science, *'sorn'* must mean matter, or substance, or physical object. You were right, all along, Martha. A civilization like this would certainly leave something like this, that would be self-explanatory."

"This'll wipe a little more of that superior grin off Tony Lattimer's face," Fitzgerald was saying, as they went down the motionless escalator to the floor below. "Tony wants to be a big shot. When you want to be a big shot, you can't bear the possibility of anybody else being a bigger big shot, and whoever makes a start on reading this language will be the biggest big shot archaeology ever saw."

That was true. She hadn't thought of it, in that way, before, and now she tried not to think about it. She didn't want to be a big shot. She wanted to be able to read the Martian language, and find things out about the Martians.

Two escalators down, they came out on a mezzanine around a wide central hall on the street level, the floor forty feet below them and the ceiling thirty feet above. Their lights picked out object after object below – a huge group of sculptured figures in the middle; some kind of a motor vehicle jacked up on trestles for repairs; things that looked like machine-guns and auto-cannon; long tables, tops littered with a dust-covered miscellany; machinery; boxes and crates and containers.

They made their way down and walked among the clutter, missing a hundred things for every one they saw, until they found an escalator to the basement. There were three basements, one under another, until at last they stood at the bottom of the last escalator, on a bare concrete floor, swinging the portable floodlight over stacks of boxes and barrels and drums, and heaps of powdery dust. The boxes were plastic – nobody had ever found anything made of wood in the city – and the barrels and drums were of metal or glass or some glasslike substance. They were outwardly intact. The powdery heaps might have been anything organic, or anything containing fluid. Down here, where wind and dust could not reach, evaporation had been the only force of destruction after the minute life that caused putrefaction had vanished.

They found refrigeration rooms, too, and using Martha's ice axe and the pistollike vibratool Sachiko carried on her belt, they pounded and pried one open, to find desiccated piles of what had been vegetables, and leathery chunks of meat. Samples of that stuff, rocketed up to the ship, would give a reliable estimate, by radio-carbon dating, of how long ago this building had been occupied. The refrigeration unit, radically different from anything their own culture had produced, had been electrically powered. Sachiko and Penrose, poking into it, found the switches still on; the machine had only ceased to function when the power-source, whatever that had been, had failed.

The middle basement had also been used, at least toward the end, for storage; it was cut in half by a partition pierced by but one door. They took half an hour to force this, and were on the point of sending above for heavy equipment when it yielded enough for them to squeeze through. Fitzgerald, in the lead with the light, stopped short, looked around, and then gave a groan that came through his helmet-speaker like a foghorn.

"Oh, no! *No!*"

"What's the matter, Ivan?" Sachiko, entering behind him, asked anxiously.

He stepped aside. "Look at it, Sachi! Are we going to have to do all that?"

Martha crowded through behind her friend and looked around, then stood motionless, dizzy with excitement. Books. Case on case of books, half an acre of cases, fifteen feet to the ceiling. Fitzgerald, and Penrose, who had pushed in behind her, were talking in rapid excitement; she only heard the sound of their voices, not their words. This must be the main stacks of the university library – the entire literature of the vanished race of Mars. In the center, down an aisle between the cases, she could see the hollow square of the librarians' desk, and stairs and a dumb-waiter to the floor above.

She realized that she was walking forward, with the others, toward this. Sachiko was saying: "I'm the lightest; let me go first." She must be talking about the spidery metal stairs.

"I'd say they were safe," Penrose answered. "The trouble we've had with doors around here shows that the metal hasn't deteriorated."

In the end, the Japanese girl led the way, more catlike than ever in her caution. The stairs were quite sound, in spite of their fragile appearance, and they all followed her. The floor above was a duplicate of the room they had entered, and seemed to contain about as many books. Rather than waste time forcing the door here, they returned to the middle basement and came up by the escalator down which they had originally descended.

The upper basement contained kitchens – electric stoves, some with pots and pans still on them – and a big room that must have been, originally, the students' dining room, though when last used it had been a workshop. As they expected, the library reading room was on the street-level floor, directly above the stacks. It seemed to have been converted into a sort of common living room for the building's last occupants. An adjoining auditorium had been made into a chemical works; there were vats and distillation apparatus, and a metal fractionating tower that extended through a hole knocked in the ceiling seventy feet above. A good deal of plastic furniture of the sort they had been finding everywhere in the city was stacked about, some of it broken up, apparently for reprocessing. The other rooms on the street floor seemed also to have been devoted to manufacturing and repair work; a considerable industry, along a number of lines, must have been carried on here for a long time after the university had ceased to function as such.

On the second floor, they found a museum; many of the exhibits remained, tantalizingly half-visible in grimed glass cases. There had been administrative offices there, too. The doors of most of them were closed, and they did not waste time trying to force them, but those that were open had been turned into living quarters. They made notes, and rough floor plans, to guide them in future more thorough examination; it was almost noon before they had worked their way back to the seventh floor.

Selim von Ohlmhorst was in a room on the north side of the building, sketching the position of things before examining them and collecting them for removal. He had the floor checkerboarded with a grid of chalked lines, each numbered.

"We have everything on this floor photographed," he said. "I have three gangs – all the floodlights I have – sketching and making measurements. At the rate we're going, with time out for lunch, we'll be finished by the middle of the afternoon."

"You've been working fast. Evidently you aren't being high-church about a 'qualified archaeologist' entering rooms first," Penrose commented.

"Ach, childishness!" the old man exclaimed impatiently. "These officers of yours aren't fools. All of them have been to Intelligence School and Criminal Investigation School. Some of the most careful amateur archaeologists I ever knew were retired soldiers or policemen.

But there isn't much work to be done. Most of the rooms are either empty or like this one – a few bits of furniture and broken trash and scraps of paper. Did you find anything down on the lower floors?"

"Well, yes," Penrose said, a hint of mirth in his voice. "What would you say, Martha?"

She started to tell Selim. The others, unable to restrain their excitement, broke in with interruptions. Von Ohlmhorst was staring in incredulous amazement.

"But this floor was looted almost clean, and the buildings we've entered before were all looted from the street level up," he said, at length.

"The people who looted this one lived here," Penrose replied. "They had electric power to the last; we found refrigerators full of food, and stoves with the dinner still on them. They must have used the elevators to haul things down from the upper floor. The whole first floor was converted into workshops and laboratories. I think that this place must have been something like a monastery in the Dark Ages in Europe, or what such a monastery would have been like if the Dark Ages had followed the fall of a highly developed scientific civilization. For one thing, we found a lot of machine guns and light auto-cannon on the street level, and all the doors were barricaded. The people here were trying to keep a civilization running after the rest of the planet had gone back to barbarism; I suppose they'd have to fight off raids by the barbarians now and then."

"You're not going to insist on making this building into expedition quarters, I hope, colonel?" von Ohlmhorst asked anxiously.

"Oh, no! This place is an archaeological treasure-house. More than that; from what I saw, our technicians can learn a lot, here. But you'd better get this floor cleaned up as soon as you can, though. I'll have the subsurface part, from the sixth floor down, airsealed. Then we'll put in oxygen generators and power units, and get a couple of elevators into service. For the floors above, we can use temporary airsealing floor by floor, and portable equipment; when we have things atmosphered and lighted and heated, you and Martha and Tony Lattimer can go to work systematically and in comfort, and I'll give you all the help I can spare from the other work. This is one of the biggest things we've found yet."

Tony Lattimer and his companions came down to the seventh floor a little later.

"I don't get this, at all," he began, as soon as he joined them. "This building wasn't stripped the way the others were. Always, the procedure seems to have been to strip from the bottom up, but they seem to have stripped the top floors first, here. All but the very top. I found out what that conical thing is, by the way. It's a wind-rotor, and under it there's an electric generator. This building generated its own power."

"What sort of condition are the generators in?" Penrose asked.

"Well, everything's full of dust that blew in under the rotor, of course, but it looks to be in pretty good shape. Hey, I'll bet that's it! They had power, so they used the elevators to haul stuff down. That's just what they did. Some of the floors above here don't seem to have been touched, though." He paused momentarily; back of his oxy-mask, he seemed to be grinning. "I don't know that I ought to mention this in front of Martha, but two floors above – we hit a room – it must have been the reference library for one of the departments – that had close to five hundred books in it."

The noise that interrupted him, like the squawking of a Brobdingnagian parrot, was only Ivan Fitzgerald laughing through his helmet-speaker.

Lunch at the huts was a hasty meal, with a gabble of full-mouthed and excited talking. Hubert Penrose and his chief subordinates snatched their food in a huddled consultation at one end of the table; in the afternoon, work was suspended on everything else and the fifty-odd men and women of the expedition concentrated their efforts on the University. By the middle of the afternoon, the seventh floor had been completely examined, photographed and sketched, and the murals in the square central hall covered with protective tarpaulins, and Laurent Gicquel and his airsealing crew had moved in and were at work. It had been decided to seal the central hall at the entrances. It took the French-Canadian engineer most of the afternoon to find all the ventilation-ducts and plug them. An elevator-shaft on the north side was found reaching clear to the twenty-fifth floor; this would give access to the top of the building; another shaft, from the center, would take care of the floors below. Nobody seemed willing to trust the ancient elevators, themselves; it was the next evening before a couple of cars and the necessary machinery could be fabricated in the machine shops aboard the ship and sent down by landing-rocket. By that time, the airsealing was finished, the nuclear-electric energy-converters were in place, and the oxygen generators set up.

Martha was in the lower basement, an hour or so before lunch the day after, when a couple of Space Force officers came out of the elevator, bringing extra lights with them. She was still using oxygen-equipment; it was a moment before she realized that the newcomers had no masks, and that one of them was smoking. She took off her own helmet-speaker, throat-mike and mask and unslung her tank-pack, breathing cautiously. The air was chilly, and musty-acrid with the odor of antiquity – the first Martian odor she had smelled – but when she lit a cigarette, the lighter flamed clear and steady and the tobacco caught and burned evenly.

The archaeologists, many of the other civilian scientists, a few of the Space Force officers and the two news-correspondents, Sid Chamberlain and Gloria Standish, moved in that evening, setting up cots in vacant rooms. They installed electric stoves and a refrigerator in the old Library Reading Room, and put in a bar and lunch counter. For a few days, the place was full of noise and activity, then, gradually, the Space Force people and all but a few of the civilians returned to their own work. There was still the business of airsealing the more habitable of the buildings already explored, and fitting them up in readiness for the arrival, in a year and a half, of the five hundred members of the main expedition. There was work to be done enlarging the landing field for the ship's rocket craft, and building new chemical-fuel tanks.

There was the work of getting the city's ancient reservoirs cleared of silt before the next spring thaw brought more water down the underground aqueducts everybody called canals in mistranslation of Schiaparelli's Italian word, though this was proving considerably easier than anticipated. The ancient Canal-Builders must have anticipated a time when their descendants would no longer be capable of maintenance work, and had prepared against it. By the day after the University had been made completely habitable, the actual work there was being done by Selim, Tony Lattimer and herself, with half a dozen Space Force officers, mostly girls, and four or five civilians, helping.

*T*hey worked up from the bottom, dividing the floor-surfaces into numbered squares, measuring and listing and sketching and photographing. They packaged samples of organic matter and sent them up to the ship for Carbon-14 dating and analysis; they opened cans and jars and bottles, and found that everything fluid in them had evaporated, through the porosity of glass and metal and plastic if there were no other way. Wherever they looked, they found evidence of activity suddenly suspended and never resumed. A vise with a bar of metal in it, half cut through and the hacksaw beside it. Pots and pans with hardened remains of food in them; a leathery cut of meat on a table, with the knife ready at hand. Toilet articles on washstands; unmade beds, the bedding ready to crumble at a touch but still retaining the impress of the sleeper's body; papers and writing materials on desks, as though the writer had gotten up, meaning to return and finish in a fifty-thousand-year-ago moment.

It worried her. Irrationally, she began to feel that the Martians had never left this place; that they were still around her, watching disapprovingly every time she picked up something they had laid down. They haunted her dreams, now, instead of their enigmatic writing. At first, everybody who had moved into the University had taken a separate room, happy to escape the crowding and lack of privacy of the huts. After a few nights, she was glad when Gloria Standish moved in with her, and accepted the newswoman's excuse that she felt lonely without somebody to talk to before falling asleep. Sachiko Koremitsu joined them the next evening, and before going to bed, the girl officer cleaned and oiled her pistol, remarking that she was afraid some rust may have gotten into it.

The others felt it, too. Selim von Ohlmhorst developed the habit of turning quickly and looking behind him, as though trying to surprise somebody or something that was stalking him. Tony Lattimer, having a drink at the bar that had been improvised from the librarian's desk in the Reading Room, set down his glass and swore.

"You know what this place is? It's an archaeological *Marie Celeste!*" he declared. "It was occupied right up to the end – we've all seen the shifts these people used to keep a civilization going here – but what was the end? What happened to them? Where did they go?"

"You didn't expect them to be waiting out front, with a red carpet and a big banner, *Welcome Terrans,* did you, Tony?" Gloria Standish asked.

"No, of course not; they've all been dead for fifty thousand years. But if they were the last of the Martians, why haven't we found their bones, at least? Who buried them, after they were dead?" He looked at the glass, a bubble-thin goblet, found, with hundreds of others like it, in a closet above, as though debating with himself whether to have another drink. Then he voted in the affirmative and reached for the cocktail pitcher. "And every door on the old ground level is either barred or barricaded from the inside. How did they get out? And why did they leave?"

The next day, at lunch, Sachiko Koremitsu had the answer to the second question. Four or five electrical engineers had come down by rocket from the ship, and she had been spending the morning with them, in oxy-masks, at the top of the building.

"Tony, I thought you said those generators were in good shape," she began, catching sight of Lattimer. "They aren't. They're in the most unholy mess I ever saw. What happened, up there, was that the supports of the wind-rotor gave way, and weight snapped the main shaft, and smashed everything under it."

"Well, after fifty thousand years, you can expect something like that," Lattimer retorted. "When an archaeologist says something's in good shape, he doesn't necessarily mean it'll start as soon as you shove a switch in."

"You didn't notice that it happened when the power was on, did you," one of the engineers asked, nettled at Lattimer's tone. "Well, it was. Everything's burned out or shorted or fused together; I saw one busbar eight inches across melted clean in two. It's a pity we didn't find things in good shape, even archaeologically speaking. I saw a lot of interesting things, things in advance of what we're using now. But it'll take a couple of years to get everything sorted out and figure what it looked like originally."

"Did it look as though anybody'd made any attempt to fix it?" Martha asked.

Sachiko shook her head. "They must have taken one look at it and given up. I don't believe there would have been any possible way to repair anything."

"Well, that explains why they left. They needed electricity for lighting, and heating, and all their industrial equipment was electrical. They had a good life, here, with power; without it, this place wouldn't have been habitable."

"Then why did they barricade everything from the inside, and how did they get out?" Lattimer wanted to know.

"To keep other people from breaking in and looting. Last man out probably barred the last door and slid down a rope from upstairs," von Ohlmhorst suggested. "This Houdini-trick doesn't worry me too much. We'll find out eventually."

"Yes, about the time Martha starts reading Martian," Lattimer scoffed.

"That may be just when we'll find out," von Ohlmhorst replied seriously. "It wouldn't surprise me if they left something in writing when they evacuated this place."

"Are you really beginning to treat this pipe dream of hers as a serious possibility, Selim?" Lattimer demanded. "I know, it would be a wonderful thing, but wonderful things don't happen just because they're wonderful. Only because they're possible, and this isn't. Let me quote that distinguished Hittitologist, Johannes Friedrich: 'Nothing can be translated out of nothing.' Or that later but not less distinguished

Hittitologist, Selim von Ohlmhorst: 'Where are you going to get your bilingual?'"

"Friedrich lived to see the Hittite language deciphered and read," von Ohlmhorst reminded him.

"Yes, when they found Hittite-Assyrian bilinguals." Lattimer measured a spoonful of coffee-powder into his cup and added hot water. "Martha, you ought to know, better than anybody, how little chance you have. You've been working for years in the Indus Valley; how many words of Harappa have you or anybody else ever been able to read?"

"We never found a university, with a half-million-volume library, at Harappa or Mohenjo-Daro."

"And, the first day we entered this building, we established meanings for several words," Selim von Ohlmhorst added.

"And you've never found another meaningful word since," Lattimer added. "And you're only sure of general meaning, not specific meaning of word-elements, and you have a dozen different interpretations for each word."

"We made a start," von Ohlmhorst maintained. "We have Grotefend's word for 'king.' But I'm going to be able to read some of those books, over there, if it takes me the rest of my life here. It probably will, anyhow."

"You mean you've changed your mind about going home on the *Cyrano*?" Martha asked. "You'll stay on here?"

The old man nodded. "I can't leave this. There's too much to discover. The old dog will have to learn a lot of new tricks, but this is where my work will be, from now on."

Lattimer was shocked. "You're nuts!" he cried. "You mean you're going to throw away everything you've accomplished in Hittitology and start all over again here on Mars? Martha, if you've talked him into this crazy decision, you're a criminal!"

"Nobody talked me into anything," von Ohlmhorst said roughly. "And as for throwing away what I've accomplished in Hittitology, I don't know what the devil you're talking about. Everything I know about the Hittite Empire is published and available to anybody. Hittitology's like Egyptology; it's stopped being research and archaeology and become scholarship and history. And I'm not a scholar or a historian; I'm a pick-and-shovel field archaeologist – a highly skilled and specialized grave-robber and junk-picker – and there's more pick-and-shovel work on this planet than I could do in a hundred lifetimes. This is something new; I was a fool to think I could turn my back on it and go back to scribbling footnotes about Hittite kings."

"You could have anything you wanted, in Hittitology. There are a dozen universities that'd sooner have you than a winning football team. But no! You have to be the top man in Martiology, too. You can't leave that for anybody else –" Lattimer shoved his chair back and got to his feet, leaving the table with an oath that was almost a sob of exasperation.

Maybe his feelings were too much for him. Maybe he realized, as Martha did, what he had betrayed. She sat, avoiding the eyes of the others, looking at the ceiling, as embarrassed as though Lattimer had flung something dirty on the table in front of them. Tony Lattimer had, desperately, wanted Selim to go home on the *Cyrano.* Martiology was a new field; if Selim entered it, he would bring with him the reputation he had already built in Hittitology, automatically stepping into the leading role that Lattimer had coveted for himself. Ivan Fitzgerald's words echoed back to her – when you want to be a big shot, you can't bear the possibility of anybody else being a bigger big shot. His derision of her own efforts became comprehensible, too. It wasn't that he was convinced that she would never learn to read the Martian language. He had been afraid that she would.

Ivan Fitzgerald finally isolated the germ that had caused the Finchley girl's undiagnosed illness. Shortly afterward, the malady turned into a mild fever, from which she recovered. Nobody else seemed to have caught it. Fitzgerald was still trying to find out how the germ had been transmitted.

They found a globe of Mars, made when the city had been a seaport. They located the city, and learned that its name had been Kukan – or something with a similar vowel-consonant ratio. Immediately, Sid Chamberlain and Gloria Standish began giving their telecasts a Kukan dateline, and Hubert Penrose used the name in his official reports. They also found a Martian calendar; the year had been divided into ten more or less equal months, and one of them had been Doma. Another month was Nor, and that was a part of the name of the scientific journal Martha had found.

Bill Chandler, the zoologist, had been going deeper and deeper into the old sea bottom of Syrtis. Four hundred miles from Kukan, and at fifteen thousand feet lower altitude, he shot a bird. At least, it was a something with wings and what were almost but not quite feathers, though it was more reptilian than avian in general characteristics. He and Ivan Fitzgerald skinned and mounted it, and then dissected the carcass almost tissue by tissue. About seven-eighths of its body capacity was lungs; it certainly breathed air containing at least half enough oxygen to support human life, or five times as much as the air around Kukan.

That took the center of interest away from archaeology, and started a new burst of activity. All the expedition's aircraft – four jetticopters and three wingless airdyne reconnaissance fighters – were thrown into intensified exploration of the lower sea bottoms, and the bio-science boys and girls were wild with excitement and making new discoveries on each flight.

The University was left to Selim and Martha and Tony Lattimer, the latter keeping to himself while she and the old Turco-German worked together. The civilian specialists in other fields, and the Space Force people who had been holding tape lines and making sketches and snapping cameras, were all flying to lower Syrtis to find out how much oxygen there was and what kind of life it supported.

Sometimes Sachiko dropped in; most of the time she was busy helping Ivan Fitzgerald dissect specimens. They had four or five species of what might loosely be called birds, and something that could easily be classed as a reptile, and a carnivorous mammal the size of a cat with birdlike claws, and a herbivore almost identical with the piglike thing in the big *Darfhulva* mural, and another like a gazelle with a single horn in the middle of its forehead.

The high point came when one party, at thirty thousand feet below the level of Kukan, found breathable air. One of them had a mild attack of *sorroche* and had to be flown back for treatment in a hurry, but the others showed no ill effects.

The daily newscasts from Terra showed a corresponding shift in interest at home. The discovery of the University had focused attention on the dead past of Mars; now the public was interested in Mars as a possible home for humanity. It was Tony Lattimer who brought archaeology back into the activities of the expedition and the news at home.

Martha and Selim were working in the museum on the second floor, scrubbing the grime from the glass cases, noting contents, and grease-penciling numbers; Lattimer and a couple of Space Force officers were going through what had been the administrative offices on the other side. It was one of these, a young second lieutenant, who came hurrying in from the mezzanine, almost bursting with excitement.

"Hey, Martha! Dr. von Ohlmhorst!" he was shouting. "Where are you? Tony's found the Martians!"

Selim dropped his rag back in the bucket; she laid her clipboard on top of the case beside her.

"Where?" they asked together.

"Over on the north side." The lieutenant took hold of himself and spoke more deliberately. "Little room, back of one of the old faculty offices – conference room. It was locked from the inside, and we had to burn it down with a torch. That's where they are. Eighteen of them, around a long table –"

Gloria Standish, who had dropped in for lunch, was on the mezzanine, fairly screaming into a radiophone extension:

". . . Dozen and a half of them! Well, of course they're dead. What a question! They look like skeletons covered with leather. No, I do not know what they died of. Well, forget it; I don't care if Bill Chandler's found a three-headed hippopotamus. Sid, don't you get it? We've found the *Martians!*"

She slammed the phone back on its hook, rushing away ahead of them.

Martha remembered the closed door; on the first survey, they hadn't attempted opening it. Now it was burned away at both sides and lay, still hot along the edges, on the floor of the big office room in front. A floodlight was on in the room inside, and Lattimer was going around looking at things while a Space Force officer stood by the door. The center of the room was filled by a long table; in armchairs around it sat the eighteen men and women who had occupied the room for the last fifty millennia. There were bottles and glasses on the table in front of them, and, had she seen them in a dimmer light, she would have thought that they were merely dozing over their drinks. One had a knee hooked over his chair-arm and was curled in foetuslike sleep. Another had fallen forward onto the table, arms extended, the emerald set of a ring twinkling dully on one finger. Skeletons covered with leather, Gloria Standish had called them, and so they were – faces like skulls, arms and legs like sticks, the flesh shrunken onto the bones under it.

"Isn't this something!" Lattimer was exulting. "Mass suicide, that's what it was. Notice what's in the corners?"

Braziers, made of perforated two-gallon-odd metal cans, the white walls smudged with smoke above them. Von Ohlmhorst had noticed them at once, and was poking into one of them with his flashlight.

"Yes; charcoal. I noticed a quantity of it around a couple of hand-forges in the shop on the first floor. That's why you had so much trouble breaking in; they'd sealed the room on the inside." He straightened and went around the room, until he found a ventilator, and peered into it. "Stuffed with rags. They must have been all that were left, here. Their power was gone, and they were old and tired, and all around them their world was dying. So they just came in here and lit the charcoal, and sat drinking together till they all fell asleep. Well, we know what became of them, now, anyhow."

Sid and Gloria made the most of it. The Terran public wanted to hear about Martians, and if live Martians couldn't be found, a room full of dead ones was the next best thing. Maybe an even better thing; it had been only sixty-odd years since the Orson Welles invasion-scare. Tony Lattimer, the discoverer, was beginning to cash in on his attentions to Gloria and his ingratiation with Sid; he was always either making voice-and-image talks for telecast or listening to the news from the home planet. Without question, he had become, overnight, the most widely known archaeologist in history.

"Not that I'm interested in all this, for myself," he disclaimed, after listening to the telecast from Terra two days after his discovery. "But this is going to be a big thing for Martian archaeology. Bring it to the public attention; dramatize it. Selim, can you remember when Lord Carnarvon and Howard Carter found the tomb of Tutankhamen?"

"In 1923? I was two years old, then," von Ohlmhorst chuckled. "I really don't know how much that publicity ever did for Egyptology. Oh, the museums did devote more space to Egyptian exhibits, and after a museum department head gets a few extra showcases, you know how hard it is to make him give them up. And, for a while, it was easier to get financial support for new excavations. But I don't know how much good all this public excitement really does, in the long run."

"Well, I think one of us should go back on the *Cyrano,* when the *Schiaparelli* orbits in," Lattimer said. "I'd hoped it would be you; your voice would carry the most weight. But I think it's important that one of us go back, to present the story of our work, and what we have accomplished and what we hope to accomplish, to the public and to the universities and the learned societies, and to the Federation Government. There will be a great deal of work that will have to be done. We must not allow the other scientific fields and the so-called practical interests to monopolize public and academic support. So, I believe I shall go back at least for a while, and see what I can do –"

Lectures. The organization of a Society of Martian Archaeology, with Anthony Lattimer, Ph.D., the logical candidate for the chair. Degrees, honors; the deference of the learned, and the adulation of the lay public. Positions, with impressive titles and salaries. Sweet are the uses of publicity.

She crushed out her cigarette and got to her feet. "Well, I still have the final lists of what we found in *Halvhulva* – Biology – department to check over. I'm starting on Sornhulva tomorrow, and I want that stuff in shape for expert evaluation."

That was the sort of thing Tony Lattimer wanted to get away from, the detail-work and the drudgery. Let the infantry do the slogging through the mud; the brass-hats got the medals.

She was halfway through the fifth floor, a week later, and was having midday lunch in the reading room on the first floor when Hubert Penrose came over and sat down beside her, asking her what she was doing. She told him.

"I wonder if you could find me a couple of men, for an hour or so," she added. "I'm stopped by a couple of jammed doors at the central hall. Lecture room and library, if the layout of that floor's anything like the ones below it."

"Yes. I'm a pretty fair door-buster, myself." He looked around the room. "There's Jeff Miles; he isn't doing much of anything. And we'll put Sid Chamberlain to work, for a change, too. The four of us ought to get your doors open." He called to Chamberlain, who was carrying his tray over to the dish washer. "Oh, Sid; you doing anything for the next hour or so?"

"I was going up to the fourth floor, to see what Tony's doing."

"Forget it. Tony's bagged his season limit of Martians. I'm going to help Martha bust in a couple of doors; we'll probably find a whole cemetery full of Martians."

Chamberlain shrugged. "Why not. A jammed door can have anything back of it, and I know what Tony's doing – just routine stuff."

Jeff Miles, the Space Force captain, came over, accompanied by one of the lab-crew from the ship who had come down on the rocket the day before.

"This ought to be up your alley, Mort," he was saying to his companion. "Chemistry and physics department. Want to come along?"

The lab man, Mort Tranter, was willing. Seeing the sights was what he'd come down from the ship for. She finished her coffee and cigarette, and they went out into the hall together, gathered equipment and rode the elevator to the fifth floor.

The lecture hall door was the nearest; they attacked it first. With proper equipment and help, it was no problem and in ten minutes they had it open wide enough to squeeze through with the floodlights. The room inside was quite empty, and, like most of the rooms behind closed doors, comparatively free from dust. The students, it appeared, had sat with their backs to the door, facing a low platform, but their seats and the lecturer's table and equipment had been removed. The two side walls bore inscriptions: on the right, a pattern of concentric circles which she recognized as a diagram of atomic structure, and on the left a complicated table of numbers and words, in two columns. Tranter was pointing at the diagram on the right.

"They got as far as the Bohr atom, anyhow," he said. "Well, not quite. They knew about electron shells, but they have the nucleus pictured as a solid mass. No indication of proton-and-neutron structure. I'll bet, when you come to translate their scientific books, you'll find that they taught that the atom was the ultimate and indivisible particle. That explains why you people never found any evidence that the Martians used nuclear energy."

"That's a uranium atom," Captain Miles mentioned.

"It is?" Sid Chamberlain asked, excitedly. "Then they did know about atomic energy. Just because we haven't found any pictures of A-bomb mushrooms doesn't mean –"

She turned to look at the other wall. Sid's signal reactions were setting away from him again; uranium meant nuclear power to him, and the two words were interchangeable. As she studied the arrangement of the numbers and words, she could hear Tranter saying:

"Nuts, Sid. We knew about uranium a long time before anybody found out what could be done with it. Uranium was discovered on Terra in 1789, by Klaproth."

There was something familiar about the table on the left wall. She tried to remember what she had been taught in school about physics, and what she had picked up by accident afterward. The second column was a continuation of the first: there were forty-six items in each, each item numbered consecutively –

"Probably used uranium because it's the largest of the natural atoms," Penrose was saying. "The fact that there's nothing beyond it there shows that they hadn't created any of the transuranics. A student could go to that thing and point out the outer electron of any of the ninety-two elements."

Ninety-two! That was it; there were ninety-two items in the table on the left wall! Hydrogen was Number One, she knew; One, *Sarfaldsorn.* Helium was Two; that was *Tirfaldsorn.* She couldn't remember which element came next, but in Martian it was *Sarfalddavas. Sorn* must mean matter, or substance, then. And *davas*; she was trying to think of what it could be. She turned quickly to the others, catching hold of Hubert Penrose's arm with one hand and waving her clipboard with the other.

"Look at this thing, over here," she was clamoring excitedly. "Tell me what you think it is. Could it be a table of the elements?"

They all turned to look. Mort Tranter stared at it for a moment.

"Could be. If I only knew what those squiggles meant –"

That was right; he'd spent his time aboard the ship.

"If you could read the numbers, would that help?" she asked, beginning to set down the Arabic digits and their Martian equivalents. "It's decimal system, the same as we use."

"Sure. If that's a table of elements, all I'd need would be the numbers. Thanks," he added as she tore off the sheet and gave it to him.

Penrose knew the numbers, and was ahead of him. "Ninety-two items, numbered consecutively. The first number would be the atomic number. Then a single word, the name of the element. Then the atomic weight –"

She began reading off the names of the elements. "I know hydrogen and helium; what's *tirfalddavas*, the third one?"

"Lithium," Tranter said. "The atomic weights aren't run out past the decimal point. Hydrogen's one plus, if that double-hook dingus is a plus sign; Helium's four-plus, that's right. And lithium's given as seven, that isn't right. It's six-point nine-four-oh. Or is that thing a Martian minus sign?"

"Of course! Look! A plus sign is a hook, to hang things together; a minus sign is a knife, to cut something off from something – see, the little loop is the handle and the long pointed loop is the blade. Stylized, of course, but that's what it is. And the fourth element, kiradavas; what's that?"

"Beryllium. Atomic weight given as nine-and-a-hook; actually it's nine-point-oh-two."

Sid Chamberlain had been disgruntled because he couldn't get a story about the Martians having developed atomic energy. It took him a few minutes to understand the newest development, but finally it dawned on him.

"Hey! You're reading that!" he cried. "You're reading Martian!"

"That's right," Penrose told him. "Just reading it right off. I don't get the two items after the atomic weight, though. They look like months of the Martian calendar. What ought they to be, Mort?"

Tranter hesitated. "Well, the next information after the atomic weight ought to be the period and group numbers. But those are words."

"What would the numbers be for the first one, hydrogen?"

"Period One, Group One. One electron shell, one electron in the outer shell," Tranter told her. "Helium's period one, too, but it has the outer – only – electron shell full, so it's in the group of inert elements."

"Trav, Trav. Trav's the first month of the year. And helium's *Trav, Yenth*; *Yenth* is the eighth month."

"The inert elements could be called Group Eight, yes. And the third element, lithium, is Period Two, Group One. That check?"

"It certainly does. *Sanv, Trav*; *Sanv's* the second month. What's the first element in Period Three?"

"Sodium. Number Eleven."

That's right; it's *Krav, Trav.* Why, the names of the months are simply numbers, one to ten, spelled out.

"Doma's the fifth month. That was your first Martian word, Martha," Penrose told her. "The word for five. And if *davas* is the word for metal, and *sornhulva* is chemistry and / or physics, I'll bet Tadavas Sornhulva is literally translated as: Of-Metal Matter-Knowledge. Metallurgy, in other words. I wonder what Mastharnorvod means." It surprised her that, after so long and with so much happening in the meantime, he could remember that. "Something like 'Journal,' or 'Review,' or maybe 'Quarterly.'"

"We'll work that out, too," she said confidently. After this, nothing seemed impossible. "Maybe we can find –" Then she stopped short. "You said 'Quarterly.' I think it was 'Monthly,' instead. It was dated for a specific month, the fifth one. And if *nor* is ten, Mastharnorvod could be 'Year-Tenth.' And I'll bet we'll find that *masthar* is the word for year." She looked at the table on the wall again. "Well, let's get all these words down, with translations for as many as we can."

"Let's take a break for a minute," Penrose suggested, getting out his cigarettes. "And then, let's do this in comfort. Jeff, suppose you and Sid go across the hall and see what you find in the other room in the way of a desk or something like that, and a few chairs. There'll be a lot of work to do on this."

Sid Chamberlain had been squirming as though he were afflicted with ants, trying to contain himself. Now he let go with an excited jabber.

"This is really it! *The* it, not just it-of-the-week, like finding the reservoirs or those statues or this building, or even the animals and the dead Martians! Wait till Selim and Tony see this! Wait till Tony sees it; I want to see his face! And when I get this on telecast, all Terra's going to go nuts about it!" He turned to Captain Miles. "Jeff, suppose you take a look at that other door, while I find somebody to send to tell Selim and Tony. And Gloria; wait till she sees this –"

"Take it easy, Sid," Martha cautioned. "You'd better let me have a look at your script, before you go too far overboard on the telecast. This is just a beginning; it'll take years and years before we're able to read any of those books downstairs."

"It'll go faster than you think, Martha," Hubert Penrose told her. "We'll all work on it, and we'll teleprint material to Terra, and people there will work on it. We'll send them everything we can . . . everything we work out, and copies of books, and copies of your word-lists –"

And there would be other tables – astronomical tables, tables in physics and mechanics, for instance – in which words and numbers were equivalent. The library stacks, below, would be full of them. Transliterate them into Roman alphabet spellings and Arabic numerals, and somewhere, somebody would spot each numerical significance, as Hubert Penrose and Mort Tranter and she had done with the table of elements. And pick out all the chemistry textbooks in the Library; new words would take on meaning from contexts in which the names of elements appeared. She'd have to start studying chemistry and physics, herself –

Sachiko Koremitsu peeped in through the door, then stepped inside.

"Is there anything I can do – ?" she began. "What's happened? Something important?"

"Important?" Sid Chamberlain exploded. "Look at that, Sachi! We're reading it! Martha's found out how to read Martian!" He grabbed Captain Miles by the arm. "Come on, Jeff; let's go. I want to call the others –" He was still babbling as he hurried from the room.

Sachi looked at the inscription. "Is it true?" she asked, and then, before Martha could more than begin to explain, flung her arms around her. "Oh, it really is! You are reading it! I'm so happy!"

She had to start explaining again when Selim von Ohlmhorst entered. This time, she was able to finish.

"But, Martha, can you be really sure? You know, by now, that learning to read this language is as important to me as it is to you, but how can you be so sure that those words really mean things like hydrogen and helium and boron and oxygen? How do you know that their table of elements was anything like ours?"

Tranter and Penrose and Sachiko all looked at him in amazement.

"That isn't just the Martian table of elements; that's *the* table of elements. It's the only one there is." Mort Tranter almost exploded. "Look, hydrogen has one proton and one electron. If it had more of either, it wouldn't be hydrogen, it'd be something else. And the same with all the rest of the elements. And hydrogen on Mars is the same as hydrogen on Terra, or on Alpha Centauri, or in the next galaxy –"

"You just set up those numbers, in that order, and any first-year chemistry student could tell you what elements they represented." Penrose said. "Could if he expected to make a passing grade, that is."

The old man shook his head slowly, smiling. "I'm afraid I wouldn't make a passing grade. I didn't know, or at least didn't realize, that. One of the things I'm going to place an order for, to be brought on the *Schiaparelli,* will be a set of primers in chemistry and physics, of the sort intended for a bright child of ten or twelve. It seems that a Martiologist has to learn a lot of things the Hittites and the Assyrians never heard about."

Tony Lattimer, coming in, caught the last part of the explanation. He looked quickly at the walls and, having found out just what had happened, advanced and caught Martha by the hand.

"You really did it, Martha! You found your bilingual! I never believed that it would be possible; let me congratulate you!"

He probably expected that to erase all the jibes and sneers of the past. If he did, he could have it that way. His friendship would mean as little to her as his derision – except that his friends had to watch their backs and his knife. But he was going home on the *Cyrano,* to be a big shot. Or had this changed his mind for him again?

"This is something we can show the world, to justify any expenditure of time and money on Martian archaeological work. When I get back to Terra, I'll see that you're given full credit for this achievement –"

On Terra, her back and his knife would be out of her watchfulness.

"We won't need to wait that long," Hubert Penrose told him dryly. "I'm sending off an official report, tomorrow; you can be sure Dr. Dane will be given full credit, not only for this but for her previous work, which made it possible to exploit this discovery."

"And you might add, work done in spite of the doubts and discouragements of her colleagues," Selim von Ohlmhorst said. "To which I am ashamed to have to confess my own share."

"You said we had to find a bilingual," she said. "You were right, too."

"This is better than a bilingual, Martha," Hubert Penrose said. "Physical science expresses universal facts; necessarily it is a universal language. Heretofore archaeologists have dealt only with pre-scientific cultures."

The Keeper

When he heard the deer crashing through brush and scuffling the dead leaves, he stopped and stood motionless in the path. He watched them bolt down the slope from the right and cross in front of him, wishing he had the rifle, and when the last white tail vanished in the grey-brown woods he drove the spike of the ice-staff into the stiffening ground and took both hands to shift the weight of the pack. If he'd had the rifle, he could have shot only one of them. As it was, they were unfrightened, and he knew where to find them in the morning.

Ahead, to the west and north, low clouds massed; the white front of the Ice-Father loomed clear and sharp between them and the blue of the distant forests. It would snow, tonight. If it stopped at daybreak, he would have good tracking, and in any case, it would be easier to get the carcasses home over snow. He wrenched loose the ice-staff and started forward again, following the path that wound between and among and over the irregular mounds and hillocks. It was still an hour's walk to Keeper's House, and the daylight was fading rapidly.

Sometimes, when he was not so weary and in so much haste, he would loiter here, wondering about the ancient buildings and the long-vanished people who had raised them. There had been no woods at all, then; nothing but great houses like mountains, piling up toward the sky, and the valley where he meant to hunt tomorrow had been an arm of the sea that was now a three days' foot-journey away. Some said that the cities had been destroyed and the people killed in wars – big wars, not squabbles like the fights between sealing-companies from different villages. He didn't think so, himself. It was more likely that they had all left their homes and gone away in starships when the Ice-Father had been born and started pushing down out of the north. There had been many starships, then. When he had been a boy, the old men had talked about a long-ago time when there had been hundreds of them visible in the sky, every morning and evening. But that had been long ago indeed. Starships came but seldom to this world, now. This world was old and lonely and poor. Like poor lonely old Raud the Keeper.

He felt angry to find himself thinking like that. Never pity yourself, Raud; be proud. That was what his father had always taught him: "Be proud, for you are the Keeper's son, and when I am gone, you will be the Keeper after me. But in your pride, be humble, for what you will keep is the Crown."

The thought of the Crown, never entirely absent from his mind, wakened the anxiety that always slept lightly if at all. He had been away all day, and there were so many things that could happen. The path seemed longer, after that; the landmarks farther apart. Finally, he came out on the edge of the steep bank, and looked down across the brook to the familiar low windowless walls and sharp-ridged roof of Keeper's House; and when he came, at last, to the door, and pulled the latchstring, he heard the dogs inside – the soft, coughing bark of Brave, and the anxious little whimper of Bold – and he knew that there was nothing wrong in Keeper's House.

The room inside was lighted by a fist-sized chunk of lumicon, hung in a net bag of thongs from the rafter over the table. It was old – cast off by some rich Southron as past its best brilliance, it had been old when he had bought it from Yorn Nazvik the Trader, and that had been years ago. Now its light was as dim and yellow as firelight. He'd have to replace it soon, but this trip he had needed new cartridges for the big rifle. A man could live in darkness more easily than he could live without cartridges.

The big black dogs were rising from their bed of deerskins on the stone slab that covered the crypt in the far corner. They did not come to meet him, but stayed in their place of trust, greeting him with anxious, eager little sounds.

"Good boys," he said. "Good dog, Brave; good dog, Bold. Old Keeper's home again. Hungry?"

They recognized that word, and whined. He hung up the ice-staff on the pegs by the door, then squatted and got his arms out of the pack-straps.

"Just a little now; wait a little," he told the dogs. "Keeper'll get something for you."

He unhooked the net bag that held the lumicon and went to the ladder, climbing to the loft between the stone ceiling and the steep snow-shed roof; he cut down two big chunks of smoked wild-ox beef – the dogs liked that better than smoked venison – and climbed down.

He tossed one chunk up against the ceiling, at the same time shouting: "Bold! Catch!" Bold leaped forward, sinking his teeth into the meat as it was still falling, shaking and mauling it. Brave, still on the crypt-slab, was quivering with hunger and eagerness, but he remained in place until the second chunk was tossed and he was ordered to take it. Then he, too, leaped and caught it, savaging it in mimicry of a kill. For a while, he stood watching them growl and snarl and tear their meat, great beasts whose shoulders came above his own waist. While they lived to guard it, the Crown was safe. Then he crossed to the hearth, scraped away the covering ashes, piled on kindling and logs and fanned the fire alight. He lifted the pack to the table and unlaced the deerskin cover.

Cartridges in plastic boxes of twenty, long and thick; shot for the duck-gun, and powder and lead and cartridge-primers; fills for the fire-lighter; salt; needles; a new file. And the deerskin bag of trade-tokens. He emptied them on the table and counted them – tokens, and half-tokens and five-tokens, and even one ten-token. There were always less in the bag, after each trip to the village. The Southrons paid less and less, each year, for furs and skins, and asked more and more for what they had to sell.

He put away the things he had brought from the village, and was considering whether to open the crypt now and replace the bag of tokens, when the dogs stiffened, looking at the door. They got to their feet, neck-hairs bristling, as the knocking began.

He tossed the token-bag onto the mantel and went to the door, the dogs following and standing ready as he opened it.

The snow had started, and now the ground was white except under the evergreens. Three men stood outside the door, and over their shoulders he could see an airboat grounded in the clearing in front of the house.

"You are honored, Raud Keeper," one of them began. "Here are strangers who have come to talk to you. Strangers from the Stars!"

He recognized the speaker, in sealskin boots and deerskin trousers and hooded overshirt like his own – Vahr Farg's son, one of the village people. His father was dead, and his woman was the daughter of Gorth Sledmaker, and he was a house-dweller with his woman's father. A worthless youth, lazy and stupid and said to be a coward. Still, guests were guests, even when brought by the likes of Vahr Farg's son. He looked again at the airboat, and remembered seeing it, that day, made fast to the top-deck of Yorn Nazvik's trading-ship, the Issa.

"Enter and be welcome; the house is yours, and all in it that is mine to give." He turned to the dogs. "Brave, Bold; go watch."

Obediently, they trotted over to the crypt and lay down. He stood aside; Vahr entered, standing aside also, as though he were the host, inviting his companions in. They wore heavy garments of woven cloth and boots of tanned leather with hard heels and stiff soles, and as they came in, each unbuckled and laid aside a belt with a holstered negatron pistol. One was stocky and broad-shouldered, with red hair; the other was slender, dark haired and dark eyed, with a face as smooth as a woman's. Everybody in the village had wondered about them. They were not of Yorn Nazvik's crew, but passengers on the *Issa.*

"These are Empire people, from the Far Stars," Vahr informed him, naming their names. Long names, which meant nothing; certainly they were not names the Southrons from the Warm Seas bore. "And this is Raud the Keeper, with whom your honors wish to speak."

"Keeper's House is honored. I'm sorry that I have not food prepared; if you can excuse me while I make some ready. . . ."

"You think these noblemen from the Stars would eat your swill?" Vahr hooted. "Crazy old fool, these are –"

The slim man pivoted on his heel; his open hand caught Vahr just below the ear and knocked him sprawling. It must have been some kind of trick-blow. That or else the slim stranger was stronger than he looked.

"Hold your miserable tongue!" he told Vahr, who was getting to his feet. "We're guests of Raud the Keeper, and we'll not have him insulted in his own house by a cur like you!"

The man with red hair turned. "I am ashamed. We should not have brought this into your house; we should have left it outside." He spoke the Northland language well, "It will honor us to share your food, Keeper."

"Yes, and see here," the younger man said, "we didn't know you'd be alone. Let us help you. Dranigo's a fine cook, and I'm not bad, myself."

He started to protest, then let them have their way. After all, a guest's women helped the woman of the house, and as there was no woman in Keeper's House, it was not unfitting for them to help him.

"Your friend's name is Dranigo?" he asked. "I'm sorry, but I didn't catch yours."

"I don't wonder; fool mouthed it so badly I couldn't understand it myself. It's Salvadro."

They fell to work with him, laying out eating-tools – there were just enough to go around – and hunting for dishes, of which there were not. Salvadro saved that situation by going out and bringing some in from the airboat. He must have realized that the lumicon over the table was the only light beside the fire in the house, for he was carrying a globe of the luminous plastic with him when he came in, grumbling about how dark it had gotten outside. It was new and brilliant, and the light hurt Raud's eyes, at first.

"Are you truly from the Stars?" he asked, after the food was on the table and they had begun to eat. "Neither I nor any in the village have seen anybody from the Stars before."

The big man with the red hair nodded. "Yes. We are from Dremna."

Why, Dremna was the Great World, at the middle of everything! Dremna was the Empire. People from Dremna came to the cities of Awster and fabulous Antark as Southron traders from the Warm Seas came to the villages of the Northfolk. He stammered something about that.

"Yes. You see, we. . . ." Dranigo began. "I don't know the word for it, in your language, but we're people whose work it is to learn things. Not from other people or from books, but new things, that nobody else knows. We came here to learn about the long-ago times on this world, like the great city that was here and is now mounds of stone and earth. Then, when we go back to Dremna, we will tell other people what we have found out."

Vahr Farg's son, having eaten his fill, was fidgeting on his stool, looking contemptuously at the strangers and their host. He thought they were fools to waste time learning about people who had died long ago. So he thought the Keeper was a fool, to guard a worthless old piece of junk.

Raud hesitated for a moment, then said: "I have a very ancient thing, here in this house. It was worn, long ago, by great kings. Their names, and the name of their people, are lost, but the Crown remains. It was left to me as a trust by my father, who was Keeper before me and to whom it was left by his father, who was Keeper in his time. Have you heard of it?"

Dranigo nodded. "We heard of it, first of all, on Dremna," he said. "The Empire has a Space Navy base, and observatories and relay stations, on this planet. Space Navy officers who had been here brought the story back; they heard it from traders from the Warm Seas, who must have gotten it from people like Yorn Nazvik. Would you show it to us, Keeper? It was to see the Crown that we came here."

Raud got to his feet, and saw, as he unhooked the lumicon, that he was trembling. "Yes, of course. It is an honor. It is an ancient and wonderful thing, but I never thought that it was known on Dremna." He hastened across to the crypt.

The dogs looked up as he approached. They knew that he wanted to lift the cover, but they were comfortable and had to be coaxed to leave it. He laid aside the deerskins. The stone slab was heavy, and he had to strain to tilt it up. He leaned it against the wall, then picked up the lumicon and went down the steps into the little room below, opening the wooden chest and getting out the bundle wrapped in bearskin. He brought it up again and carried it to the table, from which Dranigo and Salvadro were clearing the dishes.

"Here it is," he said, untying the thongs. "I do not know how old it is. It was old even before the Ice-Father was born."

That was too much for Vahr. "See, I told you he's crazy!" he cried. "The Ice-Father has been here forever. Gorth Sledmaker says so," he added, as though that settled it.

"Gorth Sledmaker's a fool. He thinks the world began in the time of his grandfather." He had the thongs untied, and spread the bearskin, revealing the blackened leather box, flat on the bottom and domed at the top. "How long ago do you think it was that the Ice-Father was born?" he asked Salvadro and Dranigo.

"Not more than two thousand years," Dranigo said. "The glaciation hadn't started in the time of the Third Empire. There is no record of this planet during the Fourth, but by the beginning of the Fifth Empire, less than a thousand years ago, things here were very much as they are now."

"There are other worlds which have Ice-Fathers," Salvadro explained. "They are all worlds having one pole or the other in open water, surrounded by land. When the polar sea is warmed by water from the tropics, snow falls on the lands around, and more falls in winter than melts in summer, and so is an Ice-Father formed. Then, when the polar sea is all frozen, no more snow falls, and the Ice-Father melts faster than it grows, and finally vanishes. And then, when warm water comes into the polar sea again, more snow falls, and it starts over again. On a world like this, it takes fifteen or twenty thousand years from one Ice-Father to the next."

"I never heard that there had been another Ice-Father, before this one. But then, I only know the stories told by the old men, when I was a boy. I suppose that was before the first people came in starships to this world."

The two men of Dremna looked at one another oddly, and he wondered, as he unfastened the brass catches on the box, if he had said something foolish, and then he had the box open, and lifted out the Crown. He was glad, now, that Salvadro had brought in the new lumicon, as he put the box aside and set the Crown on the black bearskin. The golden circlet and the four arches of gold above it were clean and bright, and the jewels were splendid in the light. Salvadro and Dranigo were looking at it wide-eyed. Vahr Farg's son was open-mouthed.

"Great Universe! Will you look at that diamond on the top!" Salvadro was saying.

"That's not the work of any Galactic art-period," Dranigo declared. "That thing goes back to the Pre-Interstellar Era." And for a while he talked excitedly to Salvadro.

"Tell me, Keeper," Salvadro said at length, "how much do you know about the Crown? Where did it come from; who made it; who were the first Keepers?"

He shook his head. "I only know what my father told me, when I was a boy. Now I am an old man, and some things I have forgotten. But my father was Runch, Raud's son, who was the son of Yorn, the son of Raud, the son of Runch." He went back six more generations, then faltered and stopped. "Beyond that, the names have been lost. But I do know that for a long time the Crown was in a city to the north of here, and before that it was brought across the sea from another country, and the name of that country was Brinn."

Dranigo frowned, as though he had never heard the name before. "Brinn." Salvadro's eyes widened. "Brinn, Dranigo! Do you think that might be Britain?"

Dranigo straightened, staring, "It might be! Britain was a great nation, once; the last nation to join the Terran Federation, in the Third Century Pre-Interstellar. And they had a king, and a crown with a great diamond. . . ."

"The story of where it was made," Rand offered, "or who made it, has been lost. I suppose the first people brought it to this world when they came in starships."

"It's more wonderful than that, Keeper," Salvadro said. "It was made on this world, before the first starship was built. This world is Terra, the Mother-World; didn't you know that, Keeper? This is the world where Man was born."

He hadn't known that. Of course, there had to be a world like that, but a great world in the middle of everything, like Dremna. Not this old, forgotten world.

"It's true, Keeper," Dranigo told him. He hesitated slightly, then cleared his throat. "Keeper, you're young no longer, and some day you must die, as your father and his father did. Who will care for the Crown then?"

Who, indeed? His woman had died long ago, and she had given him no sons, and the daughters she had given him had gone their own ways with men of their own choosing and he didn't know what had become of any of them. And the village people – they would start picking the

Crown apart to sell the jewels, one by one, before the ashes of his pyre stopped smoking.

"Let us have it, Keeper," Salvadro said. "We will take it to Dremna, where armed men will guard it day and night, and it will be a trust upon the Government of the Empire forever."

He recoiled in horror. "Man! You don't know what you're saying!" he cried. "This is the Crown, and I am the Keeper; I cannot part with it as long as there is life in me."

"And when there is not, what? Will it be laid on your pyre, so that it may end with you?" Dranigo asked.

"Do you think we'd throw it away as soon as we got tired looking at it?" Salvadro exclaimed. "To show you how we'll value this, we'll give you . . . how much is a thousand imperials in trade-tokens, Dranigo?"

"I'd guess about twenty thousand."

"We'll give you twenty thousand Government trade-tokens," Salvadro said. "If it costs us that much, you'll believe that we'll take care of it, won't you?"

Raud rose stiffly. "It is a wrong thing," he said, "to enter a man's house and eat at his table, and then insult him."

Dranigo rose also, and Salvadro with him. "We had no mind to insult you, Keeper, or offer you a bribe to betray your trust. We only offer to help you fulfill it, so that the Crown will be safe after all of us are dead. Well, we won't talk anymore about it, now. We're going in Yorn Nazvik's ship, tomorrow; he's trading in the country to the west, but before he returns to the Warm Seas, he'll stop at Long Valley Town, and we'll fly over to see you. In the meantime, think about this; ask yourself if you would not be doing a better thing for the Crown by selling it to us."

They wanted to leave the dishes and the new lumicon, and he permitted it, to show that he was not offended by their offer to buy the Crown. He knew that it was something very important to them, and he admitted, grudgingly, that they could care for it better than he. At least, they would not keep it in a hole under a hut in the wilderness, guarded only by dogs. But they were not Keepers, and he was. To them, the Crown would be but one of many important things; to him it was everything. He could not imagine life without it.

He lay for a long time among his bed-robes, unable to sleep, thinking of the Crown and the visitors. Finally, to escape those thoughts, he began planning tomorrow morning's hunt.

He would start out as soon as the snow stopped, and go down among the scrub-pines; he would take Brave with him, and leave Bold on guard at home. Brave was more obedient, and a better hunter. Bold would jump for the deer that had been shot, but Brave always tried to catch or turn the ones that were still running.

He needed meat badly, and he needed more deerskins, to make new clothes. He was thinking of the new overshirt he meant to make as he fell asleep. . . .

It was past noon when he and Brave turned back toward Keeper's House. The deer had gone farther than he had expected, but he had found them, and killed four. The carcasses were cleaned and hung from trees, out of reach of the foxes and the wolves, and he would take Brave back to the house and leave him on guard, and return with Bold and the sled to bring in the meat. He was thinking cheerfully of the fresh meat when he came out onto the path from the village, a mile from Keeper's House. Then he stopped short, looking at the tracks.

Three men – no, four – had come from the direction of the village since the snow had stopped. One had been wearing sealskin boots, of the sort worn by all Northfolk. The others had worn Southron boots, with ribbed plastic soles. That puzzled him. None of the village people wore Southron boots, and as he had been leaving in the early morning, he had seen Yorn Nazvik's ship, the *Issa,* lift out from the village and pass overhead, vanishing in the west. Possibly these were deserters. In any case, they were not good people. He slipped the heavy rifle from its snow-cover, checked the chamber, and hung the empty cover around his neck like a scarf. He didn't like the looks of it.

He liked it even less when he saw that the man in sealskin boots had stopped to examine the tracks he and Brave had made on leaving, and had then circled the house and come back, to be joined by his plastic-soled companions. Then they had all put down their packs and their ice-staffs, and advanced toward the door of the house. They had stopped there for a moment, and then they had entered, come out again, gotten their packs and ice-staffs, and gone away, up the slope to the north.

"Wait, Brave," he said. "Watch."

Then he advanced, careful not to step on any of the tracks until he reached the doorstep, where it could not be avoided.

"Bold!" he called loudly. "Bold!"

Silence. No welcoming whimper, no padding of feet, inside. He pulled the latchstring with his left hand and pushed the door open with his foot, the rifle ready. There was no need for that. What welcomed him, within, was a sickening stench of burned flesh and hair.

The new lumicon lighted the room brilliantly; his first glance was enough. The slab that had covered the crypt was thrown aside, along with the pile of deerskins, and between it and the door was a shapeless black heap that, in a dimmer light, would not have been instantly recognizable as the body of Bold. Fighting down an impulse to rush in, he stood in the door, looking about and reading the story of what had happened. The four men had entered, knowing that they would find Bold alone. The one in the lead had had a negatron pistol drawn, and when Bold had leaped at them, he had been blasted. The blast had caught the dog from in front – the chest-cavity was literally exploded, and the neck and head burned and smashed unrecognizably. Even the brass studs on the leather collar had been melted.

That and the ribbed sole-prints outside meant the same thing – Southrons. Every Southron who came into the Northland, even the common crewmen on the trading ships, carried some kind of an energy-weapon. They were good only for fighting – one look at the body of Bold showed what they did to meat and skins.

He entered, then, laying his rifle on the table, and got down the lumicon and went over to the crypt. After a while, he returned, hung up the light again, and dropped onto a stool. He sat staring at the violated crypt and tugging with one hand at a corner of his beard, trying desperately to think.

The thieves had known exactly where the Crown was kept and how it was guarded; after killing Bold, they had gone straight to it, taken it and gone away – three men in plastic-soled Southron boots and one man in soft boots of sealskins, each with a pack and an ice-staff, and two of them with rifles.

Vahr Farg's son, and three deserters from the crew of Yorn Nazvik's ship.

It hadn't been Dranigo and Salvadro. They could have left the ship in their airboat and come back, flying low, while he had been hunting. But they would have grounded near the house, they would not have carried packs, and they would have brought nobody with them.

He thought he knew what had happened. Vahr Farg's son had seen the Crown, and he had heard the two Starfolk offer more trade-tokens for it than everything in the village was worth. But he was a coward; he would never dare to face the Keeper's rifle and the teeth of Brave and Bold alone. So, since none of the village folk would have part in so shameful a crime against the moral code of the Northland, he had talked three of Yorn Nazvik's airmen into deserting and joining him.

And he had heard Dranigo say that the *Issa* would return to Long Valley Town after the trading voyage to the west. Long Valley was on the other side of this tongue of the Ice-Father; it was a good fifteen days' foot-journey around, but by climbing and crossing, they could easily be there in time to meet Yorn Nazvik's ship and the two Starfolk. Well, where Vahr Farg's son could take three Southrons, Raud the Keeper could follow.

Their tracks led up the slope beside the brook, always bearing to the left, in the direction of the Ice-Father. After an hour, he found where they had stopped and unslung their packs, and rested long enough to smoke a cigarette. He read the story they had left in the snow, and then continued, Brave trotting behind him pulling the sled. A few snowflakes began dancing in the air, and he quickened his steps. He knew, generally, where the thieves were going, but he wanted their tracks unobliterated in front of him. The snow fell thicker and thicker, and it was growing dark, and he was tiring. Even Brave was stumbling occasionally before Raud stopped, in a hollow among the pines, to build his tiny fire and eat and feed the dog. They bedded down together, covered by the same sleeping robes.

When he woke, the world was still black and white and grey in the early dawn-light, and the robe that covered him and Brave was powdered with snow, and the pine-branches above him were loaded and sagging.

The snow had completely obliterated the tracks of the four thieves, and it was still falling. When the sled was packed and the dog harnessed to it, they set out, keeping close to the flank of the Ice-Father on their left.

It stopped snowing toward mid-day, and a little after, he heard a shot, far ahead, and then two more, one upon the other. The first shot would be the rifle of Vahr Farg's son; it was a single-loader, like his own. The other two were from one of the light Southron rifles, which fired a dozen shots one after another. They had shot, or shot at, something like a deer, he supposed. That was sensible; it would save their dried meat for the trip across the back of the Ice-Father. And it showed that they still didn't know he was following them. He found their tracks, some hours later.

Toward dusk, he came to a steep building-mound. It had fared better than most of the houses of the ancient people; it rose to twenty times a man's height and on the southeast side it was almost perpendicular. The other side sloped, and he was able to climb to the top, and far away, ahead of him, he saw a tiny spark appear and grow. The fire could not be more than two hours ahead.

He built no fire that evening, but shared a slab of pemmican with Brave, and they huddled together under the bearskin robe. The dog fell asleep at once. For a long time, Raud sat awake, thinking.

At first, he considered resting for a while, and then pressing forward and attacking them as they slept. He had to kill all of them to regain the Crown; that he had taken for granted from the first. He knew what would happen if the Government Police came into this. They would take one Southron's word against the word of ten Northfolk, and the thieves would simply claim the Crown as theirs and accuse him of trying to steal it. And Dranigo and Salvadro – they seemed like good men, but they might see this as the only way to get the Crown for themselves. . . . He would have to settle the affair for himself, before the men reached Long Valley town.

If he could do it here, it would save him and Brave the toil and danger of climbing the Ice-Father. But could he? They had two rifles, one an autoloader, and they had in all likelihood three negatron pistols. After the single shot of the big rifle was fired, he had only a knife and a hatchet and the spiked and pickaxed ice-staff, and Brave. One of the thieves would kill him before he and Brave killed all of them, and then the Crown would be lost. He dropped into sleep, still thinking of what to do.

He climbed the mound of the ancient building again in the morning, and looked long and carefully at the face of the Ice-Father. It would take the thieves the whole day to reach that place where the two tongues of the glacier split apart, the easiest spot to climb. They would not try to climb that evening; Vahr, who knew the most about it, would be the last to advise such a risk. He was sure that by going up at the nearest point he could get to the top of the Ice-Father before dark, and drag Brave up after him. It would be a fearful climb, and he would have most of a day's journey after that to reach the head of the long ravine up which the thieves would come, but when they came up, he could be there waiting for them. He knew what the old rifle could do, to an inch, and there were places where the thieves would be coming up where he could stay out of blaster-range and pick them all off, even with a single-loader.

He knew about negatron pistols, too. They shot little bullets of energy; they were very fast, and did not drop, like a real bullet, so that no judgment of range was needed. But the energy died quickly; the negatrons lived only long enough to go five hundred paces and no more. At eight hundred, he could hit a man easily. He almost felt himself pitying Vahr Farg's son and his companions.

When he reached the tumble of rocks that had been dragged along with and pushed out from the Ice-Father, he stopped and made up a pack – sleeping robes, all his cartridges, as much pemmican as he could carry, and the bag of trade-tokens. If the chase took him to Long Valley Town, he would need money. He also coiled about his waist a long rawhide climbing-rope, and left the sled-harness on Brave, simply detaching the traces.

At first, they walked easily on the sloping ice. Then, as it grew steeper, he fastened the rope to the dog's harness and advanced a little at a time, dragging Brave up after him. Soon he was forced to snub the rope with his ice-staff and chop steps with his hatchet. Toward noon – at least he thought it was noon – it began snowing again, and the valley below was blotted out in a swirl of white.

They came to a narrow ledge, where they could rest, with a wall of ice rising sheerly above them. He would have to climb that alone, and then pull Brave up with the rope. He started working his way up the perpendicular face, clinging by the pick of his ice-staff, chopping footholds with the hatchet; the pack and the slung rifle on his back pulled at him and threatened to drag him down. At length, he dragged himself over the edge and drove the ice-staff in.

"Up, Brave!" he called, tugging on the rope. "Good dog, Brave; come up!"

Brave tried to jump and slipped back. He tried again, and this time Raud snubbed the rope and held him. Below the dog pawed frantically, until he found a paw-hold on one of the chopped-out steps. Raud hauled on the rope, and made another snub.

It seemed like hours. It probably was; his arms were aching, and he had lost all sense of time, or of the cold, or the danger of the narrow ledge; he forgot about the Crown and the men who had stolen it; he even forgot how he had come here, or that he had ever been anywhere else. All that mattered was to get Brave up on the ledge beside him.

Finally Brave came up and got first his fore-paws and then his body over the edge. He lay still, panting proudly, while Raud hugged him and told him, over and over, that he was a good dog. They rested for a long time, and Raud got a slab of pemmican from the pack and divided it with Brave.

It was while they rested in the snow, munching, that he heard the sound for the first time. It was faint and far away, and it sounded like thunder, or like an avalanche beginning, and that puzzled him, for this was not the time of year for either. As he listened, he heard it again, and this time he recognized it – negatron pistols. It frightened him; he wondered if the thieves had met a band of hunters. No; if they were fighting Northfolk, there would be the reports of firearms, too. Or might they be fighting among themselves? Remembering the melted brass studs on Bold's collar, he became more frightened at the thought of what a negatron-blast could do to the Crown.

The noise stopped, then started again, and he got to his feet, calling to Brave. They were on a wide ledge that slanted upward toward the north. It would take him closer to the top, and closer to where Vahr and his companions would come up. Together, they started up, Raud probing cautiously ahead of him with the ice-staff for hidden crevasses. After a while, he came to a wide gap in the ice beside him, slanting toward the top, its upper end lost in swirling snow. So he and Brave began climbing, and after a while he could no longer hear the negatron pistols.

When it was almost too dark to go farther, he suddenly found himself on level snow, and here he made camp, digging a hole and lining it with the sleeping robes.

The sky was clear when he woke, and a pale yellow light was glowing in the east. For a while he lay huddled with the dog, stiff and miserable, and then he forced himself to his feet. He ate, and fed Brave, and then checked his rifle and made his pack.

He was sure, now, that he had a plan that would succeed. He could reach the place where Vahr and the Southrons would come up long before they did, and be waiting for them. In his imagination, he could see them coming up in single file, Vahr Farg's son in the lead, and he could imagine himself hidden behind a mound of snow, the ice-staff upright to brace his left hand and the forestock of the rifle resting on his outthrust thumb and the butt against his shoulder. The first bullet would be for Vahr. He could shoot all of them, one after another, that way. . . .

He stopped, looking in chagrined incredulity at the trucks in front of him – the tracks he knew so well, of one man in sealskin boots and three men with ribbed plastic soles. Why, it couldn't be! They should be no more than halfway up the long ravine, between the two tongues of the Ice-Father, ten miles to the north. But here they were, on the back of the Ice-Father and crossing to the west ahead of him. They must have climbed the sheer wall of ice, only a few miles from where he had dragged himself and Brave to the top. Then he remembered the negatron-blasts he had heard. While he had been chopping footholds with a hatchet, they had been smashing tons of ice out of their way.

"Well, Brave," he said mildly. "Old Keeper wasn't so smart, after all, was he? Come on, Brave."

The thieves were making good time. He read that from the tracks – straight, evenly spaced, no weary heel-dragging. Once or twice, he saw where they had stopped for a brief rest. He hoped to see their fire in the evening.

He didn't. They wouldn't have enough fuel to make a big one, or keep it burning long. But in the morning, as he was breaking camp, he saw black smoke ahead.

A few times, he had been in air-boats, and had looked down on the back of the Ice-Father, and it had looked flat. Really, it was not. There were long ridges, sheer on one side and sloping gently on the other, where the ice had overridden hills and low mountains, or had cracked and one side had pushed up over the other. And there were deep gullies where the prevailing winds had scooped away loose snow year after year for centuries, and drifts where it had piled, many of them higher than the building-mounds of the ancient cities. But from a distance, as from above, they all blended into a featureless white monotony.

At last, leaving a tangle of cliffs and ravines, he looked out across a broad stretch of nearly level snow and saw, for the first time, the men he was following. Four tiny dots, so far that they seemed motionless, strung out in single file. Instantly, he crouched behind a swell in the surface and dragged Brave down beside him. One of them, looking back, might see him, as he saw them. When they vanished behind a snow-hill, he rose and hastened forward, to take cover again. He kept at this all day; by alternately resting and running, be found himself gaining on them, and toward evening, he was within rifle-range. The man in the lead was Vahr Farg's son; even at that distance he recognized him easily. The others were Southrons, of course; they wore quilted garments of cloth, and quilted hoods. The man next to Vahr, in blue, carried a rifle, as Vahr did. The man in yellow had only an ice-staff, and the man in green, at the rear, had the Crown on his pack, still in the bearskin bundle.

He waited, at the end of the day, until he saw the light of their fire. Then he and Brave circled widely around their camp, and stopped behind a snow-ridge, on the other side of an open and level stretch a mile wide. He dug the sleeping-hole on the crest of the ridge, making it larger than usual, and piled up a snow breastwork in front of it, with an embrasure through which he could look or fire without being seen.

Before daybreak, he was awake and had his pack made, and when he saw the smoke of the thieves' campfire, he was lying behind his breastwork, the rifle resting on its folded cover, muzzle toward the smoke. He lay for a long time, watching, before he saw the file of tiny dots emerge into the open.

They came forward steadily, in the same order as on the day before, Vahr in the lead and the man with the Crown in the rear. The thieves suspected nothing; they grew larger and larger as they approached, until they were at the range for which he had set his sights. He cuddled the butt of the rifle against his cheek. As the man who carried the Crown walked under the blade of the front sight, he squeezed the trigger.

The rifle belched pink flame and roared and pounded his shoulder. As the muzzle was still rising, he flipped open the breech, and threw out the empty. He inserted a fresh round.

There were only three of them, now. The man with the bearskin bundle was down and motionless. Vahr Farg's son had gotten his rifle unslung and uncovered. The Southron with the other rifle was slower; he was only getting off the cover as Vahr, who must have seen the flash, fired hastily. Too hastily; the bullet kicked up snow twenty feet to the left. The third man had drawn his negatron pistol and was trying to use it; thin hairlines of brilliance were jetting out from his hand, stopping far short of their mark.

Raud closed his sights on the man with the autoloading rifle; as he did, the man with the negatron pistol, realizing the limitations of his weapon, was sweeping it back and forth, aiming at the snow fifty yards in front of him. Raud couldn't see the effect of his second shot – between him and his target, blueish light blazed and twinkled, and dense clouds of steam rose – but he felt sure that he had missed. He reloaded, and watched for movements on the edge of the rising steam.

It cleared, slowly; when it did, there was nothing behind it. Even the body of the dead man was gone. He blinked, bewildered. He'd picked that place carefully; there had been no gully or ravine within running distance. Then he grunted. There hadn't been – but there was now. The negatron pistol again. The thieves were hidden in a pit they had blasted, and they had dragged the body in with them.

He crawled back to reassure Brave, who was guarding the pack, and to shift the pack back for some distance. Then he returned to his embrasure in the snow-fort and resumed his watch. For a long time, nothing happened, and then a head came briefly peeping up out of the pit. A head under a green hood. Raud chuckled mirthlessly into his beard. If he'd been doing that, he'd have traded hoods with the dead man before shoving up his body to draw fire. This kept up, at intervals, for about an hour. He was wondering if they would stay in the pit until dark.

Then Vahr Farg's son leaped out of the pit and began running across the snow. He had his pack, and his rifle; he ran, zigzag, almost directly toward where Raud was lying. Raud laughed, this time in real amusement. The Southrons had chased Vahr out, as a buck will chase his does in front of him when he thinks there is danger in front. If Vahr wasn't shot, it would be safe for them to come out. If he was, it would be no loss, and the price of the Crown would only have to be divided in two, rather than three, shares. Vahr came to within two hundred yards of Raud's unseen rifle, and then dropped his pack and flung himself down behind it, covering the ridge with his rifle.

Minutes passed, and then the Southron in yellow came out and ran forward. He had the bearskin bundle on his pack; he ran to where Vahr lay, added his pack to Vahr's, and lay down behind it. Raud chewed his underlip in vexation. This wasn't the way he wanted it; that fellow had a negatron pistol, and he was close enough to use it effectively. And he was sheltered behind the Crown; Raud was afraid to shoot. He didn't miss what he shot at – often. But no man alive could say that he never missed.

The other Southron, the one in blue with the autoloading rifle, came out and advanced slowly, his weapon at the ready. Raud tensed himself to jump, aimed carefully, and waited. When the man in blue was a hundred yards from the pit, he shot him dead. The rifle was still lifting from the recoil when he sprang to his feet, turned, and ran. Before he was twenty feet away, the place where he had been exploded; the force of the blast almost knocked him down, and steam blew past and ahead of him. Ignoring his pack and ice-staff, he ran on, calling to Brave to follow. The dog obeyed instantly; more negatron-blasts were thundering and blazing and steaming on the crest of the ridge. He swerved left, ran up another slope, and slid down the declivity beyond into the ravine on the other side.

There he paused to eject the empty, make sure that there was no snow in the rifle bore, and reload. The blasting had stopped by then; after a moment, he heard the voice of Vahr Farg's son, and guessed that the two surviving thieves had advanced to the blasted crest of the other ridge. They'd find the pack, and his tracks and Brave's. He wondered whether they'd come hunting for him, or turn around and go the other way. He knew what he'd do, under the circumstances, but he doubted if Vahr's mind would work that way. The Southron's might; he wouldn't want to be caught between blaster-range and rifle-range of Raud the Keeper again.

"Come, Brave," he whispered, looking quickly around and then starting to run.

Lay a trail down this ravine for them to follow. Then get to the top of the ridge beside it, double back, and wait for them. Let them pass, and shoot the Southron first. By now, Vahr would have a negatron pistol too, taken from the body of the man in blue, but it wasn't a weapon he was accustomed to, and he'd be more than a little afraid of it.

The ravine ended against an upthrust face of ice, at right angles to the ridge he had just crossed; there was a V-shaped notch between them. He turned into this; it would be a good place to get to the top. . . .

He found himself face to face, at fifteen feet, with Vahr Farg's son and the Southron in yellow, coming through from the other side. They had their packs, the Southron had the bearskin bundle, and they had drawn negatron pistols in their hands.

Swinging up the rifle, he shot the Southron in the chest, making sure he hit him low enough to miss the Crown. At the same time, he shouted:

"Catch, Brave!"

Brave never jumped for the deer or wild-ox that had been shot; always for the one still on its feet. He launched himself straight at the throat of Vahr Farg's son – and into the muzzle of Vahr's blaster. He died in a blue-white flash.

Raud had reversed the heavy rifle as Brave leaped; he threw it, butt-on, like a seal-spear, into Vahr's face. As soon as it was out of his fingers, he was jumping forward, snatching out his knife. His left hand found Vahr's right wrist, and he knew that he was driving the knife into Vahr's body, over and over, trying to keep the blaster pointed away from him and away from the body of the dead Southron. At last, the negatron-pistol fell from Vahr's fingers, and the arm that had been trying to fend off his knife relaxed.

He straightened and tried to stand – he had been kneeling on Vahr's body, he found – and reeled giddily. He got to his feet and stumbled to the other body, kneeling beside it. He tried for a long time before he was able to detach the bearskin bundle from the dead man's pack. Then he got the pack open, and found dried venison. He started to divide it, and realized that there was no Brave with whom to share it. He had just sent Brave to his death.

Well, and so? Brave had been the Keeper's dog. He had died for the Crown, and that had been his duty. If he could have saved the Crown by giving his own life, Raud would have died too. But he could not – if Raud died the Crown was lost.

The sky was darkening rapidly, and the snow was whitening the body in green. Moving slowly, he started to make camp for the night.

It was still snowing when he woke. He started to rise, wondering, at first, where Brave was, and then he huddled back among the robes – his own and the dead men's – and tried to go to sleep again. Finally, he got up and ate some of his pemmican, gathered his gear and broke camp. For a moment, and only a moment, he stood looking to the east, in the direction he had come from. Then he turned west and started across the snow toward the edge of the Ice-Father.

The snow stopped before he reached the edge, and the sun was shining when he found a slanting way down into the valley. Then, out of the north, a black dot appeared in the sky and grew larger, until he saw that it was a Government airboat – one of the kind used by the men who measured the growth of the Ice-Father. It came curving in and down toward him, and a window slid open and a man put his head out.

"Want us to lift you down?" he asked. "We're going to Long Valley Town. If that's where you're going, we can take you the whole way."

"Yes. That's where I'm going." He said it as though he were revealing, for the first time, some discovery he had just made. "For your kindness and help, I thank you."

In less time than a man could walk two miles with a pack, they were letting down in front of the Government House in Long Valley Town.

He had never been in the Government House before. The walls were clear glass. The floors were plastic, clean and white. Strips of bright new lumicon ran around every room at the tops of all the walls. There were no fires, but the great rooms were as warm as though it were a midsummer afternoon.

Still carrying his pack and his rifle, Raud went to a desk where a Southron in a white shirt sat.

"Has Yorn Nazvik's ship, the *Issa*, been here lately?" he asked.

"About six days ago," the Southron said, without looking up from the papers on his desk. "She's on a trading voyage to the west now, but Nazvik's coming back here before he goes south. Be here in about ten days." He looked up. "You have business with Nazvik?"

Raud shook his head. "Not with Yorn Nazvik, no. My business is with the two Starfolk who are passengers with him. Dranigo and Salvadro."

The Southron looked displeased. "Aren't you getting just a little above yourself, old man, calling the Prince Salsavadran and the Lord Dranigrastan by their familiar names?" he asked.

"I don't know what you're talking about. Those were the names they gave me; I didn't know they had any others."

The Southron started to laugh, then stopped.

"And if I may ask, what is your name, and what business have you with them?" he inquired.

Raud told him his name. "I have something for them. Something they want very badly. If I can find a place to stay here, I will wait until they return –"

The Southron got to his feet. "Wait here for a moment, Keeper," he said. "I'll be back soon."

He left the desk, going into another room. After a while, he came back. This time he was respectful.

"I was talking to the Lord Dranigrastan – whom you know as Dranigo – on the radio. He and the Prince Salsavadran are lifting clear of the *Issa* in their airboat and coming back here to see you. They should be here in about three hours. If, in the meantime, you wish to bathe and rest, I'll find you a room. And I suppose you'll want something to eat, too. . . ."

He was waiting at the front of the office, looking out the glass wall, when the airboat came in and grounded, and Salvadro and Dranigo jumped out and came hurrying up the walk to the doorway.

"Well, here you are, Keeper," Dranigo greeted him, clasping his hand. Then he saw the bearskin bundle under Raud's arm. "You brought it with you? But didn't you believe that we were coming?"

"Are you going to let us have it?" Salvadro was asking.

"Yes; I will sell it to you, for the price you offered. I am not fit to be Keeper any longer. I lost it. It was stolen from me, the day after I saw you, and I have only yesterday gotten it back. Both my dogs were killed, too. I can no longer keep it safe. Better that you take it with you to Dremna, away from this world where it was made. I have thought, before, that this world and I are both old and good for nothing anymore."

"This world may be old, Keeper," Dranigo said, "but it is the Mother-World, Terra, the world that sent Man to the Stars. And you – when you lost the Crown, you recovered it again."

"The next time, I won't be able to. Too many people will know that the Crown is worth stealing, and the next time, they'll kill me first."

"Well, we said we'd give you twenty thousand trade-tokens for it," Salvadro said. "We'll have them for you as soon as we can draw them from the Government bank, here. Or give you a check and let you draw them as you want them." Raud didn't understand that, and Salvadro didn't try to explain. "And then we'll fly you home."

He shook his head. "No, I have no home. The place where you saw me is Keeper's House, and I am not the Keeper anymore. I will stay here and find a place to live, and pay somebody to take care of me. . . ."

With twenty thousand trade-tokens, he could do that. It would buy a house in which he could live, and he could find some woman who had lost her man, who would do his work for him. But he must be careful of the money. Dig a crypt in the corner of his house for it. He wondered if he could find a pair of good dogs and train them to guard it for him. . . .

CPSIA information can be obtained at www.ICGtesting.com
Printed in the USA
BVOW061250040412

286822BV00003B/133/A